Heart's Thief

Books by Emma Prince

Highland Bodyguards Series:
The Lady's Protector (Book 1)
Heart's Thief (Book 2)
Book 3 (Finn's Story) coming December 2016!

The Sinclair Brothers Trilogy:
Highlander's Ransom (Book 1)
Highlander's Redemption (Book 2)
Highlander's Return (Bonus Novella, Book 2.5)
Highlander's Reckoning (Book 3)

Viking Lore Series:
Enthralled (Viking Lore, Book 1)
Shieldmaiden's Revenge (Viking Lore, Book 2)
The Bride Prize (Viking Lore, Book 2.5)
Desire's Hostage (Viking Lore, Book 3)
Thor's Wolf (Viking Lore, Book 3.5)—
a Kindle Worlds novella

Other Books:
Wish upon a Winter Solstice
(A Highland Holiday Novella)

Heart's Thief

Highland Bodyguards

Book 2

By
Emma Prince

Heart's Thief
(Highland Bodyguards, Book 2)
Copyright © 2016 by Emma Prince
Print Edition

For Scott. Always.

Chapter One

Early August, 1315
Lochmaben, Scottish Lowlands

"What the bloody hell happened?"

Colin MacKay kept his features carefully smooth at King Robert the Bruce's angry bellow.

The Bruce yanked off his nasal helm and hurled it across the tent. The helm slammed into the tent's canvas wall with a muffled thump, then thudded to the hard packed dirt floor.

"Carlisle shouldnae have been so difficult to take," the Bruce snapped. He began to pace the length of the tent, which served as the humble headquarters for the King of Scotland.

Colin slid a glance at Finn Sutherland, who stood silently at his side. Finn shook his head, the slightest of movements. Colin knew his friend well enough to comprehend the warning in the gesture.

"The ladders should have been enough. The trebuchet should have been enough." The Bruce reached the tent's back wall and spun on his heels. He pinned them with hard eyes. "Speak, damn ye!"

Finn, one of the bravest, fiercest men Colin had ever known, shifted uncomfortably under the King's glare. Dark brows lowered, Finn pressed his lips together, remaining silent.

"We couldnae have accounted for this cursed rain, sire."

The words were barely out of Colin's mouth before he regretted them. Only the weak blamed factors like the weather for their failures.

From the dark look on the Bruce's face, his King agreed with that sentiment.

Aye, the rain had been their bane all summer. With the wind at his back after the victory at Bannockburn last year, the Bruce had been storming through the Lowlands and even into northern England, reclaiming castles and towns that Longshanks had pried away from Scotland years ago.

But after months of victories against Longshanks's ineffectual son, King Edward II of England, the weather itself seemed to turn against the Scottish cause. Nigh incessant rains had slowed the Bruce's army as it moved across the Lowlands. Crops drooped and molded, making the task of feeding Scotland's soldiers all the more difficult.

And now they had suffered their greatest setback in years. Carlisle Castle sat in the northernmost corner of Cumberland, practically a stone's throw from the stretches of Lowlands the Bruce had reclaimed for Scotland. The castle would have been a jewel in the

Bruce's crown, proof of his army's strength and a not-so-subtle threat that would have spread from the Borderlands all the way to Edward in the south.

The castle should have fallen quickly and easily to the Bruce's army, ten thousand men strong. But after less than a fortnight of sieging, the Bruce had been forced to abandon his efforts and return to Lochmaben.

"The ladders would have worked if it hadnae been for the boggy ground," Colin tried again. Though it was a weak excuse, he needed to at least attempt to soothe the Bruce's rage. There were too many other fronts of the battle, and too much at stake, to waste time on fits of frustration.

The Bruce had been about to pace his next length of the tent when he rounded on Colin.

Good. Colin could take the King's anger, let him burn himself out, and then help him move on to their next challenge.

"Aye, the ladders should have worked. But it was rash no' to bring the siege machines. We wouldnae have wasted five days building new ones."

It had been a strategic decision on the Bruce's part to leave their trebuchet and siege towers in Lochmaben. He'd wanted to move quickly, to strike Carlisle in a surprise attack. But when the ladders had sunken into the marshy ground surrounding the castle, unable to gain purchase, the error of favoring speed over the war machines' strength had become clear.

The army had hastily built a siege tower to scale

the castle's walls, but that too had become stuck in the mud, rendering it useless. And though the trebuchet had fired on Carlisle's walls relentlessly for several days, little more than a few chips had been made.

"Mayhap if we had led with the tactic we used at Edinburgh Castle..." Finn offered. At the Bruce's withering look, though, Finn fell silent once more.

Colin exhaled slowly under the hard-eyed stare of his King. "I dinnae ken what to say, Robert. We tried the ladders. We tried the trebuchet and the tower. We tried scaling the back wall, as we did at Edinburgh, but they were prepared for it. I ken ye dinnae want to hear this, but mayhap we willnae take Carlisle."

At the use of his given name, the Bruce's anger deflated slightly. Though he was King of all Scotland, the Bruce preferred for his most trusted inner circle of warriors and advisors to call him Robert—they were family, he insisted. Their lives were in each other's hands. No one took that more seriously than the King himself.

The Bruce raked a hand through his graying russet-brown hair. He seemed to notice for the first time that he, like Colin and Finn standing before him, was soaking wet and covered in mud. They'd ridden hard from Carlisle that very afternoon, though the sting of defeat no doubt overrode the Bruce's physical discomforts at the moment.

"Forgive me, Colin, Finn."

The Bruce suddenly seemed far more tired than

Colin could ever remember seeing him. Only a few weeks past, the King had turned forty-one, but his energy and focus had grown along with the Scottish cause's successes over the last several years. In defeat, the lines on his face looked deeper, his body more bent with time and this loss on the way to freedom.

The King moved behind his wooden desk, pulling out a chair. "Please, sit," he said, motioning to two other chairs near the desk.

As Colin eased himself into one of the chairs, he too suddenly felt the effects of nine long years of warfare. More than just the weight of his chainmail over his soaked tunic was making his bones ache.

"Walter! Warmed wine, please," the Bruce called to the man stationed outside the tent.

The three of them waited in silence only broken by the muted drizzle of rain against the tent's canvas roof.

As Walter entered quietly with three goblets of wine, the Bruce seemed lost in thought, his auburn brows drawn together.

When the tent flap slipped closed behind Walter, Colin cleared his throat. "Training for the Corps is going well."

The Bruce looked up from his wine. "Ah. I forgot to ask about that."

A fortnight ago, Colin and Finn had been called from Roslin Castle in the Highlands by a missive that told them to meet the Bruce in Lochmaben with all haste. They'd barely had time to don their chainmail before the Bruce had led his army from Lochmaben to Carlisle with Colin and Finn at his side.

The Bodyguard Corps, as the men were coming to call themselves, was a project of particular interest to the Bruce. Almost a year ago, the Bruce and his inner circle, including Colin, had come up with the idea of a secret group of elite warriors who would serve as bodyguards to those targeted by the English.

A new era of warfare was dawning. After being trounced by the Scots at Bannockburn, the English were now resorting to striking at individual targets important to the Scottish cause of independence—even women and children. Those in the Corps were training hard in the Highlands to rise to this new challenge.

Though he'd been distracted by the sour events of the last ten days, Colin was sure the Bruce would appreciate an update on the Corps. If naught else, it would hopefully take his mind off Carlisle.

"Robert Sinclair takes great pleasure in torturing us," Colin said, lifting his mouth into a smile he knew would put his King at ease. "And Ansel Sutherland joins us most days for training."

"Ansel and Lady Isolda are well?" the Bruce asked, still staring despondently into his wine.

"Aye, verra well. He again sends his thanks for allowing his family to live so close to Roslin Castle. Isolda is carrying a bairn to join young John in the fall."

"The Corps is still small, but we are ready and awaiting yer orders," Finn added.

The Bruce swirled the wine in his goblet and sighed. "Thank ye both."

A long silence stretched. Disquiet tickled up Colin's spine even as he took a long sip of the warmed wine.

He'd always been able to read people effortlessly. Normally all it took to put others at ease was a grin or a lightly spoken word. Something must truly still bother the Bruce. He was not only unaffected by Colin's disarming smile, but was also uninterested in the Bodyguard Corps, his most personal project.

"Something troubles ye, Robert," Colin ventured, his low voice breaking the silence.

The Bruce leaned back in his chair, exhaling through his nose. "It is just… How did those bloody English ken how to defend against our men scaling the walls as we did in Edinburgh? How did they ken to stock the castle with enough boulders and arrows to outlast a siege ten times longer than we gave them?" He shook his head slowly in disbelief.

There it was. It was not merely the sting of defeat that needled at the King. But could he be seriously considering foul play?

Colin set his goblet on the Bruce's desk slowly. "What are ye saying? That they kenned we were coming?"

A flash of urgency lit the Bruce's dark eyes as he too set his wine aside. "Doesnae that explain everything? No' the rain, of course," he said with a wave of his hand. "But the rest of it. How did they ken that we would attempt to distract them on the west wall while a group scaled the east wall?"

Finn cocked a dark brow but remained silent. To say the man wasn't much for words was a vast understatement, so as usual, it fell to Colin to speak.

"Word of how we took Edinburgh spread quickly. It is no' beyond reason to think that those in Carlisle had heard of our tactic and kenned to watch for it."

The Bruce propped his elbows on his desk. "Aye, mayhap. But what of the fact that they were clearly prepared? I would almost believe that their stones bred and multiplied behind the castle's walls. And their arrows and spears seemed nigh endless."

That was true enough. The Bruce's army had been the recipient of a relentless hail of attack from the castle's longbowmen. Hurled rocks had kept them from getting near any of the three gates. Even without the rain turning the ground to mush, the Bruce's forces would have been hard-pressed to scale their ladders under such constant fire.

"And there were so bloody *few* of them," the Bruce went on before Colin could gather his thoughts. The Bruce smacked the wooden desk with his hand. "Only a few hundred men to guard the walls against our force of thousands. There is something foul afoot, I swear it."

This was a dangerous line of thought for a King. If the Bruce were to constantly look for conspiracy behind his failures, soon he would believe that he couldn't trust anyone. Nevertheless, Colin couldn't deny that everything the Bruce said pointed to black dealings.

"Spies?" he murmured at last. "Or a traitor in our midst?"

As if to underscore the dark possibility, a low growl of thunder rumbled through the tent.

The Bruce looked between Colin and Finn slowly.

"Nay, no' a traitor," he said at last. "Only a small handful of men even kenned about the plan against Carlisle, and I cannae believe one of them would aid the English."

"We have spies in the English court," Finn said lowly. "Is it so hard to imagine that Edward may have infiltrated our camp? A spy doesnae have to be in yer inner circle to hear things."

The Bruce tugged on his russet beard, which was liberally slashed with gray. Rainwater from the trek between Carlisle and Lochmaben trickled onto the desk below the King's beard, but he barely seemed to notice.

"I hardly spoke of my plans at all, except—" The King's eyes locked on Colin and then Finn once more. Realization dawned slowly across his face. "Except that in the missive I sent to Roslin Castle to call ye both down, I mentioned Carlisle."

"Robert, ye cannae think that *we*—"

"Nay, Finn, nay. But think, man. The letter traveled a great distance. It could have been intercepted at any point along the way."

Colin shook his head slowly, confusion clouding his thoughts. "But your missive arrived intact, the seal unbroken. Obviously it wasnae stolen."

"No' stolen, aye, but might someone have read it somehow?"

There were ways to open a letter without breaking the wax seal, of course. The most likely culprit would be the messenger himself, though the Bruce was extremely careful in selecting his carriers.

"Ye think someone opened yer missive, read it, resealed it, and allowed it to be delivered while the culprit himself passed the information on to Andrew Harclay?"

Harclay was the constable of Carlisle, as well as the sheriff of Cumberland. He'd been the one to set up the resistance to the Bruce's siege. Despite having only a few hundred men to the Bruce's ten thousand, he'd somehow managed to turn the Bruce away.

"That would explain Harclay's preparedness," the Bruce said. "Though I can tell from yer frown that ye find my theory far-fetched, Colin."

Colin quickly smoothed his features. It was unlike him to lose control like that. "I agree that the English were strangely prepared," he replied. "Bloody hell, it seemed as though they had every blacksmith and fletcher in the city making arrows and spears in the week before we arrived. And they must have had piles of rocks as high as the walls stacked every few yards behind the parapets. I am just…"

"Ye are just cautious to let yer King dissolve into conspiracy theories—which is why I keep ye at my side, Colin," the Bruce said, a faint smile touching his lips behind his beard.

"Aye," Colin said simply with a sigh.

"Hear me out, lads," the Bruce said softly. "I am no' chasing ghosts or imagining my friends are my enemies—hell, I've got enough enemies as it is already. Harclay would benefit from intercepting a missive that alluded to an attack on his castle, but I doubt he would have the means to gather such information—especially if he would need to have people working for him here in Scotland. But the Earl of Lancaster certainly has that kind of power and reach. As does King Edward."

"Ye think Lancaster or Edward is behind this?" Finn asked, his brows dropping.

"Edward has all but ceded the Lowlands to us, but he still has a vested interest in protecting his border. Losing any more castles to me in the Borderlands weakens his position with his nobles, who are already calling for his removal," the Bruce said. "And Lancaster has holdings in both Cumberland and Northumberland. He cannae risk losing land to me, for if he did, he would be forced to either side with Edward against me, or side with me and reveal his treason to Edward."

The Bruce was right about one thing—he had enemies aplenty. Lancaster had approached the Bruce in secret last year, proposing an alliance against Edward, his English King. Unbeknownst to Lancaster, the Bruce discovered, with the help of Ansel Sutherland, that Lancaster was actually attempting to take out both King Edward and the Bruce. Apparently the enemy of the Bruce's enemy was still his enemy.

"The truth is, it doesnae matter who is behind the interception of my missives," the Bruce went on with a wave of his hand. "Any one of my enemies would benefit. What matters is that my communications arenae secure."

Dread tightened Colin's stomach. There was truth to the Bruce's words. And that meant that the entire cause for Scottish independence was in danger. Information could be more powerful than an army of thousands—their failure at Carlisle had just proven that.

Colin glanced at Finn again. Finn was the most wary, skeptical man Colin had ever known. He'd even accused the wife of their close friend Garrick Sinclair of being an English assassin when she'd saved the Bruce's life many years ago.

With one look, Colin knew the truth, though. Finn nodded slightly. He believed the Bruce's theory.

"What will ye do, Robert?" Colin asked quietly.

Thunder once again cut the silence as the Bruce steepled his fingers in thought.

"The most obvious explanation is that a messenger has been compromised," the King said. "I dinnae wish to believe it is possible, but there it is."

"Test the man, then," Finn said. "Send the same messenger you sent to fetch us on some errand or other. Have the man watched for signs that he is either reading the missive you give him, or letting someone else read it."

"Aye, that's all well and good," the Bruce replied. "I had the same thought. Osborn was the man I sent for ye. He was to leave on the morrow with another missive, this one for my brother."

"There's yer test, then," Finn said. "Give him the letter for your brother. Ye'll ken soon enough if Osborn can be trusted."

The Bruce stood suddenly, shoving back his chair. "It is no' so simple as that. I dinnae have time to play nursemaid to Osborn. Besides, the missive for my brother is no' some bit of frivolity. He and his men are on the front lines in Ireland. If another one of my missives is compromised, it could cost him his life— and all our efforts in Ireland."

Finn shifted, his chainmail scraping against his chair.

An idea began to sprout in Colin's mind. "What if...what if ye sent Osborn with a dummy message—a bit of frivolity, as ye say, or even just a blank piece of parchment with yer seal on it?"

"And the message that must reach my brother in Ireland?" the Bruce shot back.

"Send it with me." The last piece fell into place in Colin's mind. "I can keep an eye on Osborn. Ye ken I'll be able to tell if he is hiding something or if he is innocent."

The Bruce nodded slowly, so Colin went on. "Ye can give me the real missive to yer brother. If Osborn is dirty, we'll ken it, but he willnae compromise any more of your correspondence. If he's clean, we'll ken that as well. And either way, I'll ensure that yer brother gets yer letter."

Colin realized suddenly that he had risen to his feet as he spoke. He felt Finn's eyes on him and turned to find his friend's brows lifted quizzically.

A similarly surprised expression rested on the King's features. "One of my best warriors, turned into a nanny goat and letter carrier?"

Colin couldn't help the wry chuckle that rose in his throat. "Aye, if that's what ye need from me."

The Bruce grinned briefly, but then let it fade. "Are ye serious, lad?" he asked softly. "Without telling ye too much, I can say that the contents of the letter to my brother is of grave importance. Thousands of lives hang in the balance."

Ignoring the aches in his body, the chill in his bones, and the cutting weight of his chainmail, Colin straightened and locked eyes with his King.

"I've served ye for nine years now, sire," he said, emphasizing the Bruce's title. "I have been honored to be included in yer inner circle, and honored again to join the Bodyguard Corps. This is what I have trained for—to assess and weed out dangers against ye, and to protect our cause in any and every way I can."

A keen flicker now lit the Bruce's eyes. A small smile played at the corners of his lips as his normal sharpness seemed to return at last. "Aye, aye," he murmured, his mind clearly racing over Colin's words.

"Ye are a member of the Bodyguard Corps," Finn said with a rare smirk. "Whose body will ye be guarding, then?"

"Osborn's, mayhap," Colin shot back. "Or my own if necessary. Besides, the point of the Corps is to protect what is most valuable to our cause. Why cannae it be a missive?"

Finn's lips twisted into something dangerously close to a smile. Colin narrowed his eyes on his friend, but before he could put Finn in his place, the Bruce cut in.

"Ye'll leave on the morrow for Portpatrick," he declared. "I'll tell Osborn that ye are accompanying him to Ireland to join my brother's army, but naught else. Ye'd best find some dry clothes and try to get some rest."

Finn rose beside him and they both gave the King quick bows. As the two slipped from the Bruce's tent and into the relentless rain, Finn pounded his shoulder.

"I cannae say I'm jealous that ye will be playing nursemaid to a grown man, but good on ye for it nonetheless."

Colin's chest swelled at the rare praise from Finn.

Despite the cold and dampness that had long ago

seeped into his bones, his blood warmed at what lay ahead of him. It was his first solo mission as part of the Corps.

Aye, he would do his King proud—and he would do himself proud.

Chapter Two

"**S**abine! Come!"

Even muffled through the thick wooden door, Sabine jumped at Fabian's voice.

As she quietly opened the door and slipped through, Miles slid past her on his way out.

Sabine lifted a silent brow in askance at Miles. Though his brusque, almost indifferent treatment of her in the field could hardly be misconstrued as a friendship, Miles was one of the few people she ever saw with regularity—other than Fabian.

Miles gave her a quick nod in response to her unspoken question. She breathed an inaudible sigh of relief as she stepped fully into the chamber, closing the door behind her. Fabian wasn't in one of his moods, which meant that he wouldn't hurt her—probably.

"Ah, there you are, my dear."

Nay, he was definitely not in one of his moods—or rather, he wasn't gripped by nigh blinding rage that caused him to lash out at anyone close to him. This kind, happy phase wasn't so different, though, for it would pass soon enough, just as the dark moods did.

"Fabian," she said, bobbing into a little curtsy.

He rose from behind an enormous oak desk that was covered in loose scraps of parchment, as always. With outstretched arms, he came around the desk, a smile curving his mouth behind his perfectly trimmed goatee.

Fabian took her in a gentle hug, patting her shoulders. "I'm glad to see you returned from the field," he said, pulling back. His face grew serious, his slim gray eyebrows drawing down. "But it will not be a long visit, I'm afraid. I have another assignment for you."

Sabine lifted her lips into a smile, forcing it to reach her eyes. "No need to apologize. You know I prefer to stay busy."

In a strange way, it was almost easier to deal with Fabian in one of his dark moods. At least then she knew what he was about. In times like these, Sabine had to use every drop of skill she possessed, every ounce of watchfulness and care.

"Aye, indeed," he replied, smiling again. "Good girl."

He stepped back around his desk and took up his seat once more, smoothing his silk vest. "How did your last assignment go?"

Sabine reached inside the cinched bodice of her dress and removed three folded missives.

"The seals?" Fabian asked sharply as she extended them across his desk.

"Unbroken, as requested."

"Good girl," he repeated.

Despite herself, she felt a swell of pride at her work. She'd done everything right, and Fabian was pleased.

Fabian fingered the three missives for a moment before setting them on his desk along with all the other slips of parchment. Though she wasn't sure how, the piles and stacks made sense to him.

"Our client will be most gratified," he said, leaning back in his chair.

He waved for her to take a seat as well, and she carefully lowered herself into a chair upholstered in red silk that matched his own.

"Regarding this new assignment," he said, leaning back in his seat. "This one will not be a take, but a memorize. You haven't gotten rusty, have you?"

"Nay, of course not," she replied quickly. She would never let a skill so valuable as being able to read and memorize a missive erode due to lack of use. Even when she went months without such an assignment, she practiced on her own so as never to fall out of the habit.

"Ah, of course you haven't," Fabian said, granting her another kindly smile. "Good, because you'll need to be ready to depart today."

"Where am I going?"

"My lookout has sent word that a messenger left Lochmaben this morning headed west. You'll intercept them in Dumfries."

"*Them?*"

Fabian exhaled, sliding a hand along gray hair that

used to be brown. "My source says that he recognized the messenger immediately—in fact, he intercepted one of the man's missives not long ago. But apparently the messenger is traveling with some sort of brute."

Unease slid down Sabine's spine to pool in her belly. "And I am to deal with the brute as well as the messenger?"

He waved his hand dismissively. "I wouldn't ask such a thing of you, my dear. Your strengths are your stealth and that lovely face of yours, not your ability to fight. It is more than likely that the thug is simply accompanying the messenger because their destination is the same."

Sabine nodded, but before she could ask her next question, Fabian went on.

"Of course, there is a more troubling possibility as well. The brute may have been sent to protect the messenger. In that case, it is probably because the roads have become so dangerous in the last few years."

"Or because what the messenger carries is extremely valuable," Sabine said softly.

Fabian's dark eyes lit up with pleasure. "Aye, exactly, my darling. This is why you are my dearest treasure. This assignment will take special care. As always, you'll need to avoid raising the messenger's suspicion. The missive must appear untampered with. The client was very specific about this—he doesn't wish anyone to know that he has gained this information. And you'll have to steer clear of the messenger's thug as well."

Sabine swallowed but gave Fabian a nod. "I can do it."

"Of course you can, darling. I have complete faith in you, which is just what I told the client. He is a very powerful man, and this is…important to him."

Important meant that the client was paying handsomely for the information Sabine was to retrieve, she knew.

"I'll expect you back in a sennight with the contents of the missive in that clever little head of yours," Fabian said, a cool smile touching his lips. "Miles will be in Dumfries as well, but you shouldn't need him. In fact, it would be best if you didn't contact anyone, for this assignment requires the most delicate and discreet of touches. That is why I am sending you."

Sabine nodded again. "I won't let you down."

Almost unconsciously, she touched the thin chain around her neck. Concealed under her bodice hung a gold ring set with a small emerald. It was too dangerous to display the ring in the field, but she always wore it on that chain so that she would never forget what it represented.

Fabian must have noticed her motion, for his smile softened. He lifted his hand to show her the matching ring on the middle finger of his right hand.

"I believe in you," he said, bringing his ringed hand to his heart. "Now go. You have work to do."

Chapter Three

C olin cursed his squelching boots as he crossed the inn's common room.

He cursed the relentless rain that had pounded them all the way from Lochmaben.

He cursed the thick mud that had made the roads nigh impassable.

He cursed the fact that what should have been an easy half-day ride to Dumfries had turned into a miserable day-and-a-half slog.

But most of all, he cursed himself for his foolish pride.

He dropped onto a stool in front of a high counter that served as the inn's main table. A few shorter tables and chairs sprinkled the dim common room, where a handful of the inn's other patrons sat hunched over their mugs of ale, some talking quietly.

The small fire on the other side of the room didn't exude enough warmth to cut through Colin's damp tunic or breeches. Thank God he didn't have to wear heavy chainmail for this mission.

Still, wearing clothes in the style of the English chafed. He cursed yet again, this time for the fact that he couldn't wear the MacKay clan colors here in the Lowlands without drawing unwanted attention.

A stout older woman, no doubt the innkeeper's wife, bustled by, her graying head down and her face creased with a frown.

Colin forced a smile to his mouth despite the foul words that clung to the tip of his tongue.

"Excuse me, madam," he said.

The woman grunted as she glanced at him, but then her foot faltered. She came to a sudden halt, her eyes rounding and a silly smile coming to her lips.

"Oh, ah, forgive me, milord. I didn't see ye there," she sputtered, gazing at him.

Aye, his smile still worked as well as ever.

"That's quite all right. I ken ye are busy this eve." He waved at the half-empty room, pushing sympathy into his eyes. "I only wonder if I may bother ye for a mug of ale and a warm meal. It is another miserable, damp night out."

"Oh aye!" the woman said eagerly. "Right away, milord."

She hurried around the counter and through a swinging door that led to the attached kitchen. Once she was out of sight, Colin let his smile drop as he surveyed the room.

The few men who sat in the common room looked as bedraggled as Colin felt. Most had mud on their boots, as he did, and their simple homespun tunics looked damp. One man stood before the fire, warming his hands, while the others nursed their mugs sullenly.

So, he wasn't the only one in a foul mood over the weather. But while these men were likely worrying about crops or the increase in wool prices over the last few months, Colin had more reason to be cross than they did.

This whole bloody mission was already a bust— and only a day and a half in, at that.

Within hours of meeting Osborn, Colin sensed instinctually that his suspicions about the messenger were unfounded. The man was overly talkative, aye, but entirely guileless. Though Osborn had already demonstrated a fine opinion of himself, Colin didn't believe for a second that the messenger possessed the skill or wits to knowingly compromise the Bruce's missives.

Even with Osborn out of the equation, that still left the possibility that he'd been waylaid on his way to deliver the King's message without even realizing it. Osborn had claimed that he didn't remember aught suspicious or untoward happening on his journey to the Highlands to deliver the missive about Carlisle to Colin and Finn, but then again, sometimes a man could be hit over the head so soundly that he couldn't even recall it.

That possibility meant that Colin still needed to keep his eyes and ears open—and remain close to Osborn. But so far all he'd seen last night on the road and now tonight in this inn outside Dumfries was a load of wet, grumpy farmers and merchants.

Worse, in the short time Colin had been in Osborn's presence, he'd learned that for the first time in his life, he couldn't get another person to do what he wished using his charm.

No matter how many times Colin lightly teased, or gently suggested, or hinted, or outright ordered Osborn to cease his incessant chatter, the man simply wouldn't shut his trap.

Aye, working as a messenger was certainly lonely work. It meant traveling long stretches alone, with only innkeepers and stable hands to talk with. Still, Colin had never met a man so oblivious to those around him.

Mayhap it grated so much because Colin prided himself on being able to charm people into doing as he wished—or that his abilities were completely wasted on Osborn.

He would have been saved a great deal of trouble if he had met Osborn when the man brought the missive to the Highlands requesting Colin and Finn at the Bruce's side a fortnight ago. But alas, Osborn hadn't been ordered to wait for a response, so he'd delivered the message to Robert Sinclair and returned to the Lowlands before Colin had even laid eyes on him.

Regardless, he was stuck with the man for what would no doubt be a very long fortnight. Ireland had never seemed so far away as it did now.

Speak of the devil.

Osborn came tromping down the inn's stairs, his hands looped in his belt and an inexplicably easy grin on his face. Though the mop of brown hair on his head was still damp from their travels, he'd changed into a dry tunic and breeches.

"Ah, there ye are, Colin!" he said loudly. A few of the other patrons lifted their heads at the intrusion.

Osborn strode over and plunked himself down on a stool at Colin's side. Rubbing his large, red-tipped nose with the back of his hand, he glanced around the room.

"Quiet tonight, eh?"

"Indeed," Colin replied. It was all he could do to smooth the grimace from his face. Aye, his gentle, kindly prodding hadn't worked to get Osborn to shut up, but at least he could avoid openly scowling at the man.

"Ye're wet as a dog, man! Are ye sure ye dinnae wish to change in our chamber? Surely ye have some dry clothes in that saddlebag of yers. I daresay ye'll catch yer death sitting here in damp garments."

By God, even the man's Lowland lilt grated on Colin's nerves. He nodded, pressing his lips together to keep from snapping at the messenger.

Clearly, Osborn didn't notice the fact that Colin was barely holding on to his temper by a thread, for he went on.

"I take it ye havenae done much traveling, based on the fact that ye are still sitting here in those soggy clothes. Heed my advice, laddie, for I am an expert of sorts. I've traveled all over Scotland in the service of King Robert the Bruce." Osborn leaned in, rounding his beady eyes for effect. "And even into parts of England, though I dinnae like to brag about it."

"I've traveled a piece myself," Colin managed through gritted teeth. "Ye neednae lecture me, friend."

The Bruce had thought it best not to alert Osborn to the fact that Colin was actually one of the King's most trusted warriors. Colin now saw the wisdom in the Bruce's withholding, for though there wasn't a malicious bone in Osborn's body, the less the man knew, the better. The messenger had only been told that the Bruce was sending Colin to assist his brother in Ireland. Colin might as well accompany Osborn, who was going there anyway with a missive from the King—or so he thought.

"Oh, aye, ye've traveled from the Highlands, judging from that brogue of yers," Osborn said with a wave of his hand. "But I have gleaned some of the finer skills over the years."

It was a finer skill, in need of careful gleaning, not to sit in wet clothes?

Colin was saved from having to fake another neutral response, for just then, the innkeeper's wife swung through the kitchen door with a mug of ale and a bowl of steaming stew. She beamed at Colin as she set the meal before him on the counter. He slipped on his practiced smile, meant especially to charm women.

"Thank ye, madam. Ye are most kind."

The woman flushed and began to simper, but Osborn cut her off.

"There ye are, wench! I've been sitting here for several minutes without any ale to wet my whistle or a bowl of stew to warm my belly. See to it now, if ye please."

The innkeeper's wife's smile faltered as she turned to Osborn. "Forgive me, milord," she said icily, narrowing her eyes at him. "I was just seeing to yer friend, here."

She spun on her heels, giving Osborn her back before he could reprimand her again.

Bloody hell, the man was as tactless as a fly in a cup of fine whisky.

As usual, Osborn didn't seem to notice the woman's curtness. He began whistling softly, for apparently he felt that any and all silences must be filled.

Colin took a long drag of ale. Was he losing his edge? His inability to subtly manipulate Osborn into a pliant charge was unsettling.

Mayhap he'd been spending too much time in the company of taciturn warriors. For most of the last nine years that he'd been in the Bruce's service, he'd worked in the King's inner circle, usually in small teams with men who would rather exchange sword blows than pleasantries.

Colin had always been a bit different from the others, though. Aye, he was as skilled as any of the Bruce's other elite warriors—he'd proven it enough on the practice field as well as in battle. But while Finn Sutherland would probably rather have a tooth pulled than prattle on with the likes of Osborn, Colin had always had a knack with people.

With a joke or a pound on the back, he made men feel welcome, relaxed. And with a smile or a wink, women turned soft and supple, as the innkeeper's wife had.

Aye, he'd been told by many a lass over the years that he was a handsome devil, but it was more than that. It was listening with an easy smile, all the while sharply observing the person across from him for clues on how to act, how to steer them toward what he wanted.

He'd always had such a skill. Or rather, he'd always found that reading people came easily to him. He didn't use to think of it as a skill—more like a natural way with people. But ever since Joan's betrayal, he saw it for what it truly was—a tool to be used in the service of the Scottish cause. Or a weapon.

He quickly shoved away the dark memories. Now was not the time to think on the events of eight years past. He still had a mission to complete, even if half of that mission was to play nanny goat to Osborn.

As the innkeeper's wife arrived with a second bowl of stew and a mug of ale for Osborn, the icy look still in her eyes as she served him, a muffled sound drew Colin's attention once more to the stairs.

The sound grew more distinct as someone began

descending the steps—sniffles interspersed with little sobs.

A woman's green-dyed skirts emerged from the shadowy stairwell. The material swayed around slim hips as she continued down the stairs. Hips gave way to a narrow waist, and then a snugly laced bodice. The curve of petite but shapely breasts rose above the bodice's scooped neck. A thin metal chain was clasped around a delicate neck, disappearing between those pert breasts.

With another step, the woman's head came into view. Unbound dark brown hair framed a pale face. She held a kerchief to her nose, obscuring the lower half of her face, but wide hazel eyes took in the common room. Those tear-brimmed eyes darted to each of the tables, finally landing on the counter where Colin and Osborn sat.

Heat, slow and familiar, settled low in Colin's belly. The lass was undeniably attractive, if a bit thin. Still, her delicately feminine curves and wide, innocent eyes could entice many a man.

The woman muffled another little sniffle behind the kerchief. She dipped her head so that her eyes landed on the floor, her dark hair sliding down around her face like a veil.

Colin realized that the room had fallen still at her arrival. A quick glance told him that he hadn't been the only one to notice the lass's bonny features.

A woman in an inn wasn't so unusual that all the

other patrons should be staring quite so slack-jawed at her, however. Colin reminded himself that the men around him were simple farmers and merchants unused to a pretty young lass's company.

He'd have to make a point of leaving her alone. Even from the brief contact their eyes had made, he sensed that she was not one for a quick and easy dalliance. A lass in tears almost always meant more trouble than she was worth.

Besides, he had better things to do than indulge in a wee bit of distraction. Though he knew that Osborn was incapable of deceit, the messenger still might be targeted by one of King Edward or Lancaster's lackeys.

As he turned back to his ale and stew, a flicker of movement caught the corner of his eye. The lass had settled herself on one of the stools a few feet down from Osborn.

"My, my, little missy," Osborn said, leaning toward the lass. "Ye have been through quite a tribulation, from the looks of ye."

The lass sobbed again, dabbing the kerchief at her eyes. "Oh, aye, indeed," she replied, her voice soft with a Lowland lilt.

"Wench!" Osborn called. The innkeeper's wife reemerged from the kitchen, her hands planted on her ample hips and her eyes shooting daggers at Osborn. "Wench, please serve this young lass." Osborn removed an extra coin from the pouch on his belt. "On me."

Impossibly, the lass's eyes rounded even more. "Oh, ye are too kind, milord."

"Och. I ken a good lass in trouble when I see one. What has ye in a twist?"

Colin almost rolled his eyes at Osborn's obliviousness, but managed to keep his features smooth and his gaze solidly fastened on the stretch of counter in front of him. Without knowing aught of the lass, it was fairly obvious that she was likely looking for a free meal—and Osborn was the fool to deliver it.

The lass lowered her kerchief, and Colin caught a flash of red lips in the corner of his eye. "Naught to burden ye with, milord, I am sure. I am just a silly, silly lass, that is all. And now I will pay the price for my foolishness."

As the innkeeper's wife set ale and stew in front of the lass, Osborn slid one stool closer to her. "Come now, ye are no doubt being too hard on yerself. What is yer name, then?"

"Sabine. Sabine Armstrong," the lass replied.

"Well, Sabine, I am Harold Osborn, though everyone simply calls me Osborn."

The lass giggled softly as if the messenger had just said something witty. "Verra well, Osborn. I thank ye again for the meal. My great aunt Edith always says almost everything can be fixed with a warm, full belly."

Suddenly Sabine was whimpering into her kerchief again.

"What is it, missy?" Osborn asked, scooting over

another stool. "Is yer great aunt unwell?"

"Oh, nay!" Sabine moaned. "Edith is in fine health. In fact, she is resting abovestairs. It is just…"

Colin polished off his bowl of stew, all the while trying to ignore Osborn as he attempted to coax information out of the girl. With a smile and a wink at the innkeeper's wife, he had another mug of ale placed before him.

Mayhap instead of scorning Osborn for a fool, he should be thanking this Sabine lass for taking the man off his hands for a few minutes. Though Osborn's incessant prattle, even when directed at someone else, still grated on his nerves, at least Colin didn't have to feign good humor for the time being.

"…parents died of the fever, great aunt Edith took me in. So ye see, I am verra naughty for no' being grateful to her." Sabine said, dabbing at her eyes once more. "But I cannae forgive her for what she has planned."

"And what is that? Surely she has yer best interests at heart if she has raised ye all these years, as ye say." Osborn waved for another ale for himself and Sabine. The innkeeper's wife grudgingly fetched them, setting them down with more force than necessary onto the countertop.

Sabine launched into her tale, telling Osborn in a hushed, plaintive voice that Edith had dragged her from their home outside Caerlaverock to come to Dumfries.

"I've never even seen a town as grand as Dumfries before—and now I never will," Sabine said, her voice dropping dejectedly.

"I dinnae see why, lassie! We are practically in Dumfries now! Just convince yer dear old Edith to let ye have a look tomorrow. Who kens, perhaps the rains will finally clear up."

Osborn tried to console Sabine as a fresh wave of sobs overtook her. Not so subtly, Osborn slid over the final stool that separated him from the lass and took one of her hands in his.

"Nay, she will not relent," Sabine said. "For ye see, she is going to deliver me to Lincluden Abbey to live with…" She dragged in a ragged breath. "To live with *nuns!*"

Another round of tears and Osborn's awkward attempts to simultaneously soothe and seduce the lass ensued.

Colin turned on his stool so that he could lean against the counter and survey the room. A few patrons had left in the time since Sabine had made her teary appearance, but more had arrived. Now nearly every table was occupied.

The volume in the room had increased as well, and not entirely because of the lass's sobs and Osborn's chattering. The evening had begun in earnest now, which meant that several of the men in the common room were making it their mission to drink as much ale as their coin purses allowed.

A few had taken up a game of dice at one table, while others had turned their attention to cards. Although some still shot lingering looks at Sabine, most seemed to accept that Osborn had claimed a first crack at the lass.

"…only a wee mistake. But she willnae listen. She thinks I am some sort of…*harlot* because…well, because of Thomas. And Henry. And Randolf. And William—but that was only once!"

Without looking, Colin could practically hear Osborn's eyes bulging out of his head.

"Ye mean…ye mean yer dear old Edith is sending ye to a nunnery for being…indiscreet with the lads? Wench! More ale, if ye please!"

"Aye," Sabine said. "But I loved each one, I swear! They were verra kind to me, ye ken. I just wanted to show them what they meant to me."

Colin nearly snorted. Mayhap he had been wrong. The lass wasn't playing Osborn for a free meal—she was just as foolhardy as the messenger. Somehow, Osborn had stumbled upon his perfect match.

Osborn leaned closer to the lass, pouring a cascade of reassurances for her wee transgressions and condolences for her fate with each breath.

How was it that Osborn, the oblivious, chatter-mouthed fool, was having the luckiest night of his life while Colin was left to play nursemaid? And how had Colin convinced himself that this was the best use of his skill, his training, and his dedication to the Bruce's cause?

He shifted slightly on his stool. The waxed parchment wrapped around the King's missive made the faintest crinkling noise, reassuring him that it was still in place where it lay sewn into his tunic's double-layered wool. He'd placed the missive directly over his heart. Someone would have to kill him to get it. Aye, he reminded himself, this was the reason he was here.

"...only have one night left before I am to be shut away in the nunnery for the rest of my life," Sabine was saying. She hiccupped, then giggled behind her hand. How many mugs of ale had Osborn offered her? And how many had the messenger had himself?

Colin leaned over, grabbing a fistful of Osborn's sleeve.

"We need to leave early tomorrow," he said lowly to the messenger.

Osborn swayed slightly on his stool. "Och, I ken that. I take my job verra seriously, thank ye verra much." The words ran together slightly, but Osborn managed to yank his sleeve free of Colin's grasp.

"Dinnae make a fool of yerself," Colin shot back.

"Just because ye are jealous," Osborn whispered loudly, "doesnae mean ye must ruin *my* good fortune, Colin."

Colin would have been sorely tested not to punch Osborn's red, bulbous nose in that moment, except that he sensed a pair of eyes on them.

He turned to find a cloaked man sitting in one of

the common room's dim corners. The man was watching them intently—or more precisely, he was staring at Osborn.

Unease lanced through Colin's gut. Even with an increasingly raucous and crowded room, the man sat quietly, a mug of ale untouched on a small table next to him.

Could this be the very scenario the Bruce feared? Mayhap this shadowy stranger was waiting for Osborn to drink himself silly before making a move.

Colin glanced away casually, keeping his features relaxed. He feigned taking a sip of ale, lazily scanning the room once more. As his eyes skittered across the cloaked figure in the corner, he again found the man's gaze locked on Osborn.

Something was off. The familiar heat of battle surged in his veins as he stood. If the man was a spy and missive thief, he would get far more than he bargained for this eve.

He strode with deadly calm across the crowded common room. Halfway to the man in the corner, he heard a stool clatter to the ground behind him, followed by Sabine's giggle.

A glance over his shoulder revealed Osborn looping his arm around the lass.

"Our chamber will be occupied for the evening, friend," Osborn slurred, a crooked grin on his face. "See ye in the morn."

Muttering a curse, Colin turned back to the corner.

The cloaked man was gone.

Chapter Four

S abine staggered under the weight of Osborn's arm. She forced a flirtatious giggle from her throat as she struggled to keep her footing on the stairs.

"I hope yer room isnae far," she panted, half pulling him up the remaining steps.

"Just there." Osborn pointed a swaying finger at one of the wooden doors down the hallway.

Sabine helped him stumble to the door and waited as he shoved it open. As he fumbled with a flint to light the single candle in the room, she closed the door behind her, drawing in a steadying breath.

As the candle caught and flickered to life, Osborn seemed to lose his courage.

"Och, lassie." He wiped the palms of his hands on his breeches, wetting his lips with his tongue. "Ye look verra fine in the candlelight."

"Thank ye," she said absently, her hand slipping into the folds of her skirt. As her fingers brushed the heavy hilt of her dagger, a strange calm came over her. She knew how to do this.

She stepped forward slowly. "Do I have a treat for ye," she drawled in her well-practiced Lowland accent.

"Close yer eyes."

A lopsided, almost sweet smile touched Osborn's lips as his lids drifted closed. He swayed on his feet. By God, she likely didn't even need the dagger. He was ready to fall flat on his face from the ale already.

She'd been prepared to surreptitiously switch mugs with him all night, letting him nearly drain his own and then passing her full one to him. Instead, he'd gotten soused all by himself. She was grateful for that, for his friend's perceptive gaze had fallen on her enough times to make her sick with fear.

Sabine's Lowland accent was flawless, she knew. Her story, while melodramatic, was plausible. And her fingers were light and quick enough that she had never been caught stealing or even switching cups.

She was good at her job. And yet, Osborn's thug—Colin, she'd heard him called—set her nerves on end. Those bright blue eyes were far too intelligent for him to be considered merely a brute.

The weight of the dagger enclosed in her hand snapped her back to her task. She gripped the gilded hilt. It had been a gift from Fabian, just like the ring that dangled on the chain around her neck.

She took a careful, silent step forward until she could smell the ale wafting from Osborn's breath. With a flick of her wrist, she yanked the dagger free of her skirts.

Arm rising over her head, Sabine inhaled through her teeth. Then with all of her strength, she brought the dagger down on Osborn's head—hilt first.

The heavy hilt thumped against Osborn's skull. With hardly more than a whooshing exhale, he crumpled to the floor.

Sabine watched him in the flickering candlelight for a count of one hundred—another trick Fabian had taught her. She'd never killed before, and she didn't plan on starting tonight. It was easier, this way— cleaner. The messenger would have no memory of this in the morning, nor would she have to deal with a body.

Osborn's breathing was shallow but steady. Sabine exhaled in relief. He wouldn't be waking for a long while. When he did, he'd have a hell of a headache, but he'd likely attribute it to the ale.

Though she knew she had time, unease spurred her to set about her task quickly.

After slipping the dagger back into the folds of her skirt, she knelt over Osborn's prone form and began patting him down.

Mayhap it was the messenger's damned companion that had her pulled tighter than a bowstring. Again, she was plagued by the thought that the man was far more than a bit of hired muscle.

Apparently Fabian had briefed Miles on this assignment before speaking with her, for when she met Miles at their checkpoint in Dumfries that afternoon, he already had a description of both the messenger and his thug. He even had the name of the inn they were staying at just outside the town.

She'd slipped into the inn's second storey by a sheer stroke of luck. A ladder had been left out by the stables. Trusting that the corridor abovestairs would be quiet what with most of the patrons in the common room, she'd propped the ladder below a small window at the end of the hallway and crept up. All she'd had to do then was stash her damp cloak in a shadowy corner at the end of the corridor and make her way downstairs, dabbing a kerchief at her face.

Miles's account of the messenger had been nondescript enough: a thin man approaching middle age, short brown hair, a bulbous nose, and an ever-running mouth. But his description of Colin had hardly prepared her for what she found in the inn's common room.

Miles had said that the man was built like a warrior. He hadn't said that he was so tall and broad of shoulder, so lean and yet so muscular, that he looked like a wild lion barely caged by his simple tunic and breeches. Miles had noted blond hair, not a mane that curled around the man's wide shoulders. That tawny hair was the only part of him that looked at all soft. Miles hadn't been close enough to note the brute's eye color, yet even if he had told Sabine they were blue, it wouldn't have prepared her for the shockingly clear, vibrant gaze that had locked on her when she'd entered the common room.

Nor was she prepared for the sharpness of the assessment he gave not only her, but everyone in the room. Nay, he was not merely a hired thug. He was skilled, that much was obvious.

She'd never had to work so hard at appearing natural as she'd seduced Osborn practically right under Colin's nose. Even feigning disinterest, she'd felt his cool, piercing gaze slide to her several times.

Sabine's fingers brushed against waxed parchment and her thoughts halted abruptly. Her work required her complete focus. Fretting over some man's searching glances was how foolish little girls wasted their energy—not her.

She let her fingers probe delicately along the pocket inside Osborn's tunic. The pocket was simple enough—not sewn shut, but placed carefully over his heart, a very common place for messengers to carry their missives.

Even still, she carefully felt the depth of the pocket, letting her fingers memorize just how deeply the letter was pushed, just how far to the left edge it rested. She would have to put it back exactly as she found it. Even if Osborn wouldn't remember most of this night, Fabian had taught her to be as precise and careful as possible.

Once she was satisfied that she could put the missive back just right, she slid it from the pocket.

She could make out a red seal through the layer of waxed parchment that protected the missive from the elements. Carefully unfolding the outer layer, she brushed her fingertips along the missive.

As she carried the little packet to the table where the candle sat, she slipped the letter from its wrapping. After she placed the wax parchment on the table, she tilted the seal toward the candle to assess it.

A breath caught in her throat at what the candle-light revealed.

It was the King of Scotland's seal.

She'd never encountered it before in the field, but Fabian had sketched it, along with dozens of others, for her to memorize. Especially when her assignments involved memorization rather than retrieval of missives, the seal could often be more important than the words written within.

Though he had drilled countless different seals into her head over the years, she would never mistake this one—a knight brandishing a sword and shield on horseback—for any other than King Robert the Bruce's own mark. He was a warrior King, after all.

Fabian had been right. Whatever this missive contained was of the utmost importance if it came from the quill of a King. Her chest swelled slightly at the thought that Fabian had given her such a significant assignment.

All the more reason to do everything exactly right.

Sabine removed the dagger from her skirts once more, carefully sliding it from its gilded sheath. She held the blade over the candle's flame, turning it slowly to heat it evenly.

When the tip of the blade glowed faintly orange in the dimly lit chamber, she drew in a breath and lowered the dagger to where the missive rested on the table.

With a steady hand, she gently guided the dagger's tip along the folded parchment until it encountered the red wax seal. Carefully, she slid the blade between the parchment and the seal.

Even the slightest of tremors now could crack the seal, ruining the mission and potentially endangering her life. If whoever had paid Fabian so handsomely for the information in this missive discovered that he'd been compromised... She could only imagine what such a powerful man would do to a lowly thief like her.

Relief flooded her as the blade glided smoothly under the seal. With a faint noise, the seal popped up, opening the parchment halfway.

Sabine set the dagger aside and took the missive into her hands. With gentle fingertips, she unfolded another one of the parchment flaps, then another. At last the inside of the missive was bared to the flickering candlelight.

Her jaw slackened in shock at what she found inside.

The parchment was blank.

She turned it over, holding it to the light. The back side was blank also.

Dizzying fear stabbed through her like the hot blade she'd just wielded.

What in…

This didn't make any sense. Why did the missive bear the King of Scotland's seal but naught else? Where was the message? Why had Robert the Bruce sent an empty letter with a messenger—a messenger guarded by a sharp-eyed warrior, no less?

Her mind spun wildly, the blank sheet of parchment trembling in her fingers. She dragged in a ragged breath, trying to force herself to calm down and think clearly.

She glanced down at Osborn's still form, but he couldn't give her any answers. He'd begun snoring lightly, the sound grating on her frayed nerves.

Like a bolt of lightning, a thought struck her.

Osborn was a dupe—as was the blank missive.

"Nay," she breathed as the pieces crashed into place in her mind.

It was far worse than Fabian had suspected. He'd thought that mayhap the thug sent along with Osborn was just for extra protection—the roads were dangerous these days, and the missive was no doubt valuable.

But the blank letter implied something else.

Someone was on to them.

Someone knew that missives were being intercepted, that information was being lifted and passed along.

And not just *someone*—Robert the Bruce, King of Scotland, arguably the most powerful man in the Kingdom at the moment, knew what Fabian was up to.

She had to flee—and she had to warn Fabian.

Those two thoughts clanged through her mind so loudly that she had to resist the urge to cover her ears.

She was in lethal peril, with Osborn sprawled unconscious at her feet, the King of Scotland's missive lying open before her, and Colin sitting belowstairs at this very moment.

Fabian needed to know that they'd been compromised. She owed him her life—she owed him everything. She would do whatever it took to get word of this breach to him.

Heart hammering so hard it nigh jumped into her throat, she reached for her dagger once more. She held the tip over the candle's flame again while she deftly folded the missive with one hand.

There was still a chance that she and Fabian could slide through this ordeal without notice. But she had to do everything exactly right. Aye, the Bruce was on to them, but that didn't mean that she would confirm her presence here this night. If she placed everything back as it was, he would be left unaware that they knew he'd planted the decoy missive with Osborn.

Her thoughts snagged at that. She was tangled in an intricate and deadly web. Forcing her mind to still, she removed the dagger from the flame. For a count of three, she rested the orange tip against the backside of the King's seal. When she pulled the dagger away, the underside of the seal was soft and tacky, while its face, embossed with the armed knight, remained intact.

She pressed the seal into the parchment until it

once again held the blank sheet closed, then quickly rewrapped the missive in its waxed paper. Kneeling beside Osborn, she tucked the packet into the inside pocket where she'd found it, then stood.

There was no time to drag him to the cot a few feet away. Besides, she didn't trust the strength in her trembling limbs at the moment. So she left him lying there, still snoring softly.

All that remained was slipping away from the inn without encountering the perceptive warrior belowstairs again.

Sabine eased open the chamber's door. Finding the hallway empty, she closed the door behind her and glided toward the window she'd used to enter the inn. The sounds of merrymaking drifted to her from the common room, but the voices were faint. No alarm sounded. No one drew nigh.

She snatched her cloak from the corner and spun it around her shoulders, taking a sliver of comfort in lifting the deep hood over her head. She pulled back the wooden shutters and found the ladder right where she'd left it.

The ladder's rungs were slick with rainwater, but her feet and hands were blessedly sure as she descended. When her boots squelched in mud, she allowed herself one steadying breath. Then she darted across the dark space separating the inn from its stables.

Again, no attack was sprung on her as she slipped into the barn. A few of the horses tethered there shifted at her arrival, but they remained quiet. She found the spritely mare Fabian had allowed her to take for this assignment and made quick work of saddling and bridling her.

Just as she mounted the mare, voices rose outside the stable. Her blood froze as she strained to hear, her hands clenching around the reins.

One of the voices was clearly angry, while the other was afraid. Was one of the speakers Colin? She thought his Highland brogue drifted to her ears, but she couldn't be sure. Had he discovered what she'd done?

The voices were too distant for her to make aught out. She would just have to risk drawing their attention as she fled, for she couldn't stay cowering in the stables forever. Fabian needed her.

Nudging the mare forward, she hunched even deeper into her cloak. The mare passed through the door she'd left open. The two men were still speaking loudly to each other near the front of the inn, but Sabine didn't dare glance their way.

With a squeeze of her heels and a snap of the reins, she urged the mare into the drizzling darkness, guiding her toward Dumfries.

Chapter Five

Colin spun in a slow circle.

The man who'd been sitting in the corner a moment before, tucked deep into a dark cloak, was nowhere to be seen.

He strode toward the stairs and squinted into the shadows. He heard Osborn's slurring voice mumble something to the lass he'd taken up there, and then the soft thump of their chamber door closing behind them.

Though he doubted the man had gone up there, he climbed the stairs nonetheless and quickly scanned the corridor. Naught.

Returning to the common room, he caught sight of the innkeeper's wife squeezing between the patrons as she refilled foaming ale in awaiting mugs.

"Madam," he shouted over the now boisterous mass of men.

She bustled by him with a nod and a distracted smile. Clearly she had her hands full, but he needed answers about the suspicious man.

"Madam," he repeated, ducking his head so that there was no mistaking that she heard him. "The man in the corner a moment ago—the quiet one in the cloak—do ye ken who he was?"

She shrugged and tried to move past him, but he caught her arm. Quickly plastering a charming smile on his face, he took the pitcher of ale from her hand and refilled the nearest cup he saw.

"Just a moment of yer time, I swear," he said, still grinning. "And I promise I'll no' slow ye down in yer tasks." For good measure, he winked at her.

Her annoyance melting into a faint smile, she gazed at him for a long moment.

"The man," he prodded. "Have ye seen him before?"

"Oh!" she gave herself a little shake as if waking from a dream. "Ye mean the one who didnae even touch his ale? Nay, I havenae seen him before, though that's no' so unusual. We're only a few miles from Dumfries, and with such honest prices, we get lots of travelers passing through."

She lifted her chin with pride as she spoke.

"When did he arrive?"

"Only this afternoon—about the same time as ye and that old windbag of yers," she replied, her smile dropping at the mention of Osborn.

"Och, aye, windbag indeed," he said, widening his smile. "Ye're lucky ye dinnae have to share a chamber with him tonight—his snoring could wake the dead!"

The innkeeper's wife giggled like a wee lass. Good. He still had her on his side, which meant he should be able to get a bit more information out of her.

"And did ye happen to see which direction he arrived from? The west? The south?"

She shook her head, her brows dropping despondently as if it pained her not to be able to help him.

"Did he say aught to ye?"

"Nay, no' a word. I really must see to the others." She glanced around the common room, her hands wiping down the front of her apron, no doubt a nervous gesture.

Though he could press her further, he would only draw attention to himself, and possibly raise the woman's suspicion. Though some situations called for a harder, more direct approach to extract information, he sensed that this wasn't one of them.

"Thank ye, madam," he said, handing her back the pitcher of ale. He gave her a gallant tilt of the head and flashed another smile calculated to make her titter.

As she did just that, he pivoted and sought the inn's door. He hadn't heard the door open or close when his back had been turned to the man in the corner, but then again, the noise of the tipped over stool, Osborn's drunken shout to him, and the general revelry of the men around him might have muffled the sound.

Colin ducked out the door and into the damp night. The rain had turned into a mist now, and the air was heavy with moisture.

Naught moved around the inn. No flap of a cloak or squelching step in the mud.

He slowly walked toward the stables, the mud

sucking at his boots.

When he reached the wooden structure, he listened for movement within, but all he heard was the soft rustle of animals.

Just then, a flicker of motion caught his eye. A dark figure emerged from the shrubbery not far from the inn's front door.

As the figure stepped toward the inn, Colin darted forward. He grabbed the man by the front of his cloak, giving him a shake.

"What have we here?"

The man yelped in surprise, his cloak hood falling back. The same dark eyes, now rounded with shock rather than narrowed in observation, met Colin's hard stare.

"What are ye—"

"Who are ye?" Colin barked.

When the man only sputtered, Colin gave him another shake.

"Answer me. Who are ye?"

"M-Michael," the man managed "Michael Gordon."

The name didn't ring any bells. "Why were ye watching my friend?"

"The lass? F-forgive me, milord. I didnae ken she was yer—"

"Nay, no' the lass. The man seated next to me. Dinnae deny that ye were staring, for I saw ye. What were ye about? Who sent ye?"

"Sent me, milord?" Michael's brows collided even as his eyes remained wide. "I dinnae ken what ye mean. I wasnae *about* aught, nor was I sent."

Colin ground his teeth together, his fists tightening around Michael's wool cloak. There was a time for a light touch, for charm and friendliness, and then there was a time like this. "Dinnae toy with me, man. I'll have answers from ye one way or another. What are ye about?"

Michael's throat bobbed as he swallowed hard. "A-aye, I may have been staring, and for that I apologize, milord. But I wasnae staring at the man—or if I was, I meant naught by it. I was…"

"What?" Colin snapped.

"I was staring at the lass." Michael flinched back as if Colin had raised a fist at his face. When no blow landed, he opened one eye. "I meant no harm, I swear. I didnae ken she was yer friend."

The wheels of realization ground painfully in Colin's mind. "Ye were staring at the lass," he said flatly. "To whom ye think I have some claim."

"Was she no'… Is she no' yer…yer whore?"

"What the bloody hell gave ye that impression?"

"Well, ye were sitting next to the man whom she seemed to target. He showed her a bit of coin, which made her stay. Ye were keeping an eye on them. And then they went abovestairs."

Colin cursed. The lass's entrance, Osborn putting a coin on the counter for the innkeeper to serve her, and their drunken departure all appeared different now. Hell, even her interest in Osborn should have tipped Colin off—she was likely a prostitute looking for an easy mark.

"I was only watching to see if the man might turn the lass down. If he had…well, I would have been more than happy to take his place and—"

"Enough," Colin growled.

"When she went abovestairs with him, I came out to piss, and then ye grabbed me, and—"

Now the man was blubbering.

"I said enough," Colin repeated, but this time he lowered his voice. Slowly, he released his hold on the man's cloak, smoothing the material where he rumpled it. "Go back inside."

Michael nodded swiftly, his eyes still rounded with fear. He slipped around Colin and disappeared into the inn.

As Colin watched him go, someone emerged from the stables atop a horse. A dark cloak fluttered around a small figure. Though the light was low, he noticed a green skirt peeking out from the cloak where the figure's boots sat in the stirrups.

The figure darted off into the night headed toward Dumfries before Colin could raise his voice in a shout.

What the bloody hell was going on?

The figure on horseback must have been Sabine Armstrong, for she'd been wearing just such a green dress. But no more than ten minutes could have elapsed between when she went upstairs with Osborn to now.

If it had been another night and another mission, Colin would have laughed until tears came to his eyes at the thought that Osborn, for all his bigmouthed boasting, had only lasted a few minutes with the lass. But instead of mirth, unease swelled in his belly.

Was the lass a prostitute after all? Why had she left in such a hurry? Some unnamed instinct whispered in the back of Colin's mind that something was off.

Colin stormed back into the inn and shoved his way through the drunken men in the common room until he reached the stairs. He took them two at a time and made a direct line to the chamber he shared with Osborn.

Without preamble, he shoved the door open. A half-spent candle on a nearby table fluttered, casting flickering light over the chamber.

Osborn lay sprawled on the floor not far from the bed, snoring lightly. Naught else in the chamber was out of place.

Colin stepped forward and crouched at Osborn's side. The man might very well have simply fallen over drunk right in the middle of the floor. That would explain Sabine's hasty departure if she was indeed a prostitute.

He hefted the pouch on Osborn's belt. Several coins clinked together inside. Another bit of strangeness. Why wouldn't Sabine simply steal the coins if she was a woman for hire?

Suddenly a far darker possibility gripped him. His hand dove into Osborn's tunic, searching for the pocket where he knew the dummy letter sat.

His heart slowed briefly at the feel of the letter in its proper place. Even still, he pulled it out and quickly discarded the protective wax parchment.

Inside, the Bruce's seal was unbroken.

Colin exhaled as his finger ran over the seal. It had been foolish to suspect the lass, of course, but something about the whole night had made him as jumpy as—

He'd absently pressed on the King's seal with his thumb as he'd held the missive. Underneath the pad of his thumb, the seal had compressed ever so slightly.

He tilted the missive toward the light.

Colin's stomach plummeted to his feet.

There around the base of the seal, an extra ring of red wax had seeped out when he'd pressed on it.

The seal had been heated, the missive opened, and the seal reheated so that it could be sealed again. Bloody hell, the wax was still soft enough from the operation that the light pressure from Colin's thumb had made a mess of the careful work.

Only one person had come into the chamber with Osborn. And only one person had just fled the inn.

Sabine.

Colin tossed the letter to the ground, leaving Osborn to sleep off whatever she'd done to him. He tore through the door, then charged down the stairs and out the inn toward the stables.

What a sodding, blind fool he'd been. The whole evening, he'd been looking for some cloaked fiend or masked villain, as if whoever was spying on the Bruce's missives would announce himself so obviously.

Meanwhile, a conniving slip of a lass had waltzed right under his nose and made a fool of him.

The old wound from eight years past flared deep in his chest. He'd vowed never to be duped again—not after what Joan had done to him. And yet tonight he'd been taken in by a pair of pretty eyes and the easy flirtations of a practiced deceiver, gullible arse that he was.

As he swung onto his stallion's back, he cursed himself all over again. There was more at stake here than his wounded pride. The King had entrusted him not only to deliver a message to his brother, but also to weed out the threat of spies. And Colin had let the devious lass slip right through his fingers.

He spurred his horse hard toward Dumfries. There was still time to set his failure to rights.

He wasn't through with Sabine Armstrong just yet.

Chapter Six

Sabine reined in the exhausted mare when the River Nith came into view. Though the inn had only been a small handful of miles from Dumfries, the roads were churned into a muddy mess, making for difficult footing for the horse even as Sabine had forced her ever faster.

The river looked like a wide black ribbon where it slid silently around the town's wall. The moon gave off a diffuse, weak light from behind the bank of gray clouds overhead. Normally she would have shuddered at the clinging darkness, but tonight she was grateful for it.

Spotting Devorgilla's Bridge farther down the river, she urged the mare into a walk. When the horse's hooves clopped against the bridge's wooden planks, Sabine pulled her to a halt.

Pursing her lips, she let out a low, trilling whistle. The mare sidestepped nervously at the sound, her hooves loud again on the bridge.

Sabine waited, barely remembering to breathe. The misting rain continued to drift around her, casting everything in dim haloes. Unease sat like a stone in her belly. Where was Miles?

At last, the door on the bridge's gatehouse at the other end of the wooden expanse swung open. A large figure loomed out and began making his way across the bridge.

When Miles reached her, she allowed herself one moment of relief before fear once again pinched her chest.

"That was quick," Miles murmured, looking warily behind her. "I wasn't expecting—"

"Miles, we are all in danger," she panted.

Mile's large body stiffened as if he were about to launch an attack, but there was no one nearby. "What?"

"The missive I was sent to intercept—it bore the seal of Robert the Bruce."

He nodded, unsurprised. How much had Fabian known before sending her on this assignment? And how much had he told Miles, all the while leaving Sabine in the dark?

She shoved the questions—and the prick of hurt they caused—aside. There was no time for silliness now.

"The missive was blank," she blurted. "I think the King must know that someone has been intercepting his correspondence."

Sabine could only assume that such work had been Fabian's doing. He ran the largest organization of information gathering and selling in all of England, or so he said. And now he was expanding into Scotland—his clients were clamoring for it.

She knew she wasn't his only thief, though she'd never met anyone in his organization other than Miles. Fabian said it was safer that way. Now she wished she had known that he'd sent others before her to read the King's missives. If she had slipped up in any way, she may have lost her life—but then again, that was always the case.

This new revelation had Miles's dark eyes widening.

"I left no sign of my presence," she added quickly, "but I fear we may have been compromised. Fabian needs to know immediately."

Miles nodded swiftly. "I'll get my horse."

As Miles's footsteps faded down the bridge, Sabine couldn't help the shiver that raced up her spine. In all her years of thieving, never had she felt more exposed, more endangered, than she did right now.

She swung the mare around, her gaze searching the road she'd taken from the inn to the north of Dumfries. The road was empty and silent, as was the entire town of Dumfries beyond the city wall.

Her eyes traveled west to where the forest sat thick and black. Was someone watching her, or was it only her fear that caused the hairs on the back of her neck to stand up?

She nearly cried out with fright at the sound of horse hooves clattering at the far end of the bridge. She spun back around to find Miles riding toward her.

"If we are separated, do everything you can to reach Fabian," Miles said tersely.

"Aye, of course," she breathed.

Without another word, Miles spurred his horse east.

She could only hope that Fabian hadn't moved his headquarters yet again in the few days since he'd sent her on this assignment. She'd lost count of all his safe houses over the years. He never liked to stay in one place for too long, but sometimes that meant it was challenging to find him.

That was what Miles was supposed to be for. He was her only contact in the field. She reported to him, and then he'd lead her back to Fabian. But Miles was currently disappearing into the dark gloom ahead of her. If she didn't keep up, she'd have no certain way of getting her news to Fabian.

She leaned low over the mare's neck, squeezing her heels firmly into the animal's flanks.

Just as the mare burst forward, an enormous mounted figure lunged from the shadows directly in front of her.

The mare skidded in the mud, then reared, nearly unseating Sabine. Just as she got the mare under control, a hand shot out and snatched the reins from her grasp.

"There ye are, lass."

Panic spiked through her. The words were growled

with an unmistakable Highland brogue. *Colin.*

"I have a few questions for ye, and I'm sure ye'll provide some most interesting answers."

Chapter Seven

S abine's gaze shot past Colin's looming form. Miles and his horse were just being swallowed by the misty gloom ahead. She could call out to him, but then if Colin managed to overpower both her and Miles, word would never reach Fabian that he had been compromised.

Nay, Miles couldn't help her now. She had to help herself.

Sabine wrapped one hand around her saddle's pommel, then snatched the reins above where Colin's large hand held them.

With a deep breath and a fleeting prayer, she dug her heels into the mare's flanks hard and jerked back on the reins with all her strength.

The animal, already spooked from Colin's sudden appearance, neighed in distress and reared again. Sabine clung to the pommel for dear life. She heard Colin curse over the horse's cry, and his hand vanished from the reins.

Now his own animal danced wildly back from the rearing mare, its ears flat.

As the mare's front hooves connected with the

ground, Sabine knew she would only have this one heartbeat of distraction to escape.

Just as Colin got his steed under control, she jerked the mare around, pointing her toward the shadowy forests to the west. Sabine kicked the horse once more, slapping the reins. The mare bolted forward, unleashing all her pent energy in a swift gallop.

Though the mare had already proven herself brave-hearted and spritely, there was no way she could outrun Colin's enormous stallion on the open road, even with the mud slowing both of them down. Nay, Sabine's only chance of escape would be to lose him in the woods. She wasn't familiar with these forests, but she prayed she could evade Colin and his steed in the tightly packed trees and tangling underbrush.

Behind her, she heard Colin curse again as he gave chase. She leaned low over the mare's neck, whispering encouragements as she flew across the open space separating Dumfries's town wall and the looming forest.

Pounding hooves drew closer behind her. She dared a glance over her shoulder. Colin was hunched low, his golden hair nigh glowing in the diffuse gray light. The black stallion surged forward, closing the distance between them with each long, powerful stride.

Sabine urged the mare on, watching the forest line draw nearer. Out of the corner of her eye, she caught sight of Colin inching up on her right side. His stallion's head was even with her mare's flank, then the back of her saddle, then her neck.

Just as Colin's large hand darted out toward her reins once more, they both plunged headlong into the tree line.

Colin was forced to veer away as a row of trees whizzed by between their horses. Sabine tugged the mare to the left, putting more distance between them.

It was even darker under the cover of the trees. Strange shadows loomed toward her as she pushed her horse deeper into the woods.

The mare was forced to slow as she wove around trees and clambered over fallen logs. Shrubs clawed at Sabine's cloak and skirts. Branches whipped at her face. Her hood had fallen back in her desperate dash away from Colin, and now twigs tangled in her unbound hair.

A loud snap behind her sent her heart jumping into her throat.

"Ye'll no' lose me so easily, lass." Colin's voice echoed through the misty woods not far away.

Despite the mare's caution in the dark, uneven terrain, Sabine squeezed her heels and snapped the reins again. The horse whinnied her objection but quickened her pace.

Sabine shot a look over her shoulder. Emerging between the trees, Colin's black steed strode forward as if stepping from a nightmare. Shrubs parted around the stallion's powerful chest as Colin urged him on.

Though Colin's face was shrouded in shadow, a

chilling shudder raced through her as she felt more than saw his gaze lock on her.

The pounding of her own blood was nigh deafening, her breath ragged in her throat. Never before had she sensed her death so close at hand.

Just then, her mare placed a hoof into a bramble of ferns. What should have been solid ground under the ferns suddenly gave way. Dimly, Sabine realized that the mare had actually stepped on a rotted out fallen log.

The mare stumbled forward with a snort of surprise. Sabine was sent tumbling over the horse's neck.

As the dark forest floor raced toward her, a scream ripped from her throat. She thrust out her arms, but there wasn't enough time to catch herself. She turned, landing on her left arm and rolling to the side.

A sickening pop reverberated in her shoulder. Pain, sharp and hot, washed through her. Her head spun as her stomach lurched into her throat at the agony radiating from her left shoulder.

Colin bit out an oath not far away. She could feel the vibrations of his horse's hooves through the forest floor where she lay on her side.

God, nay. She could not give up. She would not die lying like a tattered rag doll in the muddy ferns.

Rolling to her right side, she dragged herself to her feet. Her left arm dangled limply, the shoulder hanging unnaturally low. It was likely dislocated. She could survive that—but she would not survive if she were taken down for opening the King of Scotland's missive.

Sabine reached for the mare, who had regained her footing, but the poor animal was so spooked that she nickered and sidestepped out of Sabine's reach.

Still, she refused to surrender. Clutching her limp left arm to her side, she took off on foot.

"Wait, lass!" Colin's voice behind her was no longer so hard-edged. Instead, a note of fear sliced through it.

It couldn't be that he feared for her safety, running off through the darkened woods with a dislocated shoulder. Nay, he was her enemy, she reasoned dimly through the searing pain. He was likely only worried that he would have a hard time maneuvering his horse after her.

With each pounding step, a fresh bolt of pain jolted through her. She clamped her teeth shut on a sob, holding the arm closer to her body to try to stop it from jostling.

She sensed more than heard Colin giving chase behind her, so loud was the hammering of blood in her ears. She darted and was rewarded with a muttered curse from him. Aye, she still had a chance of evading him if he remained on horseback.

As if he had read her thoughts, she heard a thump behind her that could only be the sound of Colin dismounting. Now it was her turn to curse.

She dared a glance back. He was sprinting after her, his tawny hair streaming behind him. He moved like a ghost, his feet gliding impossibly smoothly over the uneven forest floor. Nay, not like a ghost—like a lion on the hunt.

Just then her foot snagged on a protruding root. She tumbled to the ground, managing to land on her right side this time. Even still, agony tore through her like hot lightning as her left shoulder reverberated with the impact.

She couldn't suppress the sob of pain this time. She tried to roll to her feet once more, but her body screamed its protest.

Suddenly, Colin's looming form filled her vision.

"Are ye mad, lass?" he demanded. "Ye could have broken yer neck."

To her pain-addled brain, he seemed even larger and broader than he had at the inn. Somehow his shadowed figure grew and stretched before her eyes.

Her stomach lurched again, and she had to swallow hard to keep from losing its meager contents.

"Lucky for me yer head is still attached to yer shoulders," he said, his voice low and flat. "I'll have my answers now, if ye please."

Colin bent over her, his bright blue eyes materializing from the shadows. A big hand reached toward her to wrap around her left arm.

So it was to be torture, then. Fabian had warned her that if she were ever captured, death would be made slow and painful. She was the most dangerous kind of thief, after all—a thief of secrets.

If Colin intended to tweak her left arm, at least she wouldn't last long. Already, darkness that had naught to do with the night-shrouded forest was creeping in at the edges of her vision.

She had always vowed to Fabian that she would never spill his secrets, no matter what torture was applied. But now that she was nigh drowning in agony, she could only hope that unconsciousness would save her from betraying the only person who'd ever cared for her.

As Colin's hand closed around her limp arm, her ears filled with her own tormented scream.

The firm pressure of his hand suddenly vanished.

"Christ," he muttered. "Yer shoulder is dislocated."

She would have laughed at his obviousness, but she was too busy fighting against the specks of black floating in her vision and the nausea roiling in her stomach.

"Get on with it, then," she mumbled. "If you mean to have answers, do your worst."

Only after the words were out did she realize through the haze of pain that she hadn't used her Lowland accent, and instead had slipped back into her natural-born English one.

She heard him suck in a breath through his teeth.

"Ye are *English*." He spat the word out as if it tasted bitter on his tongue.

It didn't matter now, she supposed distantly. He would torture and kill her either way. But judging from the hatred in his voice at realizing she was English, mayhap he would find a way to make this worse for her.

She clenched her teeth, bracing for the fresh surge of pain she knew was coming.

But his hand closed around her good arm instead.

He pulled her to her feet before him, his eyes sharp and searching through the black spots in her vision. He swayed before her—or rather, she swayed, she realized dimly.

Suddenly she was being lifted as if she weighed naught at all. Colin tucked her against his broad chest, her hurt arm on the outside so that it could nestle limply against her torso.

"W-what are you doing?"

"Taking ye back to Ruith." His voice rumbled through his chest where her good shoulder pressed against it. "And then I'm going to find a good spot to reset yer damned shoulder."

The words were spoken with the sharpness of anger, but for some reason he seemed more annoyed than filled with vicious intent. Even still, mayhap he would draw out the pain, use the resetting of her shoulder as some twisted torture technique. She shuddered against him at the thought.

He murmured another curse, his arms tightening slightly around her.

The forest blurred as he walked. She tried to keep her eyes open, but they kept wanting to lower. Behind the darkness of her lids, however, the world spun dangerously, so she forced herself to drag them up.

A few minutes later, he set her on her feet, keeping a hand fastened on her good arm to hold her upright. With his other hand, he spun his cloak off his shoulders and tossed it onto the damp forest floor.

She heard the black stallion stamp a hoof nearby. Was this Ruith? Distantly, she wondered what had become of the brave little mare.

Then he was easing her back onto his cloak. Why was he doing all this for her? It made no sense. Was he luring her into a false sense of comfort, only to tear it all away, thus making her torture all the more brutal? That was how the world worked, after all—people were cruel and self-serving, and kindness was reserved for the fortunate, wealthy few.

Sabine groaned as she came to rest on her back. Her gaze lazily roamed the little window of overcast sky framed by dark treetops until Colin loomed over her once more.

"This will hurt a mite, lass," he said, his voice surprisingly soft.

He took hold of her left elbow and wrist, then wedged his big knee into her armpit. She sucked in a breath between clenched teeth. Aye, it hurt just to have his hands on the cursed arm.

"Can ye count backward from ten, lass?"

"Aye, of course I can count—forward and backward." It took her a moment to recognize the haughty voice as her own.

Fabian had been right—pain would loosen even the most guarded of tongues. She clamped her jaws together once more.

"Well then, get on with it," Colin shot back.

She dragged in a breath and began counting aloud. She knew what was coming—when she reached one, he would torque her aching arm. She'd heard of the counting technique. Fabian said it was used to make victims feel as if it was in their control to avoid the pain of torture. If she only answered his questions before she got to one, she could be free of the pain.

"Four...three..." Sabine swallowed and drew in a breath.

But before she reached one, his hands tightened on her. A fraction of a second later, he yanked hard on her arm, driving his knee against her armpit.

A loud thunk filled the air as her shoulder popped back into place.

Just before Sabine's mind at last slipped into blessed unconsciousness, a strange thought occurred to her.

She hadn't told him aught, and yet as her shoulder slid into place, the pain dropped off substantially.

Why would he do that? What kind of man was this Highland warrior?

Chapter Eight

It was Colin's habit to rise at dawn—too many years as a warrior meant that whether he slept in a downy bed or on the muddy ground, the first hints of morning light would rouse him.

It didn't matter that he'd only slept a few hours last night. When the sun began to warm the eastern horizon, he woke.

He tucked the length of green and blue MacKay plaid that he'd used as a bedroll back into Ruith's saddlebags. Then he set about making a fire, for although the August air did not yet hold the sting of fall, everything he wore was damp.

At least the rain had finally let up during the night. He didn't know what he would have done with the unconscious lass lying on his cloak nearby if they had been caught in a storm.

All morning, he was careful not to stare at her, yet his thoughts were consumed by her.

What was he to do with the lass?

If he rode back to Lochmaben now, he could deliver her to the Bruce. The King needed to know that his suspicions had been correct, and he'd want to find out as much as he could from the lass about who she worked for.

But then again, the lass had led him on one hell of a chase. They were more than an hour west of Dumfries now. It had taken him a day and a half just to get this far from Lochmaben. If he rode back to the King's camp, he would be setting himself back from reaching Ireland by three full days.

The Bruce had conveyed in no uncertain terms that the missive Colin carried for the King's brother, Edward Bruce, was of utmost importance—and urgency. Though Colin didn't know the exact contents of the missive, he could guess that it had something to do with a tactical decision in Edward Bruce's ongoing quest to claim Ireland in the name of the King of Scotland. Would a three-day delay cost men's lives?

His thoughts roiled throughout the morning as he slowly made camp. All the while, the lass slept.

When he could no longer find aught with which to busy his hands, he squatted across the fire from where she lay and let himself truly look at her.

In the weak gray light of the overcast day, her skin looked pale. It stood out starkly against her dark pillow of hair and their two cloaks. Her delicately carved cheeks bore no hint of a healthy flush. At least her soft, full lips were rosy.

Her slow, steady breath made her gently curved chest rise and fall rhythmically. He'd flipped the edges of her cloak over her after she'd passed out, but he imagined that the rest of her skin was just as milky white as her face.

She looked innocent in sleep. He clenched his hands against the memory of the feel of her in his arms. She'd been so slight, so fragile, despite her valiant determination to flee him.

Colin shook himself. She was a bloody spy, and an English one at that. Had he learned naught from Joan's betrayal? He thought he'd rid himself of the tendency to be blinded by a lass's beauty, and yet here he was, imagining that the wee lass lying before him was innocent.

She'd already duped him once. He'd be damned if he let her do it again.

As Colin took up a stick and began whittling it idly, he felt himself being watched. He looked across the fire to find the lass's big hazel eyes observing him guardedly.

"Morning," he said. He looked up at the heavily clouded sky. "Or rather, afternoon."

"How long did I…" Her voice was rough and low from disuse.

Colin stood, throwing the stick into the fire but keeping a firm grasp on his knife. He stepped around the fire and to Ruith's side, digging in one of the saddlebags for his waterskin.

When he turned and approached her, those green-gold eyes rounded, locking on the blade in his hand. He tossed the waterskin next to her, then resumed his crouch on the other side of the fire, taking up a new stick.

She didn't move for a long time. Colin glanced up at her, only to find confusion lurking in the depths of her eyes. Her dark brows winged down, furrowing her creamy skin. At last, she took up the waterskin with her good hand and took a long drag.

Colin watched her slim throat bob as she drank. "I had begun to worry that ye wouldnae wake at all today."

She wiped the back of her hand across her lips, still watching him nervously.

"What is yer name?"

She stared at him silently.

He sighed. How the bloody hell was he supposed to proceed with a hostile, tight-lipped Englishwoman spy?

"I take it ye are no' a Lowland Armstrong, so that much at least is established. Is yer given name really Sabine?"

She shifted slightly, wincing as she gingerly repositioned her left arm across her body.

Colin gritted his teeth. Perhaps a new approach was needed.

"Have ye ever dislocated that shoulder before?"

After a pause, she shook her head slowly, her eyes never leaving his.

At last, a response.

"It will pain ye for several days, but if I set it correctly, it shouldnae be nearly as bad as before. How does it feel?"

She swallowed, her wary eyes still pinning him. "It…is better," she said finally. "It is stiff and sore, but the sharp pain from last night is gone."

"Good. Ye'll need to wear a sling on it in the coming days."

Again, confusion, followed quickly by guardedness, flashed across her features.

Colin stood again and retrieved a few dry biscuits from his saddlebag. When he turned once more to her, terror had replaced her wariness. Her lips paled as she pressed them together, her eyes wide on the knife he still carried.

He crouched next to her, and she flinched back. "Don't—" she breathed.

"Dinnae what? Keep ye alive by feeding ye this stuff?" he snapped, holding up the biscuits.

"You mean…you aren't going to torture me?"

Christ. What had the lass been through to make her assume he would ply her flesh with his dagger? Aye, she was a criminal, but he wasn't a monster.

"Nay, I'm no' going to torture ye. I've never meted out violence on a woman—enemy or nay. I may be a Highlander, but I am no' a barbarian."

Her features softened with surprise, and she suddenly looked younger—not some seasoned criminal but a lass barely into womanhood.

"Then…then what will you do with me?"

Colin dragged a hand through his hair. Bloody hell, he was in a bind. The Bruce had given him two equally important missions, and he could only think of one way to accomplish both of them.

"I'm taking ye with me."

Her eyes rounded again, and he noticed the intricate pattern of gold flakes in their green depths. "W-where?"

"West. That's all ye need to ken for the time being."

She glanced at where Ruith stood tethered, her brows furrowing once more.

"What happened to my mare?"

"She was so spooked after she unseated ye that she took off headed back toward Dumfries. Ye're lucky ye didnae lame the poor animal. As it is, someone will be verra happy to find her."

"Then what am I to ride?"

"Ye'll ride with me. That way I can be sure ye willnae attempt some wild flight again."

The lass sat mutely while Colin broke their rudimentary camp. He kicked damp soil over the fire, tucked his blade into his boot, and tightened the flaps over Ruith's saddlebags.

He also unfastened his sword, which was strapped to the outside of one of the bags, and belted it around his waist. Though he would have liked to check the blade to make sure no moisture had gotten into the sheath, he imagined that doing so would only send the lass into a panic again.

At last he turned to her, a scrap of his MacKay plaid in his hands. Crouching, he looped the strip of plaid over her injured shoulder and under her arm. As he tied off the sling, she watched him as a doe watches a wolf.

Though he didn't seek to terrorize her, it was good that she remembered their roles—they were enemies, and she was now his captive.

He lifted her by her good elbow from the forest floor, then shook out his cloak, which had served as her bedroll.

Wrapping his hands around her waist, he lifted her onto the saddle. As she settled herself, he spun his cloak around his shoulders despite its dampness.

Damn. The material smelled of wet wool and ferns and soil, but also something soft and feminine. Was that the scent of the lass's hair?

"My name truly is Sabine, by the way."

He stilled at her quietly spoken words.

"Sabine what?"

Her good hand rose to her collarbone, where the thin chain around her neck disappeared into her bodice. "Just Sabine. I don't have any other name."

He forced his mouth into a wolfish smile, making his eyes go hard for what he had to do next. "I am Colin MacKay. Pleasure to meet ye."

Just as the corners of her rosy mouth began to relax, he produced a short length of rope and began binding her good wrist to the saddle's pommel.

"What are you doing?" she gasped.

"As I said, I cannae have ye attempting to slip away again," he replied flatly.

Outrage flared in her gaze, but she clamped her lips shut.

Colin hoisted himself into the saddle behind her, his thighs sliding around hers and her bottom fitting snugly against his groin. That soft, feminine scent wafted to his nostrils again. Aye, it was definitely drifting from Sabine's sable hair.

It would take him a fortnight to reach Ireland, deliver his missive, and return to Lochmaben where he could hand Sabine over for the King's judgement.

Only a fortnight, he told himself as he spurred Ruith forward. He could get through one fortnight.

Chapter Nine

Fabian carefully slipped another folded missive into one of the many stacks covering his desk.

That particular pile was to be delivered to the Earl of Arundel. They contained quite lurid details about one of Arundel's rival earls—something about a young male lover, as Fabian recalled overhearing.

Arundel would no doubt use the letters to blackmail his rival. Fabian smiled to himself. There was something pure about the transaction. Arundel paid Fabian. Fabian produced the missives. Then the Earl's rival paid Arundel. It was almost quaint in its simplicity.

Of course, not all of Fabian's dealings were quite so straightforward. This was the modern era, after all. Not everything could be solved by simply stealing a missive and selling its contents. Nay, these days, it was all so terribly complicated.

Fabian pinched the bridge of his nose. Now not only did he have to maintain his network of pickpockets and missive lifters, but he also had to juggle the ones who dealt purely in information. Not every situation could be solved by stealing a letter, which meant that he had to train his underlings to read, to open missives while making sure the seal was unbroken, and to be able to memorize and report back to him.

He looked across the sea of parchment before him. Even in these advanced times, he supposed he still fundamentally dealt in the simple reality of paper. He kept careful records of every favor owed him, every balance unmet, every promise whispered in gratitude or in fear.

Hopefully with Robert the Bruce stationed in Lochmaben for the foreseeable future, he wouldn't have to leave this convenient base of operations not far outside of Carlisle. It was always such a terrible head-ache to move his meticulously stacked records.

A loud rap on the door yanked Fabian from his musings.

"It is Miles, milord." The man's voice was urgent through the thick wood.

"Enter."

Mile's enormous form nigh took up the entire doorframe as he entered.

Even a quick glance at the man told Fabian something was wrong. Miles's boots and breeches were splattered with mud, his tunic and uncovered head damp. Though he was a strong, powerful man, he gasped for breath as if he'd just had to run for his life.

Miles dipped his dark head in a quick bow.

"Out with it," Fabian said sharply.

"Sabine has discovered something...most worrisome, milord."

Fabian's gut coiled with apprehension. "What happened?"

"I gave her the description and location of the Bruce's messenger and the brute riding with him yesterday afternoon. Then yestereve, she showed up at Devorgilla's Bridge and whistled for me."

Fabian rolled his wrist with impatience, urging Miles on.

"She said she had no trouble getting to the messenger, milord, but that once she opened the missive, it was blank."

Cold comprehension washed through Fabian's veins like ice water.

"She's sure it was the Bruce's missive?"

"She seemed sure, milord. She believes the Bruce is on to you, and perhaps even hoped to catch you in his trap with that blank missive."

Fabian's hand slid over his mouth to finger his neatly trimmed goatee. "Ah. And the messenger's bodyguard—he was actually the King's plant."

Miles nodded. Though the giant of a man was kept on more for his brawn than his brains, it was obvious enough that even he had managed to piece it together. Fabian muttered a curse.

"And where is Sabine now?"

"I left her behind in Dumfries. I told her to find her way to you, but I believe…"

Fabian slapped his hand on his desk, sending several scraps of parchment fluttering. "Speak!"

Miles's dark eyes turned flat. There was the obedient warrior Fabian needed. All it took was a show of anger.

"I believe the King's brute caught up with her. When I realized she wasn't behind me, I saw a rider approach her from behind."

A new fear seized Fabian's innards. "Do you think she has turned on me?"

"Nay, milord," Miles answered quickly. "Her only thought when she told me of the blank missive was to get word to you as swiftly as possible. She is still loyal."

Fabian waved his hand in annoyance. "Nay, you fool," he snapped. "I didn't believe she was working with the man already. I have her too well trained for that. I meant—do you think she *could* be turned against me? You've seen her in the field. If certain...pressures were applied, might she compromise me?"

Miles remained silent for a long moment. At last, he spoke. "I cannot be certain, milord. As you say, you have her well trained. But many things can happen in the field."

Fabian stroked his goatee in thought. Though he had once been little more than a hungry pickpocket himself, it had been years since he'd actually worked in the field.

He'd grown up in a brothel, his mother and the other whores encouraging his light fingers to lift extra coins from the patrons. Once he'd become a man himself, he'd taken over the running of the brothel and found the manipulation of people's hopes and fears much more satisfying—and lucrative—than simply picking pockets.

He'd built this network—nay, *empire*—of thieves and spies singlehandedly. The most powerful men in all of England sought him out. With his expansion into the Scottish Lowlands, his reach and his wealth were sure to double.

What was all that worth? What did Sabine know, and how much did her life cost?

Fabian exhaled slowly, disappointed at the decision he knew he had to make. He'd recruited her young— he found that children were easier to manipulate—and trained her personally. She'd been especially responsive to the idea that he cared for her, that she was special to him somehow. Many orphans were.

Sabine's sharp mind had proven suited for lessons in reading and memorization, for which he was pleased. Finding street urchins with those predilections was rare.

He'd even saved her virginity all these years in the hopes that it could be used strategically for his gain someday. He'd fantasized about earning a King's ransom if he sent her to be bedded by some powerful earl or other. The incident could be used as blackmail—or even payment, for she was a pretty young thing.

He clucked his tongue at his own hesitation. Aye, she was a sweet little pawn, but she wasn't worth all that he'd built over the years.

Sighing again, he brought his attention back to Miles.

"Both the Bruce's messenger and the bodyguard have seen her. As far as you know, she is in the thug's hands, and the Bruce knows that his missives have been compromised."

Miles nodded again mutely.

"I suppose there is only one course of action then." He smoothed his silk vest, rolling his head on his neck. "Kill her."

"Aye, milord." Miles's coarse features were impassive at the order. It wasn't his first time with such a task, after all. In this line of work, secrecy was everything—and secrecy sometimes must be paid for in blood.

"Take a man or two with you. The twins, mayhap. Go back to Dumfries and see if you can track her or the Bruce's thug down. Report back to me when the task is complete."

"Aye, milord," Miles repeated. With a quick bow, he ducked out of Fabian's chamber.

Fabian returned his attention to his stacks of secrets and promises, tidbits of information and bills for satisfied clients. A flicker of disappointment once again slid through him at the loss of such a valuable tool as Sabine, but it vanished as he lifted a new slip of parchment.

Chapter Ten

By the time blue-gray dusk fell, Sabine's shoulder pulsed with pain so great that she could feel it throbbing in her clenched teeth. With each of the horse's steps, her arm jostled, shooting aching agony into her shoulder. The sling kept her from having to hold her arm up, but it did naught to alleviate the clopping of the large stallion's hooves.

She bit the inside of her cheek to keep from moaning.

"Are we going to stop soon?" she managed when she couldn't stand the pain any longer.

"Aye, soon enough," Colin said gruffly. But suddenly he stiffened behind her. "Ye are in pain."

She was too exhausted to deny it. "Aye."

"Ye should have said something earlier, lass," he said, though there was no longer an edge to his voice.

He wrapped a hard arm around her chest, his hand closing over her injured shoulder.

She inhaled sharply, fearing a fresh wave of agony, but instead his hand supported her shoulder, smoothing the roughest of the jolts. He held her close against his chest so that her body rolled with his instead of jarring with each of the horse's steps.

She couldn't help the little whimper of relief that slipped from her lips as his fingers began to gently massage the aching joint.

How could he be so hard and so gentle at the same time? Before the pain in her shoulder had grown so overpowering, she'd been acutely aware of Colin's warm, muscular form behind her—nay, not just behind her, but *around* her. His corded thighs encased hers, the large hand holding the reins dangerously close to brushing her stomach.

And now his steely forearm pressed against her breasts as that callused hand massaged her shoulder. Another moan of relief slipped past her lips as his fingers worked magic on her sore muscles.

The black outline of a little village against the twilit sky jerked her back to reality. How could she be mewling like a well-fed kitten, melting into Colin's arms, when he was her enemy?

None of this made sense. Why hadn't he tortured her yet? And if he was to be believed, he wasn't going to torture her at all. The grudging gentleness of this Highland warrior didn't fit with everything Fabian had told her of the world. Hell, she'd seen a bit of the world herself, and Colin's kindness didn't add up.

But never mind all that. He was still holding her against her will, keeping her from Fabian. They were traveling west rather than east, where she knew Robert the Bruce had stationed himself in Lochmaben. Mayhap Colin had something worse in store for her than turning her over to his King as a missive thief.

Whatever he was up to, she was still in trouble. With any luck, Miles had already reached Fabian and told him of the Bruce's blank missive. Mayhap Fabian was already on the move again, hunkering down in some safe house or distant town where he could lie low for a while. He'd always made it clear that if she were ever compromised in the field, it would be too dangerous for him to retrieve her. She'd have to take care of herself.

She shifted a little in the saddle, accidentally shoving her bottom into the crux of his thighs. Colin exhaled sharply, his fingers stiffening on her shoulder for the briefest moment before resuming their careful massage.

Sabine cursed herself for a fool. She had to think, had to form a plan.

If Colin wasn't going to torture information out of her, he just might be lax enough to allow her to escape. She could head back toward Carlisle and see if she could pick up a trace of Fabian. With a little luck and a lot of work, she might be able to find him again.

But first she had to free herself from Colin. This little village they were riding into might provide just the opportunity.

"Are we stopping here?" she asked, cursing herself again for the thinness of her voice.

"Aye," Colin rasped, his hand dropping from her

shoulder. "If ye behave yerself, ye may even get to sleep in a bed tonight instead of on the wet ground."

He flicked the left side of her cloak over her slung shoulder, and the right side over where her wrist was bound to the saddle's pommel. "Dinnae even think of causing trouble," he murmured against her ear. "And dinnae say aught in that bloody English accent of yers."

A shiver raised the hairs on the nape of her neck, but she wasn't sure if it was from the dark warning in his voice or the way his lips had grazed her lobe when he'd spoken so softly into her ear.

She nodded curtly, not trusting her voice.

Colin guided his horse past the first row of buildings and down a narrower road into the heart of the village. A few of the huts and two-story shops glowed from the inside with candlelight, but most were dark.

An inn came into view ahead, the double doors of its common room thrown open to the mild evening air. Light and cheery noise spilled out into the muddy street as they approached.

Colin reined the stallion off to the right, where the inn's dim stables sat.

"I willnae warn ye again," he said in that low, velvety voice. He slid from the horse's back and took the reins, walking the animal, Sabine still tied to his back, toward the stables.

As they reached the stables, a lad perhaps a year or two younger than Sabine emerged from the shadows.

"Can I help ye with yer horse, milord?" the lad

asked.

"Nay, but thank ye," Colin said, his voice light and friendly all of a sudden. "My wife and I would greatly appreciate it if ye'd see the innkeeper about a room for us, though."

Sabine nigh jumped out of her skin at the word "wife," so casually spoken in his lilting brogue— referring to *her*. She swallowed her surprise quickly. She needed to keep her wits sharp if an opportunity to escape presented itself.

Colin was clearly trying to rid himself of the stable lad. So, he thought the less others saw and interacted with them, the safer he'd be from curious eyes or the risk of Sabine acting up. An idea began to form at the realization, but it would mean she'd have to act fast before her window of opportunity vanished.

As Colin led her and the stallion into the stables, the sound of hooves sucking in mud drew up behind them.

"Evening," the solitary man said cheerily, dismounting from his horse with a grunt. He landed with a splat in the mud.

Colin nodded in greeting, leading Sabine deeper into the stables.

"One room for ye inside, milord," the lad said, appearing at the stable doors next to the newcomer. "And for ye, milord? May I assist ye with yer horse or secure a room at the inn?"

This was as good an opportunity as Sabine could

hope for. Though the lad looked rather scrawny and she couldn't see in the twilight dimness if the solitary rider bore a weapon, she was unlikely to have access to anyone else for the rest of the night.

She dragged in a deep breath.

"Help me!" she shrieked, startling not only the men in the stable but the horses as well. "This man has kidnapped me and holds me against my will!"

She flicked her right shoulder back, revealing her bound wrist.

If it was a commotion she wanted, she didn't get one. Instead, the stable lad's jaw dropped open and the rider's eyes rounded in shock.

She'd been careful to use her Lowland accent, since she doubted these Scots would much care if one of their countrymen had stolen an Englishwoman. And they could see that she was tied to the saddle—couldn't they? Why were they just staring at her?

"Foolish lass," Colin growled, glaring up at her.

"Help me, please!" she tried again, turning a pleading gaze on the two at the door.

At last, they seemed to come to their senses.

"What's all this about?" the newcomer asked cautiously, taking a step forward.

Colin casually tossed back one side of his cloak to reveal the jutting hilt of his longsword.

"Leave it, friend." His voice was deceptively calm, for this close, Sabine could see that his whole body had tensed in preparation for a fight.

"He kidnapped me," Sabine said again in a rush. "He took me from my home and I dinnae ken what he'll—"

"Sabine, enough!"

"Calm down, man," the lone rider said, taking another step forward. "There is no reason why we cannae sort this out." Though his words were spoken judiciously, he too flicked back his cloak to reveal a sheathed sword.

The stable lad sidled behind the other man uncertainly, his eyes wide and shifting between Colin and Sabine.

"Bloody hell," Colin muttered, sounding suddenly resigned to something unpleasant.

Abruptly, he yanked his sword from its scabbard. He moved like lighting across the stables. A startled cry rose in Sabine's throat, but she swallowed it. This was exactly what she wanted.

Twisting in the saddle, she had to stifle another gasp of surprise. Colin's blade flashed dully in the dim light, but he wielded the hilt end at the rider. The man ducked under the hilt, which had been aimed at his skull, just as the stable lad sent up a shout for help.

Sabine's chance for escape was slipping away all too quickly. She twisted her wrist hard against the rope binding her to the pommel, but Colin's knot held. Biting back a cry of pain as the coarse rope grated against her skin, she leaned forward, this time with the intent of snatching the horse's reins with her left hand, which hung limply from its sling.

Her shoulder screamed in protest at the movement as she fumbled to reach the reins, which dangled from the horse's mouth.

Colin threw his shoulder into the rider, knocking him off balance. He raised the heavy hilt of his sword once more and brought it down on the man's head. The rider slumped to the ground with a moan, knocked out cold.

The stable lad scrambled backward, his hands raised to show that he was unarmed. With a muttered curse, Colin straightened from his fighting stance and began to re-sheathe his sword.

This was it—Sabine's last chance. She gave up on the reins and instead dug her heels into the horse's flanks, praying that she could control the enormous animal once he broke into a run. At least she was lashed to the saddle, she thought distantly.

To her horror, the horse grunted but didn't budge. She spurred it again, squeezing both her heels and knees this time. Still, the cursed animal didn't move.

"He's too well trained for that."

Her stomach dropped to the stable floor at Colin's even voice as he approached her from behind. She squeezed her eyes shut, refusing to believe that she'd failed so miserably.

"What's going on?"

Sabine froze at the sound of several people hurrying toward the stable. The lad's cry for help had brought reinforcements. She spun in the saddle to find half a dozen men crowding into the stable door.

Colin, too, had turned to find the men eyeing him where he stood not far from the rider's unconscious form.

"The lass says she needs help—claims she's been kidnapped," the stable lad said from the safety of the back of the group.

Several blades hissed as they were drawn from their sheaths.

"Let's no' do this, lads," Colin said wearily. The men only stepped farther into the stable.

Sabine forgot to urge the stallion into motion as several of the newly arrived men surged forward, swords and daggers drawn.

Colin moved like the lion she'd once idly compared him to in her mind—powerful, graceful, and most of all lethal. Yet as before, she was shocked to realize that he did not attempt to swing the sharp edge of his sword at his attackers.

He blocked a blow aimed at his sword arm, then pivoted half a heartbeat later to stop another blade from slicing his leg. Spinning, he slammed his hilt into his first attacker's nose.

Blood suddenly flowed dark and fast down the man's face. He stumbled backward, clutching his broken nose as blood dripped through his fingers.

Colin didn't slow or falter as he turned to the next man. As he smoothly fended off two others' blades, his boot shot out to deliver a powerful kick to a third's chest. The man stumbled back, gasping for breath.

Now all four of the remaining inn patrons leapt at Colin, but the narrow walkway in the middle of the stables only allowed two of them to swing their blades at him.

Sabine looked on helplessly. Only if the inn patrons took Colin out would she be able to free her wrist from the saddle and find a new blasted horse who would take her orders. Something strange pinched in her chest at the thought of one of the men piercing Colin with a blade, however.

She shoved the errant thought aside as Colin blocked another attack, then leveled a third man with a crushing punch to the jaw.

One of the three remaining inn patrons still on his feet suddenly darted forward, sword raised. With a whir of steel, he slashed the blade across Colin's chest.

Sabine shrieked with unchecked fright as the blade's motion seemed to slow just before it sliced into Colin's chest. Colin twisted and hunched his back, drawing his chest away from the line of the sword.

Nevertheless, the tip of the sword still made contact. The sound of rending fabric filled Sabine's ears as the sword snagged on Colin's tunic.

Colin stumbled backward, one hand coming to his chest, but no blood welled between his fingers.

Instead of red, Sabine's eyes fixed on a flash of white directly over Colin's heart.

What in…

She squinted in the low light. Something was tucked within the tattered folds of the woolen tunic. Something creamy white, with a waxy sheen to it.

Parchment.

Clarity, sudden and hot, washed through Sabine.

Osborn, the King of Scotland's messenger, had carried a decoy missive, with Colin as the messenger's watch dog. But there was a *real* missive to be delivered—carried by Colin himself.

Suddenly it all made sense—the fact that he was traveling west instead of east, the fact that he was dragging her along with him rather than returning her to his King. It was all so that he could deliver his missive.

The realization was followed by a second, the answering thunder to a bolt of lightning.

If Colin bore an important missive from the King of Scotland himself, then she hadn't completed her assignment yet.

Fabian's client had paid for the information sealed within the letter secreted away in Colin's tunic. She still had a chance to gather that information and report it to Fabian.

How pleased Fabian would be with her, how proud and impressed. But if she was ever going to see the inside of that piece of parchment, she couldn't flee from Colin. Nay, she needed to stay close to him now.

"Stop!"

The inn's patrons, who'd been closing in on Colin as he'd backed slowly toward the rear of the stables, started at her sudden shout.

"Stop!" Sabine repeated. "No more, I beg of ye. This was all a terrible misunderstanding."

The men gaped at her, still perched atop the black stallion, as if she had truly gone mad.

"Ye see, that man is my husband, as he said." She looked for confirmation from the stable lad, who nodded dumbly near the door. "We had a terrible row," she hurried on. "He turned my mother out of our home. I sought to exact revenge on him for his harshness, so he tied me to this saddle to prevent my troublemaking. I thought to teach him a lesson by saying he'd kidnapped me, but I never intended for anyone to get hurt."

The men continued to look at her in stunned silence, so she barreled on with the lie. "It was naught but a quarrel between husband and wife, ye understand. I beg yer forgiveness for all the trouble I've caused."

"Is this true?" one of the remaining men demanded of Colin.

"Aye," he said slowly. "My *wife* is most devious, but this is a personal matter between us. She shouldnae have dragged ye all into it." His gaze pierced her as he spoke, sending a shiver of apprehension down her spine.

The men began muttering some foul and very

pointed curses about her as they straightened, re-sheathing their weapons. They helped their injured companions toward the stable door, with two men lifting the unconscious rider from the floor by the arms.

"Get yer woman under control," snapped one of the men bluntly over his shoulder at Colin.

"Oh aye, I plan to," Colin muttered, never taking his gaze from Sabine. He smoothly slid his blade into its scabbard and shrugged his shoulders so that his cloak fell back across them, concealing the missive behind the thick wool.

"Ye'd best find some other place to sleep," the stable lad said, suddenly brave now that the threat was over.

Colin nodded wordlessly at him, then stomped to where Sabine sat atop his horse. He swung himself into the saddle behind her and snatched up the reins. When he gave the stallion a nudge, the animal immediately responded, stepping forward and through the stable door.

As Colin coaxed the horse into a trot and led them away from the little village, Sabine's left shoulder began to throb. Yet it wasn't the same pulsing pain she'd experienced earlier. Nay, it was because her shoulder was rhythmically rubbing against Colin's chest—right where she'd seen the missive.

Sabine knew it was just her imagination, but she fancied her shoulder actually growing warm with the proximity of that longed-for message.

How would she manage to get her hands on it, though? Her little stunt in the stables would undoubtedly make Colin even more guarded and cautious around her. If he kept her good hand tied, she wouldn't have a chance of even getting close to the missive.

A plan slowly took root in her mind as they rode across the darkened landscape. Besides a few defensive maneuvers with her dagger, Fabian had never taught her how to fight. That was because he always told her that her greatest asset was her beauty and charm.

How many messengers had she lured to private chambers and secret nooks using naught more than a smile and a story about wanting to take a tumble with them? How many scraps and tidbits of information had she secured over the years?

Colin suddenly reined his horse off the road and into the surrounding forest. As the dark trees closed in around them, Sabine was acutely aware of being alone with him—a powerfully built, skilled Highland warrior who was furious with her.

Nay, Colin would not be fooled as easily as the messengers she'd seduced before. Invariably, messengers were lonely, solitary men who didn't stop to question why a woman like Sabine was inviting them for a romp.

Colin, on the other hand, looked like the type of man who never lacked for female companionship. Though his features seemed perpetually set in granite, there was no denying that he was handsome and well-formed.

Even with a scowl on his face, his bright, perceptive eyes glowed like sapphires, his lips were firm but full, and his jawline was strong. Women no doubt threw themselves at him to stroke that leonine mane of golden hair sitting on his broad, muscular shoulders.

And Sabine had overheard enough women's talk over the years when she passed herself off as a servant to get close to her target. She had an idea of what a man with a honed, powerful physique could do in the bedchamber.

Aye, to woo him into a false sense of security would take every last drop of her skill. It would be harder than taming a lion. But if she succeeded, she had a chance at getting that missive—and she had never failed a mission yet.

Chapter Eleven

S he knew.

Sabine knew about the Bruce's missive.

Thought she'd masked her sudden realization swiftly, Colin had seen the flash of understanding in her hazel eyes just before she'd called a halt to the skirmish with the men in the stables.

He'd been lucky to avoid having his chest split open, but in his experience one streak of luck was always countered by a balancing weight of ill fortune. With the Bruce's missive exposed to her sharp gaze, she would no doubt try to get at its contents.

Which meant that he had to be even more vigilant around her.

What puzzled him, though, was how she hoped to put those thieving fingers on the missive. Why had she called the men off? Why not let them kill him—or at least attempt to—instead of forming a swift lie that allowed both of them to flee?

Colin's curiosity niggled at him all night. He'd picked a spot to make a rudimentary camp in the woods well off the road. The men from the inn seemed annoyed enough that after several ales, they might work up the courage to go looking for them.

The night had been quiet, however, with Sabine exchanging no more than a handful of words with him. She seemed as deep in thought as he was, though that made him nervous. What was brewing in that lovely, deceiving head of hers?

He'd kept her tied to the saddle throughout the night. When he'd dismounted, he'd unbuckled the saddle from Ruith and pulled Sabine, saddle and all, from the animal's back. She hadn't even protested when he simply set her a few paces away from the horse, leaving her to arrange both her hurt shoulder and her bound wrist in a way that would allow her to sleep.

Once dawn's weak light had woken him, he'd quickly mended his tunic. A jagged, hastily sewn line now ran directly across his chest, but at least the missive was out of sight once more. When the task was done, he waited, watching Sabine as she slept.

Again, he was struck by the unmarred innocence of her resting form. How could a spy—a liar and a thief as well—look so bewitchingly sweet in slumber?

Unbidden, his manhood stirred. His mind instantly shot back to the feel of her pressed against him on the saddle, their hips rolling together in rhythm with the horse's stride.

Shite.

He cursed his traitorous body and yanked his thoughts away from the feel of her slight, delicate form grinding against his. She was up to something, damn it. And he was going to find out what.

When the sun at last broke through the patchy clouds, she stirred.

She blinked, her green-gold eyes hazy with sleep, until they at last fastened on him. Something pinched low in his belly as their eyes locked, but he ignored it.

As if his hard, steady gaze chased away the fog of slumber, she sat up suddenly. She winced as her bound wrist stopped her progress, jarring her shoulder and forcing her to settle for propping herself on her good elbow.

"What a strange turn of events last night, wouldnae ye say, lass?" he asked calmly.

"Nay, not so strange, really," she shot back, just as placidly.

He watched her features—especially those large hazel eyes—for signs of a betrayal of her inner thoughts, but she kept her face blank. She was skilled, he'd give her that.

"Why did ye cause that scene in the stables?"

She blinked at him again, though it was not particularly coy. Rather, it was matter-of-fact. "I hope you understand why I would want to try to escape. You are indeed holding me against my will, as I said last night. I'm sure I want no part in whatever fate you have planned for me."

Christ, that might have been the most she'd said to him in the day and a half since he'd captured her—

combined. So, she was suddenly willing to talk, was she? Colin narrowed his eyes on her. There was something behind this newfound frankness, he was sure—the lass was clearly no fool.

"So ye wanted to escape, was that it?"

"Aye."

"Then why did ye call the men off with that lie about a row between husband and wife?"

A delicate pink blush crept to her cheeks. Good. The lass was not made of stone after all. But what did she hide behind that pretty flush?

"I...I realized when I saw you break that man's nose that I would have innocent men's blood on my hands for sending them after you. I thought they could best you and I could slip away, but once you began fighting, I wasn't so sure."

He smothered his desire to grin at that—of course a few inn patrons wouldn't have been able to cut him down. Nay, he had to focus on her excuse for helping him. Here was a chink in her armor that he could exploit.

"Ah. So when ye saw that man's bloody nose, ye thought better of yer little escape plan."

"Aye."

"Except that ye let the others attack me for several moments before telling them to stop."

Her lashes fluttered, and he noticed her thin throat bobbing as she swallowed. "I had to come up with a lie to stop them," she replied at last. "I couldn't think with all the noise and confusion."

"How verra interesting. Ye seem to have no problem spouting off lies any other time it serves ye."

Her blush deepened, and her eyes flashed with indignation. "Mayhap I shouldn't have told that one last night. Mayhap I should have let those men take you down after all." For one heartbeat, she seemed surprised at the words that had tumbled from her mouth, but then she smoothed her features once more.

"So ye didnae want those men's innocent blood on yer hands," he prodded, returning to his inquiry. "Ye thought of a lie that got us both out of that cursed village. But why didnae ye simply lie in such a way that ye still could have been rid of me?"

He doubted she would own up to seeing the missive, to the clear longing for its contents that had flashed in her eyes for the briefest moment before she shuttered herself once more, but perhaps she'd let something of her true motivations slip—or the reason behind her sudden willingness to talk.

"I don't know," she murmured, lowering her gaze to her lap. "I suppose...I suppose the truth is that you've been...kind to me."

He lifted an eyebrow. Aye, there was a ring of truth to the words, but he kept a sharp eye on her.

"The truth is," she hurried on, keeping her chin tucked, "that I don't understand why you haven't forced me to speak, haven't harmed or threatened me. It felt...wrong to throw you to those men."

"As I told ye before, I may be a Highlander, but I am no' a barbarian," he said. "I willnae resort to torturing an injured woman—though I will remind ye that ye dinnae ken what awaits ye tomorrow or the next day."

Colin doubted the Bruce would torture her either when he turned her over—Robert had seen what had happened physically and mentally to his sister Mary and Isabella MacDuff. The two had been captured by Longshanks, King Edward II's father, and held captive in cages outdoors and far above the ground for four long years. The Bruce loathed the use of women and children in warfare.

Still, Colin would not admit just yet that he didn't have a plan for her beyond dragging her with him to Ireland and then handing her over to the Bruce. Let her stew a bit. Mayhap then she would reveal something useful.

"I…I don't understand that," she murmured.

"What? That the English—and most Lowland Scots as well—think we Highlanders are savages?" he asked.

"Nay, I've heard that enough," she replied, one side of her mouth lifting even as she kept her gaze lowered. "But I have always been told…I've always known what would happen to me if I was ever caught."

"And who told ye that? The one ye work for?"

She stiffened slightly, and he knew he'd uncovered a small kernel of truth.

"Aye," she said softly, surprising him. "The man I work for…he raised me from childhood, trained me.

He's been the only one who has ever—"

Her voice pinched off suddenly. She shook her head as if in warning to herself, her sable hair sliding down around her pinkened cheeks.

For one long breath, Colin's chest squeezed with a strange ache. What had this wee slip of a lass been through in the short score of years she'd been alive? Who was this man who had taken her in? And what had he done to turn an innocent child into a deceitful spy?

A distant alarm bell rang in Colin's mind. Aye, the lass was up to something. The old unhealed wound left by Joan and her deviousness throbbed anew.

Inwardly, Colin smiled as realization dawned. Was this the lass's scheme, then? To pull at his heartstrings, make him feel sorry for her, and then when his guard was down, slip away with the King's missive?

It was what she'd done to Osborn, wasn't it? She'd spun some sob story about being sent to a nunnery, carefully tugging on both Osborn's sympathy and his lust. Without even trying, Sabine had already stirred Colin's desire—and now she was angling for his pity.

Sabine was watching him with those wide hazel eyes. He carefully let a minuscule ripple of compassion flicker across his face before smoothing his features once more. Those keen, bottomless eyes registered the flash of emotion, he was sure.

"I do not wish to speak of it, though," she said, drawing her dark brows together. "My shoulder aches badly this morn, and if we are to be in the saddle another day, I will need to save my energy."

"Do ye wish for me to massage it again?" Colin murmured.

Relief washed her delicate features, followed by another pretty pink blush. "A-aye, if you wouldn't mind. It helped greatly yestereve."

Colin stood slowly and stalked toward her. She craned her neck to watch him approach, looking all the world like a wounded doe gazing at an approaching wolf.

He crouched behind her, letting his knees open to encase her between them. By God, this was becoming an all-too-familiar position—her gently curved hips and bottom tucked against his manhood, their bodies pressed together, his blood pumping hotly despite his brain screaming at him to keep away.

When his hand closed around her left shoulder, she moaned. As he worked his fingers into the tight, slim muscles there, her head fell back onto his chest. Those plump lips parted on a half-groan, half-sigh. Her brows unknitted and her eyelids fluttered closed, her dark lashes resting against her creamy cheeks.

Though his manhood had already stirred to life at their first contact, when Sabine sank her teeth into her lower lip to stifle yet another breathy moan, his cursed cock surged to attention.

Colin had no doubt that she could feel his desire, pressed as it was against her bottom. Her lashes wavered open and she tilted her head up where it still rested on his chest, pinning him with those hazel eyes.

"I...I still do not understand why you are being so kind to me, but I thank you," she murmured. "You make me feel..." She let the unspoken word slip away with another little shake of her head, as if she were chastising herself for the pleasure she'd clearly taken from his touch.

Even as hot desire coursed through his veins, an icy stab of realization buried itself in Colin's gut. He'd thought he had already experienced the worst of his base lust for her. But nay, the lass had not yet even fully unleashed her plan. She wasn't just going to pull at his heartstrings. Her true scheme was to pull a string attached to an organ about two feet below his heart.

The minx was planning to seduce him.

Bloody hell.

Colin's heart hardened to stone, though he had to repress the urge to smile. Little did Sabine know that Colin would be the last man in all of England or Scotland to fall for the feminine wiles of a beautiful, innocent lass. He'd already learned that lesson the hard way.

What was more, Sabine had clearly not considered the fact that two could play at her little game. He'd been distracted and annoyed at Osborn when she'd first met him. Then after learning that she was a spy, his own anger at the bind he found himself in meant that he hadn't considered attempting to charm information out of her.

She likely thought him naught more than a warrior, but she'd never been the recipient of his true skill.

Colin slid away from Sabine, though he made a point of letting his hand linger on her, his fingertips brushing across her shoulder blade as he slowly withdrew.

"Come, lass. It is time we break camp and move on."

"Are we still riding west?"

"Aye."

He took her good elbow and lifted her to her feet, scooping up the saddle as well before it could tug on her arm. She feigned a little stumble, bumping into him and steadying herself with a small hand on his chest.

If she felt the hammering of his heart beneath his tunic, she might mistake it for passionate longing. In actuality, Colin's blood pumped at the challenge laid out before him.

Sabine was undeniably skilled. He would have to resist her enticing charms, all the while deploying his own seduction to wheedle answers from her.

Aye, he loved a good challenge, he thought as he wrapped his hands around her narrow waist to steady her.

The game was on.

Chapter Twelve

The day had been warm enough that they'd both discarded their cloaks. Sabine should have been pleased at the loss of the layer of thick wool separating them, for it meant that she could better feel Colin's desire for her. Instead, her skin itched and felt warm beneath her dress and shift—a warmth that if she were honest with herself was only partly due to the turn in the weather.

She'd never experienced a genuine attraction to one of her marks before. Then again, her marks were never brawny warriors stacked with muscle and oozing lethal grace.

They'd stayed away from roads and villages all day. Colin had murmured something about not being able to trust her to play nicely with others as he'd urged his stallion through the dense woods.

Though she'd assured him that she would not risk an escape attempt again—not until she'd secured the contents of the King's missive, that was, but she kept that to herself—he'd kept her lashed to the saddle. Even when she needed to stop and seek privacy, he simply unwound the rope from the pommel and left her wrist bound, creating a leash several feet long which he held as she sought a dense shrub.

When at last the sun dipped toward the treetops ahead of them, Colin reined in his steed and dismounted.

"Another night on the ground?" she asked, trying to lace her voice with tight dismay. In truth, she'd slept in far worse conditions than on a forest floor, but if she were going to get him to trust her, she needed him to feel compassion for her.

"Aye," Colin said, swinging down from the saddle. "How is yer shoulder?"

Sabine started. She actually hadn't thought of it much all day.

She glanced down at the sling he'd made for her. Though she'd never been farther north than she was now in the Lowlands, she knew enough about Scots to comprehend that the blue and green patterned scrap of wool was Colin's clan plaid.

"It truly does feel better—thanks to your ministrations this morning."

Colin tilted his golden head back and pinned her with his gaze where she sat atop the stallion. Those vibrant blue eyes seemed to penetrate to her very core. A slow smile curved his lips, and suddenly his whole face transformed from hard granite to honeyed sensuality.

Sabine nearly gasped, but she managed to catch her breath in her throat before revealing her shock.

He'd been undeniably handsome before—all hard lines and trained control. But now…by God, seeing him smile was like staring into the sun. He radiated a seductive heat mingled with a mischievous playfulness. Those sea-blue eyes danced suggestively, his curved lips promising wicked delight.

"I'm glad I could bring ye pleasure, lass," he murmured.

This time she couldn't stop the sudden inhale of breath through her parted lips. The wheels of her brain ground slowly as she kept mentally tripping over the word "pleasure," spoken so softly in that lilting Highland brogue.

"Oh, aye, my shoulder," she blurted at last. "Thank you again."

He sent another honeyed smile at her before wrapping his hands around her waist and pulling her from his horse's back. Heat licked at her skin where those large hands gripped her through her dress.

Had her seduction worked so quickly and easily? Was he truly already succumbing to her after little more than a few mysterious comments about her past and a couple of bats of her eyelashes at him?

It was possible. She'd taken men down quicker than this, and with less effort, though they'd been lonely and desperate for female attention.

Her thoughts churned as he went about unsaddling the horse. She was forced to stand in close proximity to him as he did, for he'd left her bound to the pommel.

That was proof aplenty that he didn't trust her enough—care for her enough—to let his guard down just yet. She'd laid the groundwork for her plan, but she still needed him to free her wrist—and that was only the first of many steps to get her close enough to the missive he carried over his heart.

While his back was turned, she gave herself a little shake. She couldn't become distracted by Colin's handsomeness or near-blinding smile. She had to remain in charge, which meant getting him to believe and trust her.

And if he were like most men, the fastest way to turn him into a bowl of willing porridge was to guide his mind toward lust.

As Colin turned toward her, an idea began to form.

"I need privacy," she said, lowering her chin demurely.

"Again?"

"Not for that," she replied quickly. "I…I have been wearing this dress and shift for three days now, and my skin is beginning to itch. If there is a stream or pond nearby, I would like to wash."

To Sabine's surprise, she only had to half fake the nervous flutter in her voice. The thought of undressing and bathing near this lion of a man sent an unnerving spike of heat into her belly. She could only hope that the thought had a similar effect on him.

As she watched, one of his golden brows lifted slowly. With any luck, his mind was running a string of images across his eyes.

Sabine was always amazed at how little she actually had to *do* when seducing a mark. Just a mere suggestion, and men's minds usually did most of the work for her.

"Verra well," he said at last. "There is a wee loch no' far from here. I'll accompany ye."

Once again, Sabine silently cursed herself for hoping that Colin would be like the other men she'd targeted. How far would she have to go with this ruse?

"You cannot!" she breathed, again only half feigning shock and embarrassment. "I...that is, I have never...I'll be—"

That slow, sensuous smile played around his lips, but his eyes, which held her in their blue depths, were like those of an animal of prey. "Ye'll be naked? Aye, but I'll no' risk ye attempting to escape again."

"As I told you before, I will not—"

"Aye, aye," he said with a dismissive tilt of his head. "Ye say ye willnae flee again. But I'm afraid ye havenae earned my trust on that just yet."

Sabine swallowed. Nay, Colin would not go down as easily as the others. Straightening her spine, she held his gaze steadily. Mayhap she could use this opportunity to her advantage. After all, if some men fell to their knees at the mere thought of a naked woman, how much more could be accomplished by actually showing some skin?

"Fine," she said. "You may accompany me. But I

would still request some privacy."

She hated the prudish edge to her voice—not exactly the note she'd been hoping to strike as she attempted to seduce him into trusting her.

He eyed her for a long moment, but to her surprise, he only nodded.

As he dug for something in one of the saddlebags, she took in their surroundings.

It was shaded beneath the pine and oak bows overhead, but the air was still warm from the sunny day. Through the trees, she thought she spied a flash of late-afternoon sun playing on water. Mayhap that was the loch Colin had mentioned.

The warmth of Colin's callused hands on her bound wrist snapped her attention back to him. With a few expert tugs and twists, he undid the knot tethering her to the saddle and the rope fell away.

She wanted to scream at how easily she was made immobile. If her left arm had been functional, she would have long ago freed herself, but as it was, she remained at Colin's mercy.

"Ye shouldnae tug against yer bindings so much," he said, his brows lowered as he inspected her red wrist, which was chafed from the coarse rope.

She would have retorted, but decided it was best to swallow the sharp words and instead focus on the task before her.

Just as she pulled her wrist from his grasp, he placed a small lump of soap into her hand.

"It doesnae have whatever scent that is in yer hair, but it will do the job."

He'd noticed the smell of her hair? Something warm coiled in her stomach even as heat went to her cheeks. "Thank you," she said quickly.

Before he could give her another one of those devastating smiles, she spun on her heels and strode toward the water. In no more than one pace, he was at her side, never letting any more than a few feet of distance open between them.

This was what she wanted, she reminded herself. This was all part of her plan. He'd soon enough lower his guard, and when he did, she could at last complete her assignment and make her way back to Fabian.

When they reached the water, though, her nervousness hitched higher. Fortunately, Colin turned and gave her his back without her having to ask.

How could she have played the harlot, the whore, the promiscuous farm girl on her way to the nunnery so many times, and yet she'd never been naked before a man?

Fabian had warned her never to take one of her ruses too far, for he said she should guard her innocence with great care. She was not a simple prostitute after all, he frequently reminded her. She was special, he said.

Yet even without Fabian's warning, Sabine wouldn't have approached that dangerous line. Men were easily controlled with seduction. Sex—even the hint or promise of it—was a tool, naught more. She saw what became of the men she charmed. They'd spill their secrets, or drink themselves silly, or simply turn their back on her, never suspecting that she could harm them. She'd vowed long ago never to be as vulnerable, as trusting, as the men she seduced.

She fumbled with the laces running down the back of her dress, twisting her good arm first over her head and then around her back to try to get at the ties. To her dawning horror, she realized that she was not going to be able to undress herself—not with her left arm in a sling.

Cursing silently, she dragged in a fortifying breath. This would work to her benefit, she reminded herself. This was all part of her scheme.

"Colin? I need help removing my gown."

Chapter Thirteen

Colin gritted his teeth at her breathy request.

By God, the lass must truly know what she was about.

Though he'd seen a crack in her resolve when he'd given her his first alluring smile, she seemed unfazed enough to continue with her own scheme.

He would just have to try harder—and keep his mind on his task even as he undressed the lass.

He turned to find her twisting to reach the laces running down her back at the loch's rocky edge.

"Easy, lass," he said, stepping toward her. "Ye'll dislocate yer other shoulder if ye keep that up."

She made a little huffing noise that sounded part defeated, part amused. "And we can't have that. Then you'd no longer be able to tie me to your saddle."

"Och, I'm sure I'd find a way to keep ye close," he said, intentionally letting his voice drop seductively.

Her back stiffened slightly at his remark, but she let her hand drop. "Please," she said softly, glancing over her shoulder. Her eyes were shadowed and unreadable, for behind her the slanting sun danced blindingly across the loch's surface.

Something about her earnest vulnerability tugged at his chest. Aye, that was exactly what she wanted, wasn't it? But he still had his own aims as well.

He untied the laces cinching the top of her dress tight over her slim form, letting his fingers play lightly along her spine.

"Thank you. I can do the rest," she said.

"No' with that hurt shoulder," he replied.

Sure enough, when she went to shrug out of the green wool, she drew in a sharp breath and froze, clearly in pain.

Colin quickly slipped the plaid sling from around her neck, then placed stilling hands on her shoulders.

"Let me. I willnae hurt ye."

After a long pause, she nodded, though he couldn't see her face from where he stood behind her.

Carefully, he eased the dress off first her uninjured shoulder. The white linen shift beneath the green wool was warm to the touch—warm from her bare skin beneath.

She pulled her right arm free of the dress, but to his surprise, she did not attempt to swat his hand away from her injured shoulder. Instead, she held herself still, hardly even breathing as he slowly peeled back the dress.

This time, she didn't lift her arm free of the dress's sleeve, for it hung limp at her side. He gingerly took her elbow, easing the strain on her shoulder, and rolled the sleeve all the way down.

When at last the most delicate work was done, she stood with her back to him, her dress peeled to her waist. Her shift, along with both creamy arms, was exposed.

Colin repressed a shocked inhale as his eyes landed on her wounded shoulder. Dark purple bruises marred her pale skin, and the shoulder looked decidedly more swollen than its healthy match. How had Sabine held back the pain that no doubt even now racked her?

He shoved down the swell of admiration. He needed information, damn it, not respect for a spy.

"Hold yer arm," he said, his voice coming out rougher than he'd intended.

Without comment, and hardly seeming to breathe, Sabine cradled her left arm in her right.

Colin gripped the dress where it bunched around her hips, willing his mind to focus. "How is it that ye came to know how to count?"

She stiffened again, but he couldn't be sure if it was from his abrupt question or the fact that he'd cupped her hips in his hands to draw down her dress.

"Count?"

"Aye. When I reset yer shoulder, ye counted backwards quite well. Most wouldnae have been able to, especially in so much pain."

Sabine audibly swallowed. He slid her dress around her bottom, clenching his hands in the wool to keep them away from the delectable curve.

"The man who trained me taught me many

things," she said at last.

"Ye said he raised ye from childhood. How old were ye when he took ye in?"

As the dress slid the rest of the way down her legs to pool around her feet, she wobbled. Instinctively, his hands shot out to her hips, steadying her.

"He…he found me wandering the streets of London when I was five. I don't remember much before him—only being very cold and hungry, and being surrounded by strange faces."

Her quiet voice, distant with memory, sent an ache into his heart. Slowly, he turned her in his grip so that she faced him.

"Is that the truth, or another one of yer lies?" he ground out, refusing to soften his gaze as he searched her face.

Pain flickered across her eyes, which shone with unusual moisture all of a sudden. "It is the truth. Fa—…the man who found me took care of me. He fed me, clothed me, and taught me more than an orphan girl could ever hope to learn. He is like a father to me."

She'd almost let the man's name slip before she'd caught herself. A name alone wouldn't unravel the entire network behind the breach in the Bruce's correspondence, but it was a start. Colin pushed on despite the hurt that still lingered in Sabine's eyes.

"He must have taught ye to read as well."

Her delicate brows rose with surprise, but she quickly smoothed them once more. "What makes you think that?"

Colin felt amusement playing around his mouth. Well, if he wanted to get more information from her, mayhap he'd have to give some as well.

"I assume yer boss has been behind the other interceptions of the Bruce's missives. Yet the letters always arrived where they were sent, their seals unbroken. I can only guess at how long this operation has been going on."

She stared at him blankly, yet a faint white line appeared around her lips as she compressed them.

"When I found Osborn unconscious in our chamber, I checked the missive he was carrying. It was sealed, of course, but the wax was still soft from where ye'd melted it on the underside."

"Ah, so that is how you knew to chase after me," she said, a weak smile quirking one side of her mouth.

"Aye. And if ye were opening missives only to reseal them and let them go on their way, it means that ye can read."

"And memorize," she added, holding his stare.

Christ, so much for seduction. He'd managed to turn this sensual moment into an interrogation. He was gaining ground, but he needed take control of the situation once more.

"What of this necklace?" he asked, sliding a finger under the thin chain around her neck. "I've seen ye touch it several times already."

Her skin was like silken cream along her collar

bone. He could feel her pulse quicken under his fingertip, but he wasn't sure if it was because she was preparing another lie or if his touch was having the intended effect.

"The man who employs me gave it to me."

Though a flush had crept up her neck and to her cheeks, Colin detected no guile in her steady gaze.

"It must be verra special to ye, then."

"Aye, it is." She withdrew slightly so that his finger slipped from the chain.

Something hung on the end of the necklace, for there was an anchoring weight to the chain, but the metal disappeared beneath the edge of her shift. The bauble at the end no doubt hung between those two pert, round breasts.

"Do ye wish for me to help ye remove yer shift as well?"

"Nay," she said quickly.

She placed one foot on the heel of the other and yanked out of her boot, then repeated the motion on the other side. Reaching under the hem of her shift with her good hand, she swiftly removed both stockings as well.

"You promised to give me some privacy," she said, looking up at him.

He didn't remember making any such promise, but he grudgingly stepped away, then turned his back on her.

At the sound of the loch waters lapping around her

legs, he clenched his fists at his sides. Images of that thin shift plastered against her lithe form barraged him.

Bloody hell.

She was better at this game than he'd thought—mayhap even better than he was.

Chapter Fourteen

S he was in over her head.

Sabine cursed herself silently for the twisting knot in her stomach. Was it simply from fear that her plan wouldn't work, or was it from Colin's devastating smile, his warm touch, and those damned piercing blue eyes that seemed to see right through her ruse?

Cool water lapped around her ankles, then her calves, then past her knees. She shouldn't have insisted that Colin turn his back, for seeing her in a wet shift just might make him pliant enough to forget that she was his captive.

But mayhap instead she was becoming the vulnerable one. She'd already said far more than she'd intended. What else would she let slip if his gaze scorched over her—or worse, if she ended up in his arms again?

Lies normally came quickly and easily to her tongue from years of practice. For some reason, though, she'd blurted the truth to him on the loch's shore. Hell, she'd nearly let Fabian's name slip.

When the loch waters reached her waist, she bent her knees and sank to her chin, letting the cool water lap at her blazing flesh. Why had she told him the truth? Why had she let her guard down for even one heartbeat?

As she dunked her head under, she let the water cool her mind as well as her body. This would be her longest and most challenging assignment ever. Normally, her point of contact—it had always been Miles—would send her to her mark in the afternoon, and by midnight she'd have the man wooed, secreted away someplace private, and then lying unconscious as she took what she was sent for.

But getting this missive from Colin wouldn't be so simple. Mayhap she'd told him the truth because with such an extended scheme, she could easily become tangled in her own lies. Aye, that sounded plausible.

Or mayhap she'd told him about her childhood and being taken under Fabian's wing because she'd known somehow that Colin's senses were sharper than her average mark's were. He would have sensed instinctively if she'd lied, but since she'd been honest—if guarded—mayhap it would increase her credibility to have spoken so earnestly.

Sabine worked the little lump of soap Colin had given her in her good hand. By God, she couldn't even be sure if she was telling *herself* the truth anymore.

Her hand trembled as she scrubbed the soap into her hair. A clean, piney scent rose from the lather.

A hot stab of recognition shot low through her belly. It was the earthy, masculine fragrance that clung to

Colin. That scent had enveloped her whenever they rode pressed together atop his stallion.

A little shiver ran through her, despite the mild water and the warm evening air. Who was playing whom now? Did Colin know the effect his smile had on her, or his penetrating gaze, or the very nearness of his powerful body? Was he using himself as a weapon against her, as she was against him?

Sabine dragged in a ragged breath as she began lathering her body through her shift. Aye, she was playing a perilous game. Yet although she racked her mind for an alternate scheme to get her hands on the missive he carried, she could draw naught else forth.

She'd been hesitant, frightened of his dangerously alluring reaction to her seduction, she realized. She felt exposed by his searching gaze, his sensuous touch, but wasn't that exactly what she wanted to produce in him?

Dunking herself once more to rinse away the soap, she steeled herself. She needed to be bolder, braver. No more shyness and silly girlish modesty. If a powerful, enthralling man like Colin was ever going to let his guard down, it would not be for a few batted lashes and confessions about her childhood. Nay, it would require something far more daring.

"Colin?" Without even trying, her voice came out low and breathy.

"Aye?" His broad back was turned to her, his tawny hair looking like rippling gold silk in the slanting evening sun.

"I...I do not have aught to dry myself with. Would you fetch me my cloak, or mayhap one of those plaids in your saddlebags?"

The muscles in his back strained against his tunic as he crossed his arms over his chest.

"Ye want me to leave ye alone out here? Do ye take me for a fool, lass?"

"I have naught but a wet shift to my name at the moment," she called back. "Do you truly think I would flee now?"

Colin's shoulders stiffened, but at last he sighed. "Verra well, but I'm taking yer dress with me."

He backed slowly to the loch's edge and picked up her discarded dress. Muttering something under his breath, he stalked into the trees where his horse stood not far away.

Sabine forced herself to wade toward the shore on suddenly wobbly legs. Her shift clung to her skin, a soft breeze making her shudder as she emerged from the water.

This was the bold action required of her, she told herself firmly as another shiver that had naught to do with the balmy evening air rippled through her. She was doing this for her assignment—not for herself.

"Yer cloak was still damp from last night, so this plaid will have to—"

Colin plowed his way through the underbrush, the blue and green wool held in his hand. As his eyes locked on her, the words died abruptly on his lips.

Sabine took the last few steps onto the shore, her shift tangling and clinging around her ankles as she gingerly found her footing on the rocks.

"*Christ.*" His hiss was sharp as his gaze scorched her. He looked suddenly like the wild lion she'd first thought him.

She glanced down at herself to see what his gaze so fiercely consumed.

Sabine couldn't suppress a gasp at what met her eyes. She might as well have been wearing naught at all, for the wet shift blended seamlessly with her pale skin. Her rosy nipples stood out clearly, puckered from the cool water. The dark triangle of hair between her legs was also plainly visible. Every inch of her was on display.

She forced her feet to remain rooted and her hands to stay at her sides, even though her left shoulder ached a bit from hanging unsupported. Lifting her chin, she met his searing gaze with smooth features.

"What are ye doing, lass?" Colin rasped. He stalked a pace closer, his chest rising and falling starkly with his ragged breathing.

"I must get out of the water if I am to dry myself, mustn't I?" Sabine surprised herself at how calm her own voice sounded. She could only hope that he didn't notice her knees beginning to tremble.

Like lightning, he closed the distance between them. "Nay, dinnae toy with me. What game are ye playing?" he demanded.

She had to tilt her head back to meet his eyes, which burned with blue flames. A little alarm bell rang distantly in a corner of her mind. Aye, he looked like a hungry predator—and she was using her flesh as the bait.

Willing herself not to cower, not to throw her arms across her body and scurry for cover like a scared little girl, Sabine held her ground, chin raised.

"Ye dinnae ken what ye are about." A hint of a question softened the edge in his voice ever so slightly. Was he giving her an out, after she so obviously threw herself at his feet?

"I know exactly what I'm doing," she lied, praying that her wide-eyed stare wouldn't give her away.

He moved so swiftly that she gasped in surprise.

The gasp suddenly froze in her lungs as his mouth claimed her lips in a demanding kiss.

Chapter Fifteen

S abine had kissed men to lure them to dark chambers and stable stalls.

She'd given pecks on the cheek, or whisper-soft brushes of her lips against theirs, with a giggle and a murmured promise of more.

But never had she kissed a man like this.

His lips were soft but firm, challenging her to back down. Yet she refused to retreat. Instead, she kissed him back, meeting his urgent need with her own.

He yanked the plaid out from between them and wrapped it around her. With a strong tug, he pulled her against him.

She gasped again when she collided with his stone wall of a torso, and he took the opportunity to invade her mouth with his tongue. The velvet heat spread down her spine and began to pool between her legs.

His tongue coaxed and caressed hers, even as every other inch of him was all hard challenge. One hand snaked up from the plaid to bury itself in the hair at her nape. He pulled slightly, suddenly in complete control of her head. He tilted her back even farther, deepening his plunder of her mouth.

Sabine realized distantly that her own hand tangled in his silken locks. She clung desperately to him, her legs turning to porridge. All rational thought had long since fled her mind, and she let instinct guide her. Arching, she pressed herself against his hard warmth.

In response, he growled low in his throat, sending vibrations through her lips. Their hips ground together, and she could feel the long, hard column of his desire through his breeches.

The ache between her legs thrummed more insistently as her nipples rasped against his tunic, her wet shift providing a scant barrier.

On a ragged pant, he tore his lips from hers. He fisted her hair even tighter, exposing her neck to his roaming mouth.

"God, what are ye doing to me, lass?" he grated out against her neck.

What was *she* doing? She was clinging on for dear life, for with every frantic heartbeat, she feared she would be swept away by the storm of her own desire.

She could only moan in response, needing more from him, yet unable to call forth the words from her passion-addled brain.

One of those big, callused hands slid from her back to her waist, then moved achingly slowly until he cupped her breast. If she'd imagined she couldn't form a thought before, now her whole mind erupted in dazzling light and heat.

Under his palm, her nipple tightened even more,

despite the warmth cocooning around them within the folds of his plaid.

Sensation like she'd never experienced before shot through her, dragging another moan from her throat. Colin's lips fastened on the sensitive skin below her ear, sending another wave of liquid heat through her veins.

Sabine's whole body trembled in Colin's embrace. Her fingers slipped from his hair to his chest as she tried to steady herself against the barrage of pleasure. Her palm flattened over his heart, which hammered erratically beneath his tunic.

Unthinking, her fingers curled in the tunic's wool as she clawed for purchase in the storm of sensation breaking within her.

The sound of crinkling parchment, muffled by wool, shattered the moment.

Colin jerked away so quickly that she stumbled back until she felt the loch's cool waters lapping at her ankles. Even as the scorching heat of his body evaporated from her, she felt a flush climbing up her neck and into her cheeks.

"Bloody hell," he snapped, narrowing his eyes on her. The blue flames had been replaced with shards of icy suspicion. "This was what ye were after all along with that little stunt, wasnae it?"

His big hand closed over his chest. For a frighteningly long moment, Sabine mistook his gesture to mean that she'd come close to stealing his *heart*. Why did that thought send her own heart slamming against her ribs? But then she realized he'd meant to indicate the missive sewn into the wool of his tunic.

"Nay, I—"

"Dinnae try to deny it. I ken ye saw it when that man nigh cleaved me in two. Yer game is up."

She opened her mouth to defend herself, but the words clogged in her throat. Aye, she'd planned on using her body to lull him into lowering his guard, yet somewhere in the middle of their kiss, she'd forgotten all about her assignment.

Shame at her failure collided with confusion at her own actions. Fabian had taught her that the mission always came first, yet she'd let herself get lost in Colin's embrace. The terrible truth was, when her hand had closed over the missive, she hadn't even been thinking of a way to get at its contents.

"But what should I expect from an English spy," Colin went on when she couldn't form a response. "Fool, I, for imagining that ye had one *innocent* hair on yer head."

If he had slapped her, the sting would have been less than his words. His overt accusation obscured a subtler one—that not only was she guilty of spying, but also that she was no better than a prostitute.

"I am *not* a whore, if that is what you are implying," she hissed.

"Nay? Then what do ye call this?" His hand made a broad arc over her, taking in her dripping hair and wet shift.

She clutched his plaid tight around her as best she could with her one good arm. Hot embarrassment flooded her. The words of rebuttal simply wouldn't come—mayhap because he was right. She'd risked her body, her innocence, for the missive that would have made Fabian so proud.

"And I am not a spy," she managed at last, suppressing a wince at her feeble redirection.

"Och, that's rich!" he snapped, taking a step toward her.

Sabine curled in on herself slightly, taking a step back into the loch. "I'm not," she replied, forcing indignation to rise above her sudden fear. "I'm a thief. I acknowledge that. I steal. I do not spy. I am simply…doing what it takes to survive in this world."

That was the line Fabian always fed her when she dared to question their actions, anyway.

"That's a bloody fine distinction, lass," Colin growled, narrowing his eyes. "Ye're a thief—but ye steal information, which I imagine ye sell to the highest bidder. Yer spying—or thieving, if ye prefer—costs men their *lives*."

She clamped her teeth shut on a retort. Her clumsy attempt at seduction had failed, but that didn't mean she would turn on Fabian. The world was a cold and cruel place, and Fabian was the only one who'd ever offered her shelter.

Colin looked half-wild with anger, yet she had no doubt that if she let something slip, he would use it against her. That was how people were—they would use you, unless you used them first.

"Ye said before that ye didnae wish to have innocent blood on yer hands," he went on. "Well, ye *do*, for the countless missives ye've intercepted and given to yer boss has resulted in the deaths of good men—good Scots who are just trying to defend their families and their land."

Unable to defend herself, she lashed out at him.

"Oh, and what of you?" she shot back even as she retreated to her shins in the loch. "You can't claim innocence either. You were using me for your own ends. You smiled at me. You kissed me. You wanted something from me, just as I wanted something from you."

Her voice rose with each accusation, one tumbling after another as her throat grew tighter. Distantly, she registered that she was losing control, but she could hardly think over the hammering of blood in her ears.

A slow, cruel smile spread across Colin's handsome features. "Oh, aye, I had my own scheme. So, we were both playing each other, but the game is over now. I'll have my answers from ye, by charms or no'."

He reached behind him and slipped something out from his belt at his lower back. "I found this among the folds of yer dress," he said. "I didnae even think to search ye for weapons, injured as ye were—and trusting fool that I am."

As his hand appeared from behind his back, the object he carried flashed blindingly in the slanting sun.

Her dagger.

Sabine's legs buckled suddenly, and she fell to her knees in the loch's shallows. She flung her good arm over her head, as she'd learned to do when Fabian was in one of his moods. It was a pity that her other arm still didn't work properly, she thought hazily, for it meant she would likely take more blows to the head.

Her mind went strangely blank then. The calm that stole over her was almost serene, except for the little part of her that always feared the pain that awaited her. No matter how many times she'd faced Fabian's black moods, that little sliver of fear never went away.

She crouched like that, trembling as she waited for the swift kick from Colin's boot or the hot slice of her own dagger against her flesh.

"What in bloody hell—"

Under her arm, she saw Colin's boots splash through the shallows toward her before she squeezed her eyes shut.

His large hand closed around her elbow. She couldn't help the frightened whimper that escaped her lips as he hauled her to her feet.

"I told ye I would never hurt ye," he said. "I was only going to demand who gave ye this weapon, and who ye've used it against."

She dared a glance at his face. Though his jaw was set so firmly that a muscle jumped in his cheek, his eyes were clouded with confusion.

Her face must have revealed something, for he blinked, sudden clarity registering in the depths of his gaze.

"Ye've been hurt before, havenae ye?" he breathed.

When she didn't answer, his grip on her elbow loosened so that he supported her, but she could have broken free if she'd wanted to.

"The man who gave ye this, and that necklace— your boss. He hurts ye."

It was as if a hot fist clutched her throat, for hardly a wisp of air could get by, let alone the words lodged there. As she held his gaze, she felt something crack and crumble in her chest. Wordlessly, she nodded.

Those sea-blue eyes clouded with a raging storm, and she almost flinched back, but his hand remained gentle on her.

At last, he let out a long, slow breath, his hand falling from her elbow.

"I'm holding on to this," he said, tucking her gilded dagger back into his belt. "Come. Ye need to dry yerself and get dressed."

Colin stepped back and held out his hand, beckoning her toward where his stallion stood through the trees.

Stunned, she slowly walked from the water and into the underbrush.

Why hadn't he struck her? And why did it seem to upset him so greatly to know that Fabian did?

She'd always believed that the pain she suffered at

Fabian's hands was just part of life—one more piece of proof that the world was a cruel place. Yet Colin had never once hurt her. In fact, his kindness threatened to unravel everything she thought she knew of people and the world.

As she wrung her hair out and slipped her dress over her damp shift, Colin set about making a fire. They moved in silence around each other until the evening faded to night. Colin stretched out a few feet from her, wrapping himself in his cloak and settling in for sleep.

Sabine lay staring at the stars speckling the black sky overhead for a long time. She rubbed her bruised left shoulder, thankful for the freedom of her unbound wrist.

Even without the rope tying her down, however, she felt tethered in place.

She'd failed in securing the missive, of that she was certain. Her plan to woo Colin into a false sense of trust had been a disaster. She had no doubt that he would never let her get near enough again for her to slip the missive away.

Aye, she'd succeeded in getting him to leave her wrist untied, but something far more confusing, far more dangerous, and far more binding held her in place where she lay an arm's length away from him.

She was beginning to care for him.

Miles swung down from his horse in front of the cheery little inn, whose double doors were open to let the cool night air in.

Rabbie and Rollo, the two hulking twin brutes he'd selected to ride with him, followed his lead, dismounting and awaiting his orders.

Miles stood motionless in the shadows for a count of one hundred slow breaths. He kept his gaze on the inn for sights and sounds of trouble, but only merry-making drifted to him.

He'd already confirmed that the girl and a fair-haired man had been glimpsed taking off east from Dumfries. This village would be right in their path if they'd continued eastward, and the inn was the only one for several miles in any direction.

It was the likeliest spot that Sabine would have gone, as Miles well knew from years of being assigned her only point of contact besides Fabian. Though she was a resourceful and clever girl, she was from the streets. She might hide in the woods for a short while, but she felt safer near towns and villages, where she so often worked.

The man was an unknown factor, however, which meant Miles needed to proceed with caution. Still, naught seemed amiss within the inn.

"Let's check the stables," he murmured to the twin shadows looming behind him, nodding with his chin off to the right.

They followed him as he moved silently toward the

shadowed structure alongside the inn. One of the doors was cracked, and the warm light from a lantern slipped out onto the muddy street.

Miles motioned for the two brutes to halt beyond the cast of light, then opened the stable door and stepped inside.

A stable lad jumped from an idle slouch and came to his feet.

"Can I help ye, milord? See to yer horse, or mayhap arrange for a room at the inn?" the lad asked.

"I'm looking for someone," Miles said, forcing his voice into a friendly Lowland lilt. "A woman with dark brown hair—a pretty thing ye'd likely no' soon forget."

Recognition fluttered across the lad's oversized features, but he hesitated.

"Mayhap a man was with her as well," Miles went on, casually dropping his hand to the coin pouch on his belt. "A big braw laddie with blond hair." He slipped a coin from the pouch and lifted it until it caught the light streaming from the lantern.

The stable lad's eyes rounded on the coin, his mouth falling open. "A-aye, I believe I know who ye speak of. They came through two nights ago, and gave us a hell of a lot of trouble—forgive my tongue, milord."

Miles waved away the boy's apology and gave him an encouraging smile.

"The man—a Highlander, I believe—roughed up several of the inn's patrons when the lass squawked something about being kidnapped. After he broke a few noses, she said it was all some jest. They didnae stay the night, needless to say."

"And which direction did they go when they left?"

"East, though no' by the road, for the next morning a few of the men who were still sore over the ruse went to the edge of town and saw tracks headed into the forest."

Miles granted the lad a warm smile and flipped him the coin. The boy caught it and eagerly tucked it into his belt.

"Thank ye, my laddie," Miles said over his shoulder as he slipped from the stables.

In the darkness outside, he halted in front of Rabbie and Rollo.

"No blood," he said, dropping his voice. "Make it look like an accident. We don't need any more questions or attention."

The twins' faces split into identical coarse smiles as they nodded their comprehension and strode into the stables behind Miles. He mounted, waiting for them to finish their task.

When they reappeared, they still bore those stupid, harsh grins.

"Mount," Miles snapped. "We ride east."

Chapter Sixteen

Colin hunched deeper into his cloak, drawing the hood lower so that rain would stop trickling down his spine.

The briefly pleasant weather had vanished the morning after they'd slept next to the loch, and once again the cursed rain had started up.

Even by Highland standards, this weather was a blasted pain in the arse.

But if Colin were honest with himself, it wasn't the incessant rain that had him in such a foul mood.

He and Sabine had spent the day and a half since their kiss beside the loch in near silence, which only left Colin's echoing, self-castigating thoughts to keep him company.

Even now, his gut twisted at the memory of that kiss. Fierce desire spiked his blood, followed quickly by rage at himself for his lack of control.

He was supposed to be the one in charge. He was supposed to be the one wooing her, charming her into lowering her guard until she let some useful tidbit about the spy organization she worked for slip out.

Instead, he'd nearly shoved her to the loch's rocky

shore and buried himself between her thighs like some wild animal.

And damn it all, but part of him still wanted to claim her right here, right now. He'd yank down her cloak's hood and sweep aside that dark mass of unbound hair, then sink his teeth into the soft skin at the nape of her neck. He'd lift her in the saddle and spin her around so that her legs wrapped around his hips and his cock drove into her—

He ground his teeth hard enough that the pain in his jaw jerked him from his fantasies. For the hundredth time in the last day and a half, he cursed himself and his wayward thoughts.

He'd never lost control like this before—first in kissing her by the loch, and now in being unable to rein in his lust for her.

That wasn't entirely true, though, which drove cold fear into the pit of his stomach. Aye, he'd lost control like this once before—and nearly lost everything else because of it, too.

Ever since that terrible day eight years ago, he'd vowed never to be caught unaware again, to always be the one in command.

He'd broken that vow. Worse, his threadbare hold on restraint threatened to snap once and for all with each passing moment in Sabine's presence.

Blessedly, the sound of rushing water ahead cut through the monotonous thrum of the rain. The River Cree couldn't be far, which meant that they were only a day or two away from Portpatrick.

With any luck, the straight separating Scotland and Ireland would be calm enough that they could make a swift, easy passage across. Then Colin could deliver his missive to the Bruce's brother and decide once and for all what to do with Sabine.

The memory of her, cowering and trembling in the loch's shallows, twisted like a knife in his heart. From the moment Colin had met her, Sabine had seemed strong and confident, scrappy and damned annoyingly determined. Seeing her recoil from him had been like a blow from a hammer to the gut.

Far more disturbing, he'd seen the truth in her eyes. The man who'd rescued her from the streets, the man whom she seemed utterly devoted to, must have been in the habit of striking her, for the way she'd ducked and covered her head spoke of experience with beatings. That bastard had made her afraid. He'd hurt her, yet she still protected him.

How he'd longed to demand answers from her, to hear from her own lips what that piece of shite for a man had done to her. But fear had shadowed those wide hazel eyes. He would never be like the man she protected. He'd never force a word from her, or give her any reason to fear him.

Yet she was still Colin's enemy—and the enemy of Robert the Bruce.

What a bloody mess he'd made.

As the river came into view, Colin's stomach

dropped.

At his string of muttered curses, Sabine stiffened in the saddle before him.

"What's wrong?" She turned her head partially toward him so that he could see the outline of her nose and soft mouth, but her eyes remained hidden behind the edge of her hood.

"The river. We need to cross it, but these cursed rains have made it swell."

Worse than made it swell, he realized as they drew nearer. The river had risen well past its natural banks, swallowing underbrush that had once been several feet above the waterline. The water rushed south, murky brown with silt and frothy white where it churned into rapids.

"Is there a bridge?"

"Nay, no' within a day's ride of here."

And Colin couldn't afford to lose another day, not when he'd already been delayed at nearly every turn. Despite the muddy roads, Sabine's attempt to escape, and having to travel through dense forests, he still calculated he could make it to Ireland in a day or two, but not with yet another setback.

He eyed the river for a long moment, considering. "We may still be able to ford it," he said at last.

Aye, the river surged by with the force of all the extra rainwater, but he'd crossed here before. The water normally didn't even reach Ruith's belly. Now it would likely swell past his flanks, but he was a powerful animal. If he could keep his footing, they'd be safely across and on their way to Portpatrick.

Sabine stiffened even more but didn't speak. Though he hadn't tied her wrist since they'd spent the night at the loch, she was still his captive. He would make the final decision, but her life rested in his hands.

Carefully, Colin unbuckled his sword from his hip and twisted in the saddle so that he could secure the weapon to one of the saddlebags. He tucked Sabine's heavy dagger, which he still carried in the back of his belt, into the bag as well. When he'd fastened the buckles snugly on both bags, assuring himself that naught would drift free, he nudged Ruith toward the river's edge.

"Hold on to the pommel," he said, leaning toward Sabine's ear to be heard over the coursing water.

Her hood bobbed quickly as her good hand darted out to grip the pommel.

With one hand tightly clenching the reins, Colin wrapped his other arm around Sabine's torso, careful to hold her hurt arm gently.

"I've got ye," he murmured next to her hood. "Ye'll no' be swept away, I promise."

He could feel a shiver race through her, and then she pressed her spine into his chest, as if drawing comfort from him.

Though Ruith nickered and hesitated at the water's edge, Colin urged him on with his heels and a sharp click of his tongue. Despite the horse's misgivings, he was trained well enough to follow Colin's order. Fast-moving water shot up around Ruith's hooves as he made his way into the river.

When the water raced around Ruith's knees, Colin could feel the stallion working for control. He urged the animal to cut a new angle toward the far shore. Though it meant a longer path, by slanting their direction slightly downriver, he hoped it would lessen the force of the water lashing them.

At the halfway point, the muddy water surged at the base of Ruith's shoulders and tugged at Colin's cloak. His knees were submerged, his feet getting battered by the water's powerful grip, but he kept his seat in the saddle, holding Sabine close to his chest.

Ruith plowed forward like a ship through a storm, somehow still managing to hold his footing. Colin urged him on, relief washing him as they began rising out of the deepest section of the river.

As Colin glanced back at the shoreline behind them to gauge their progress, though, his heart froze in his chest.

Upriver, an enormous tree trunk had been swept into the current. The log, which was so big that Colin likely couldn't have encircled it with his arms, now careened toward them.

"Hold on!" he bellowed over the roaring river.

Fighting against the sucking water, Colin dragged his right boot free of the stirrup.

If he'd had more time to think, he might not have

risked this rash plan. As it was, the enormous log would take them both out if he didn't act.

Just as the log reached them, Colin planted his boot against the wet bark and shoved with all his might.

The log spun sideways, Colin's kick enough to propel it away from them and point it downriver. But the force of the impact was so great that Colin was thrust off Ruith's back and into the river.

Just before his head was swallowed by the cold, churning waters, he heard Sabine scream in terror.

Chapter Seventeen

The river spat Colin upward on a sudden swell of water and he gasped for breath.

The enormous log shot past him, picked up by a swift current that sent it crashing against rocks and partially submerged trees as it careened farther downriver.

Once again, he was sucked under by the icy, grasping water. He hadn't seen if Sabine still sat atop Ruith or if his efforts hadn't been enough to save her.

What little air he held in his lungs was knocked free as the current brutally drove him into an enormous boulder. As his body was swept around the boulder, he forced his stunned arms to reach out for something, anything, to hold on to.

His fingers dragged against rock as he fumbled for purchase. The cold numbed the scraping pain. If he lived through this, he could worry about his fingers later.

As he fought for a hold, his palm wrapped around an apple-sized protrusion on the boulder. His wooden fingers latched onto the spur of rock, and suddenly he was jerked to a halt even as the angry river continued to rush past him.

Gritting his teeth against the clawing water, Colin dragged his other hand up to the tie holding his cloak around his neck. The cloak twisted and pulled at his throat. The sodden garment had become the river's minion in its quest to pull him under. With a jerk on the knot, the cloak came free and was instantly sucked away.

"Colin!" Sabine's terrified cry pierced his water-filled ears.

Relief crashed through him as he pried open his eyes. She still sat atop Ruith's back upriver, water cascading around the animal's powerful legs.

"Keep moving!" he shouted, muddy water invading his mouth.

Though Ruith was as sure-footed and strong as any horse Colin had ever known, even the stallion would be hard-pressed to remain in place against the rush of the river. If they continued along the angle he'd made, cutting across the river without going fully against its strength, they might have a chance to make it to the other side alive.

But Sabine didn't urge the animal on. Instead, her panicked gaze was rooted on him.

"Go!" he barked, jerking his head toward the shore-line.

At last she seemed to snap out of her daze, for she kicked Ruith, her one good hand still gripping the pommel. She leaned low over Ruith's neck to say something into his ear, but the words were swallowed by the river before they reached Colin.

Whether it was because Ruith knew his master's wishes, or that the horse's survival instinct had taken over, he obeyed Sabine's command this time and began to step carefully toward the far shoreline once again.

Even as he fastened his other hand to the little knob of rock, Colin kept his gaze locked on them until the horse had fully cleared the swollen river and was on solid, dry ground.

It was only then that he considered Sabine's options.

She'd gotten Ruith to obey her once, so she could try her luck and urge the horse on without a backward glance at Colin. She could go upriver and look for a safer place to cross, then return to Dumfries or wherever she pleased.

And even if Ruith refused to take her commands now that they were out of the river, she could simply dismount and walk back to the east. She would be rid of her captor and free to return to her employer, with none the wiser.

But to Colin's shock, Sabine slipped from Ruith's saddle and ran back to the river.

"Colin!" she cried again, her face a mask of fear. She began wading into the water, never taking her wide eyes from him.

"Stop, lass!"

Was she mad? She couldn't simply swim across the river to where he clung for dear life to the slippery, water-battered boulder.

His words seemed to jar her from her terrified torpor. She halted, knee-deep in the swirling river, the angry waters tugging mercilessly at her skirts and cloak.

Her rounded eyes darted around desperately until they landed on Ruith. She bolted from the river's edge to where the horse stood several feet away. With a yank, she pulled open one of the saddlebags and began digging frantically in it.

Colin's arms had already gone numb, but now they began to turn loose and limp from the relentless hammer of the water battering him against the boulder. With a grunt, he willed his strength into his fingertips, where he clung to the slippery little rock spur.

Blinking against the silty water, his gaze locked on Sabine once more. She'd removed a length of rope from the saddlebag, the same one he'd used to bind her wrist, and was tying it around the saddle's pommel.

Colin hadn't realized just how dim his hope of surviving the raging river had grown until it suddenly flickered to life once more.

Despite the clumsiness of having only one good hand, Sabine worked swiftly and with complete focus to secure one end of the rope to Ruith's saddle.

When she was done, she gave the end of the rope a tug hard enough to jostle the saddle on Ruith's back.

The animal only stood patiently, seeming to sense the direness of the situation.

Sabine snatched up the loose end of the rope and shot to the edge of the river once more. She quickly balled some of the rope in her grasp, then pulled back and launched it at him.

The rope splashed into the river off to Colin's left, shooting downriver and out of reach.

Sabine jerked the rope back toward her, straining against the line's extra waterlogged weight.

Again, she threw the rope toward him, this time stumbling with the effort. But the line didn't reach as far this time. It slapped into the water several feet away.

"Throw it upriver!" Colin shouted.

His left hand suddenly slipped from his hold. The surging water yanked his arm back in its attempt to sweep him away.

Sabine cried out wordlessly in fright even as she yanked the rope toward the shoreline. Her arms full of heavy, wet rope, she staggered several paces upriver along the muddy bank.

With a heave that sent her lurching to her knees into the water, Sabine hurled the rope, this time aiming well above Colin.

The river snatched the rope and tugged it along with the swift current. As Colin watched the line approach, his stomach sank.

The angle would be off. The current was carrying

the rope farther to Colin's left once more.

One of his fingers slipped from his hold on the boulder, then another. The end of the rope was almost even with him, but several feet off to the left.

As the tail end of the line slipped by, Colin knew he had to take a chance.

Gathering the last of his strength, he shoved away from the boulder and gave himself over to the river.

As the current took him, he was flung closer to the rope. With a hard kick and a stroke of his numb arms, his hand closed around the rope's end.

The rope burned against his palm as the water fought to pull him away, but somehow he managed to cling to the line. Rolling his hand, he wrapped the rope around his wrist to ease the strain against his palm.

"Go, Ruith, go!" Sabine cried.

Without hesitation, the stallion surged forward, fighting against both Colin's weight and the power of the river trying to drag him back.

One aching inch at a time, Colin was pulled toward the riverbank. His wrist, arm, and shoulder screamed in protest even as he forced his legs to kick.

Sabine grabbed hold of the rope on the shore, pulling with all her might to aid Ruith. She leaned her entire body back, her hands skidding along the sodden line and her boots slipping in the mud.

When he was only a few feet from the bank, she waded into the water once again, scrambling toward him. Colin tried to plant his feet under him, but he'd spent every drop of strength he had. His limbs had turned to sludge.

Sabine tried to lift him under the shoulders, but his weight was far too great for her frame. She fell backward in the shallows, with Colin tumbling on top of her.

She cried out again as his weight came down on her. He realized through the haze of pain and fatigue that he must have hurt her. He tried to roll away, but then her slim arm wrapped around his neck and her fingers sank into his sodden tunic.

"I thought you were lost," she choked out, her voice thick with emotion. "I thought I'd lost you."

"Nay," he mumbled, his lips and tongue slow and stiff from cold. "Ye'll no' be rid of me so easily, lass."

A noise that was half-laugh, half-sob escaped her and she clung even tighter to him.

Easing himself off her, he rolled onto his back, the river lapping futilely at his boots and the muddy bank sinking under his shoulder blades.

"Ye saved me, Sabine. Why?"

He felt her stiffen next to him. When she didn't speak for a long moment, he dragged himself up to sitting and looked down at her.

Her dark hair lay splayed in the mud, her dress and cloak tangled around her. Rosy color sat high in her cheeks, and her green-gold eyes were wide and locked on him.

If they weren't both soaking wet and covered in

mud, he might have made the mistake of noticing how ravishing she looked—and ravished as well, like she'd been fully sated by his mouth, his hands, his—

He shoved the dangerous thought aside. Aye, this was a woman of many secrets. Would he ever have answers?

"Come," he said at last, his voice tight in his throat. "We'd best get dry."

Chapter Eighteen

I t wasn't until her teeth began to chatter that Sabine realized just how deeply the cold and dampness had burrowed into her bones.

After slowly rising to his feet by the riverbank, Colin had walked Ruith away from the rushing water and into a little copse of trees that provided shelter from the misty rain that had started up once more.

Numbly, she'd followed, his question still ringing in her ears.

Why? Why had she helped him? Why had she stayed and saved his life instead of turning her back and never thinking of him again?

In her scramble for an answer, all she could come up with was that he still carried the missive she'd been sent to intercept. If he'd been swept away by the river, she would have never learned what that missive bore. She wouldn't have been able to deliver the information it contained to Fabian, which would have angered—or worse, disappointed—him.

But that answer rang false. Sabine had worked her whole life at fooling people into trusting her, believing her. Yet the only one she feared she was fooling now was herself.

She watched in silence as Colin started a fire, not feeling any of its warmth penetrate through her sodden layers of wool.

When her teeth began to clack together, either with cold or shock at what had transpired, she did not know, she looked up to find those vivid blue eyes examining her.

"Ye'd best get out of those wet clothes, lass." He tossed a damp log into the fire, never taking his gaze from her.

"I have naught else to wear."

He walked woodenly to where he'd chucked Ruith's saddlebags on the ground near their fire. After a moment of rummaging, he pulled out the same length of green and blue plaid from which he'd removed a strip for her sling.

Unthinking, she glanced down at where that scrap of fabric had wrapped around her injured arm. She hadn't worn the sling for almost two days—ever since Colin had removed it along with her dress for her bath in the loch. For some reason she didn't want to contemplate, she missed seeing its vibrant colors and feeling the soft wool that still faintly bore Colin's scent.

She forced her thoughts away from Colin's kind gesture in making her that sling. Instead, she focused on her soiled and dripping garments.

"I cannot take that. It will only become wet and muddy if I wear it now."

"No' if ye remove that dress and cloak."

Her gaze darted up to his, searching for the deceptively enthralling smile he'd used against her once before. Exhausted, cold, and wet as she was, she feared she wouldn't be able to resist him if he started his charm offensive once more.

But instead of a beguiling grin or a suggestive glint in his eyes, she found her own raw fatigue mirrored on his weary features.

"And what will you use to warm yourself?"

An invisible guard seemed to lift behind his eyes and he grew hard and flat as a stone wall.

Too late, she realized how he'd taken her question. He thought she meant to encourage him to cast off his tunic so that she could make a move for the missive.

A flood of hot pain cut through her exhaustion. Of course he didn't trust her. Why should he? Aye, she'd saved him, but she couldn't even form the words to explain why.

"I'll be fine," he said quietly.

All she could manage was a nod, the lump in her throat too large to speak around.

He held out the plaid, and she stood from the damp log she'd been sitting on to retrieve it. When her legs came under her, however, she swayed like a leaf in a stiff breeze.

Colin was there suddenly, his hands steadying her.

"Do ye need help, lass?"

She looked up at him, the tears welling in her eyes

blurring the hard, handsome lines of his face. She nodded again, blinking back her foolish emotion.

Colin undid the pin holding her cloak at her throat and let the wet material fall heavily at her feet. Then he turned her gently by the shoulders and began working the ties running down her back.

"I dinnae ken what ye were thinking, lass," he said, his voice a low caress behind her as he loosened the ties. "When ye reached the shore and leapt from Ruith's back, ye looked ready to barrel into the river and fetch me, raging current be damned."

Sabine swallowed hard, forcing her throat to slacken. "I-I don't know what I was thinking, either. I couldn't think at all when I believed you might die."

Colin's hands stilled for a moment on her back. After a long pause, he began peeling down the dress from her shoulders, just as he had by the loch when she'd thought to seduce him. How much had changed in so little time.

When his hands slid around her waist, with naught separating their skin except for her sodden shift, the thread of control she'd been clinging to finally snapped.

She spun to face him, her dress falling limply to the ground alongside her cloak. Rising on her toes, she brushed her lips against his in a questioning kiss.

The battle that waged in his depthless blue eyes took her breath away. Pain and desire, distrust and longing warred for dominance as he held her with his gaze, his hands still resting on her waist.

When at last his features turned to granite, she knew the hardened warrior in him had won out over the passionate lover she'd glimpsed by the loch.

Questions skittered through her mind as she watched him straighten and drop his hands from her waist. The easy smile, the playful glint in his eyes— she'd thought them acts before, but might they actually reveal his true nature? If so, what had turned him so cold inside, so hard and suspicious—so like her?

He reached for the length of plaid, which he'd tossed over one shoulder.

"Get some rest," he said curtly. "And stay close to the fire. Ye need to get warm."

He looped the plaid around her shoulders and wrapped her snugly in its thick, dry folds. The scent of pine—Colin's scent—drifted around her, making a tight knot low in her belly.

She did as he commanded, lowering herself to the mossy forest floor near the weak fire. Yet even as she grew warm and drowsy within the plaid, she could not tear her eyes from Colin. She watched him through her lashes, trying to burrow as deep as possible in his plaid.

He paced around their little camp, busying himself despite his obvious exhaustion. His face was set in a scowl as he restlessly moved around her.

Once he'd seen to Ruith, he spread her cloak and dress over a large rock to help them dry, then piled sodden logs near the fire. Every once in a while, she caught a shiver he no doubt tried to repress as he paced in his soaking tunic and breeches.

At last, he settled by the fire, holding his hands out to catch some of its heat. Still, he could not seem to get warm, for his large body trembled with shivers. To make matters worse, even though the misty rain let up, night began to fall in earnest.

Standing, he muttered something that sounded like a curse and finally yanked off his tunic. His skin glowed orange in the flickering firelight, which cast deep shadows across the plains and valleys of muscle stacking his torso. Gooseflesh rippled across his taut skin, confirming her fear that he'd remained too long in his cold, wet garments.

As he turned to drape the tunic next to hers on the rock, she sat up, dropping the ruse of sleep. He must have sensed her movement, for he spun quickly, his gaze hard and dark on her in the low light.

Sabine rose slowly to her feet, hugging the plaid around her shoulders. When she took a step toward him, he purposefully angled his body to block her from his tunic.

Even as the sting of his motion registered, she took another step forward, holding his gaze.

She couldn't muster the bravery to speak the truth, so she would show him instead. She didn't want the missive in this moment. She only wanted him.

Opening her arms slowly, she beckoned him wordlessly into the warmth of the plaid. She held his gaze unfalteringly, letting him glimpse the raw need swirling through her.

He stood motionless for one heartbeat, then two,

then three. Just when Sabine was ready to retreat back into herself, he stepped forward into the spread plaid.

Hard arms enveloped her, his cold skin sending shivers through her at every point of contact. She wrapped the plaid around both of them, willingly giving him her heat.

He dragged her to the ground before the fire. He turned so that she lay partially draped across his hard body, both of them bound together in the tightly wrapped plaid.

Sabine lifted her head from his chest, gazing at his hooded eyes. In the shadows cast by the fire, his features were unreadable.

His hands tightened around her, drawing a gasp from her lips. Her pulse hammered as his body heated against hers. Unbidden, her tongue darted out to wet her lips in anticipation for his kiss.

But his kiss never came.

Deliberately, he drew in a deep breath, then another. His hands unclenched from her shift and his head fell back, his gaze searching the night sky overhead.

All the events of the last few days seemed to hit Sabine at once. If she weren't so exhausted, she probably would have wept like a silly girl in Colin's arms. The warmth of his embrace and the now familiar scent of pine and male skin saved her, though.

"Good night, lass." Colin's voice rumbled against her cheek as her head relaxed against his chest and sleep stole her away.

Chapter Nineteen

When the first rays of sunshine gilded the tops of the trees overhead, Colin stirred awake.

He was wrapped in warmth, his plaid softening the forest floor.

For a moment, he thought he was in the Highlands, sleeping on the ground with his plaid as a bedroll, just as he had done countless times while fighting for the Bruce and Scottish independence.

But then he registered the arm draped over his stomach, the sable head nestled against his chest, and the slim thigh thrown over his leg.

Nay, he wasn't in the Highlands, nor was he still dreaming. Sabine lay in his arms, limp and soft in sleep.

The sweet smell of her hair drifted around him like a cloud. He could feel the curve of her breast rhythmically press against him with her slow, steady breaths.

He must have stiffened, for she shifted and nuzzled against him as if silently urging him to relax.

Dragging in a ragged breath, he forced himself to lie still, though he couldn't quite convince every part of him to soften.

Unable to move without disturbing her, he let his

eyes drink their fill.

Those full, pink lips were parted slightly. Her cheeks bore a healthy, warm glow to match her lips. Her lashes made dark fans against her skin, with her brows relaxed in innocent rest.

Innocent.

Bloody hell, why did he have to think of that word? The implications swirled through his mind, destroying the peace he'd experienced a moment before.

She claimed not to be a spy, but did it make a difference? Did being a thief of secrets make her any more innocent of treason for opening the King's missive?

And when he'd kissed her, her response had been far from innocent, yet when he'd cruelly implied that she was a prostitute, the flush that had rushed to her cheeks seemed to be more than just outrage.

Was it possible that somehow through a life of stealing and lying, seduction and evasion, Sabine had come through it all holding on to a piece of her innocence, either in body or soul?

Mayhap the better question was why Colin was so desperate to know the secrets tucked away in Sabine's heart. She was unlike anyone he'd ever known before. She rivaled him at his own game—control and manipulation through a look or a smile—yet behind those hazel eyes he sensed a deeper truth, an unfathomable pain, that remained just out of his reach.

And she'd saved his life, damn it all.

Something stretched in his chest. Some buried and

unused part of him expanded where her head rested just above his heart.

She'd been hurt, of that he was sure. Yet there was something trusting in the way she slept so soundly curled against him.

Tentatively, he lifted a hand and brushed a lock of dark hair from her cheek. She stirred against him, burrowing into his chest as if she were starved for more of his touch.

He traced her ear with the pad of his thumb, and a soft sigh fanned across his bare chest.

Heat scorched through his body at her response. By God, why did he want to give her anything and everything she desired just to hear that breathy sigh again?

He let his fingertips graze down the slim column of her neck, drawing gooseflesh across her skin in their wake.

She shivered against him and murmured something, but the words were incoherent.

His fingers played over her injured shoulder lightly. The bruises were already fading—a good sign that she was recovering quickly.

Still, irrational anger burned in his chest just at the sight of the marks marring her creamy flesh. The man to whom she was still loyal had likely left marks like that.

He'd noticed that she'd gained increasing mobility in her shoulder the last two days, though she still kept her arm tucked against her or rested it in her lap while they rode. Soon, he would have to decide if he should tie her to the saddle once more.

The thought of binding her sent a sick swell rising in his stomach, but she was still his captive. Naught had changed, despite the fact that she'd saved his life.

Sabine murmured again, and he realized that he'd frozen, his hands turning unconsciously into fists in the plaid. He softened his hands and let them run soothingly down her back. She settled against him once more like an attention-starved cat, drinking in his touches.

As one hand reached her lower back, she arched against him, her head rolling so that her lips brushed his chest.

Bloody hell, what was he doing? He hadn't kissed her last night for fear that if he started, he wouldn't be able to stop. Yet here he was, cock achingly stiff and hands all over her just to satisfy his desire to draw another contented noise from her.

"Don't stop. Please."

He started at her voice, which was far too distinct to be mistaken for a drowsy mumble. Christ, how long had she been awake while he'd indulged in touching her?

"Please," she whispered again, lifting her head and capturing him with her gaze. Her eyes were as richly green as a Highland forest, with flecks of gold like the morning sun streaming overhead.

Before his brain could tell him nay, his hand slid further down to cup her bottom. He ground his hips against her, wordlessly showing her his desire.

Aye, he wanted to pet and stroke her until she purred for him, but she needed to know what he truly longed for—to bury himself in her, claim her body with his. This was no longer about a flirtatious smile or a teasing wink. The base male animal within him wanted her, *needed* her.

If she had pulled back, he would have stopped. If she had hesitated, a hand on his chest to stay him, he would have found a way to drop his hands and move away. If there had been even a flicker of fear or uncertainty in the depths of her dark eyes, he would have cooled his blood and let her go.

Instead, she rocked forward and pressed her lips to his.

Like a wild animal being set loose, Colin unleashed his tightly reined desire.

With a low growl, he rolled over so that she was pinned beneath him. She gasped, but the sound died as he took her mouth in a commanding kiss.

Chapter Twenty

His tongue met hers in a tangle of velvety warmth when he deepened the kiss.

He dragged in a breath through his nose, growing drunk on the sweet, delicate scent of her hair and skin. Though he bore most of his weight on his elbows, he let his hips press into hers, grinding slowly against her.

One of her knees rose, giving his thigh access between her legs. A moan of pleasure quickly followed her surprised inhale as he pressed into her womanhood with his thigh.

His hand slipped down to her raised knee and gripped her hard, looping her calf over his hip to give him fuller contact with her womanhood. Just a slight shift of his hips and the hard column of his cock would grind against her heat, with naught between them but her thin shift and his cursed breeches.

A distant warning rang in the back of his mind. She was his enemy, a voice whispered, an English spy.

Was this still part of some game she played? Was she using him even now for her own aims?

And what of his own motivations? Did sating his lust for this complicated, mysterious lass help his mission? Or was he endangering himself and his King even as he plundered Sabine's mouth, wrapped her leg around his waist, and ground his cock against her womanhood?

Sabine arched beneath him with a wordless moan, and the rational whispers were drowned out with a hot rush of fresh desire.

His hand found her breast, the pert curve rising up to meet his palm immediately. He could already feel the tight pebble of her nipple through her shift. She exhaled sharply and writhed beneath him at the simple touch.

Colin couldn't help the hard-edged satisfaction that shot through him at her responsiveness. He wanted more from her, wanted to take her further into the dark waters of desire and pleasure that they waded in now.

He broke their kiss with a growl. Sabine barely had time to sigh in frustration before his mouth was trailing down her neck. Her head rolled back on the plaid as he dragged his lips to her collarbone.

She arched even higher when he brought his mouth to hover over the peak of one breast. He let a hot breath fan across the outline of her nipple beneath her shift. Then his lips came down and he laved the peak through the linen.

She gasped and cried out, her head tossing to one side and then the other as he rocked against her. Her knee tightened around his hip as she fell into rhythm with him, arching into his mouth and pressing her womanhood against his thigh.

Half-wild with need, Colin tore his mouth away and yanked down the front of Sabine's shift. He ignored the sound of a few stitches popping as he let his eyes feast on the sight of her.

Every inch of her was creamy and smooth, except for the two rosy peaks of her breasts. She shivered, though he wasn't sure if it was from the cool morning air or from the need he'd kindled within her.

Her eyes fluttered open then. Unspoken tension crackled between them like lightning.

"Do ye want this, lass?" Colin asked, holding her gaze as he ground slowly against her.

"Aye," she panted. Her bared breasts rose and fell erratically with her ragged breath, her dark eyes burning with hunger. Something vulnerable suddenly flashed across her features. "Aye…but…I have never—I should not—"

She swallowed hard, and Colin felt her tremble beneath him.

Some final shred of sanity dragged Colin back from the brink he'd nearly tumbled over just then. Yet his body throbbed with undeniable need—and not merely need to release himself, but to take Sabine with him, to see behind the walls she'd erected around herself.

"I want to give ye pleasure," he rasped, "and ye dinnae have to give me aught in return—no' yer maidenhead, no' yer touch. Naught."

"And if I *want* to touch you?"

Hot anticipation shot through his veins straight to his cock. "Ye may."

Her lashes fluttered down, but he froze, holding her motionless.

"Look at me," he ordered, his voice hard and low.

She lifted her gaze, confusion swimming in her hazel eyes.

He needed to see her, to witness the truth in her eyes as he brought her pleasure. The thought that this might be some dangerous game she played still lurked in the recesses of his mind. But he also longed to watch her let go, to witness her vulnerability in her need for him.

Slowly, he lowered his mouth to one of her exposed breasts, never breaking their eye contact. As his tongue circled her nipple, her lids drooped but she held his gaze.

Her green-gold eyes flared with yearning as he ground his thigh against the crux of her legs once more. A breathy moan escaped her lips as she undulated against him.

Aye, one could fake attraction. One could flirt and smile with manipulation in mind—Colin would know.

But a woman could not feign the flush of desire like the one that pinkened Sabine's breasts and cheeks. Nor could she feign the hot moisture that dampened her shift where his thigh pressed against her womanhood, or the instinctual arch of her back in preparation for his invasion of her body.

There was truth in her desire for him—he could see it burning in her eyes. Though she still shielded many secrets from him, this moment was real, pure, unadulterated with schemes and ploys.

Need carving deep into him, Colin reached for the hem of her shift. He longed to explore every inch of her lithe, creamy legs, but he could not manage to slow himself. He rolled slightly to free his thigh from between her legs even as his fingers rose to her womanhood.

When he touched her, she jolted, her eyes fluttering but never breaking contact with his.

"God, ye are so wet for me," he hissed, his fingers tangling in her damp curls.

He slid a finger down the seam of her sex, parting her. She started again, this time gasping as he found that spot of pure pleasure.

He teased her, circling and stroking until her knees fell apart even wider and her hips rocked against his hand of their own volition.

Keeping a thumb on that bud of pleasure, he slid a finger to her opening and slowly began to ease into her.

Just then, her hand shot out, fumbling at his groin. When her palm cupped the hard length of his cock, he groaned and cursed.

Tentatively, she ran her fingers up and down his length, as if exploring his dimensions through his straining breeches.

The last of his self-control crumbled to dust in that moment. With another curse, he yanked down the front of his breeches even as he slid his finger all the way inside her.

They both inhaled sharply in unison. The pleasure of her bare hand on his cock blurred with the feel of her sheathing his finger in her tight, wet heat. Blood hammered in his ears, deafening him to her panting gasps and his own groans.

Slowly, he began pumping his finger inside her, all the while circling his thumb over her clitoris.

"Wrap yer fingers around me," he gritted out through clenched teeth, "and slide yer hand up and down."

She obeyed immediately, matching the rhythm he set inside her.

Colin's head dropped over her, at last breaking their gaze. His mouth found one of her breasts, and her whole body began to tremble as he worked his hand and tongue in time together.

He strained against the building pleasure, willing himself to hold back the tide of release even as her gasps and moans drew him closer.

Suddenly she twisted and cried out as she tumbled over the brink of ecstasy. She squeezed her thighs against his hand, her womanhood quivering around him.

He dragged up his head just in time to catch a

glimpse of her pleasure-clouded gaze before he followed her in release. He shuddered against her hand, shoving himself hard along her palm one last time as the dam of his pleasure broke.

As he drifted back down to earth, the fog of lust at last began to clear. Sabine lay dreamily in a pillow of her own lustrous hair. Her cheeks and lips were pleasure-flushed, and her eyes drifted closed as her breathing began to slow.

Seeing her lying there in the folds of his green and blue MacKay plaid sent a stab of something primal through his chest.

He'd almost made her his, fully and completely.

In the increasingly bright light of the dawning day, he acknowledged the wisdom in not claiming her maidenhead. Even still, an irrational hunger to do so still lingered, despite the fact that he'd sated his most urgent lust.

Sabine sighed and nestled deeper into his plaid. A far darker sensation suddenly stole over him—a memory.

Joan lying in his embrace, wrapped in his MacKay plaid.

Her body welcoming him as he drove into her.

The sight of her draped in the green and blue MacKay pattern, but this time lying in the arms of his best friend.

Colin tried to shove the dark memories aside, but they still haunted him as he looked down at Sabine.

What did he truly know of this woman?

She was a spy and a master manipulator. Or was she a wounded, innocent lass caught up in her boss's schemes?

His chest tightened with fear—fear of his desire for the lass. No woman had ever tied him in knots like this—except for Joan.

And what of his vow? Though invisible, the scar Joan had left would never heal. He'd promised himself never to let another woman so close to his heart, never to risk being taken in for a fool again.

Sabine's eyes drifted open, gazing at him with unguarded trust.

"Get dressed," he said. He hadn't meant to be so curt, but confusion made his tongue sharp.

Surprise followed quickly by hurt flashed across her eyes before she dropped a veil shielding her emotions from him.

"Aye," she murmured, untangling their limbs.

As they broke camp in silence, Colin struggled for an anchor in the storm of swirling thoughts within his mind. By the time they'd mounted Ruith, though, no clarity had come.

He spurred the stallion on, leaving the little copse where they'd shared that moment of passion behind.

Chapter Twenty-One

All day Sabine had been acutely aware of Colin's hard form pressed against her atop Ruith's back.

All day she'd felt tension radiating from him just as strongly as his clean, piney scent, which clouded her thoughts with its masculine pull.

And all day she'd cursed herself for a damned fool.

This was exactly what Fabian had warned her about. If she lowered her guard, surrendered to her desire, and gave up her body to a man, he would use her and then discard her.

Fabian had been right. How stupid Sabine had been to waver in her loyalty and obedience to him. Aye, Fabian frightened her sometimes, and even hurt her when he was in one of his moods. Yet he had never turned his back on her, as Colin had after giving her the most exquisite pleasure she'd ever known.

Thank God she hadn't surrendered everything to Colin. Mayhap if she had given him her innocence, he would be far worse than cold and distant now. Mayhap he would at last torture her, beat her, carve answers out of her flesh with her own dagger, which he still withheld in his saddlebag.

Even as the dark thought skittered across her mind, a soft, chiding voice rose against it.

Colin had already had every reason, every opportunity, to hurt her. Yet he hadn't. She was his enemy, his captive, yet he had never once raised a hand against her, as Fabian did even at her slightest falter.

Something real, something frighteningly true had passed between them by the river that morning. She'd seen it in his sea-blue eyes as he'd held her rapt with his gaze, his touch. She'd seen it in the satisfaction he'd taken from her pleasure and the fulfillment of his own need.

But then he'd turned away, that stone wall dropping around him once again. Sabine tried for the hundredth time that day to swallow the burning hurt that rose from her chest into her throat, but try as she might, she could not dislodge the pain of his sudden distance.

She was being abandoned all over again, just like when she was a child. Only this time, Fabian wasn't here to rescue her. She was truly alone now.

She doubted God listened to her anymore, but she sent a silent prayer from her heart anyway.

Please God, help me see the truth.

By the time Colin reined Ruith to a halt next to a little stream tucked between two thickly wooded hills, Sabine's whole body was in knots of confusion. Though the day had started out sunny and warm, threatening clouds had moved in from the west. The air now hung heavy with the promise of yet another fierce storm as evening approached.

"We are almost to Portpatrick," Colin said as he swung down from the saddle.

He reached for her waist, but she shied away from his touch, keeping her eyes downcast. After a long pause, he let his hands drop and stepped back, giving her space to awkwardly fumble her way down from the enormous stallion's back.

"Is that where we are going, then?" she asked when her feet reached solid ground.

He stiffened, his mouth compressing into a firm line.

After a day of confusion, hurt, and tension, his refusal to give her even a faint explanation about what he had planned for her shattered her fragile resolve.

"I don't understand why you can't tell me where we are going," she snapped. The sudden flood of anger was actually a relief from the cold silence that had settled over them all day.

"I cannot escape you," she went on, motioning to her hurt arm, which hung loose at her side. Though only a bit of stiff soreness remained, she still hadn't gained back much range of motion or strength. "And though you've ceased in tying me up, you've kept so far clear of the roads that I doubt I'd reach them on foot before you could hunt me down."

Colin's golden brows dropped forebodingly, a muscle working in his jaw as he pinned her with a narrowed gaze.

At his silence, her anger hitched higher. "You know very well that I won't try to escape anyway!"

"Because ye still want to get at the contents of the missive I bear."

"Aye!" she blurted, tears of frustration burning her eyes. What spell had Colin cast on her to make her feel so precariously close to losing control?

"So, we are to speak the truth at last." His voice was low and deceptively level.

"Why not?" she shot back, her voice rising dangerously with emotion. "Aye, I want that missive. You know I am a thief. You know what I am after."

"Do I?" he snapped. "Forgive me, but I cannae tell what ye want at all or what ye are doing."

He took a step toward her, and instinctively she backed up until she bumped into Ruith's flank. Thunder suddenly rolled in the distance, an ominous warning of the approaching storm.

"What were those murmurs for me to keep touching ye this morning?" he went on. "Was that for the missive as well?"

"Aye—nay!" Anger blurred with confusion in her churning stomach. "I-I don't know!"

He took another step forward, his large form practically pinning her against Ruith. A fierce storm raged in his eyes as he held her with his gaze.

"That is the problem, lass," he ground out. "Ye dinnae ken. Ye dinnae ken why ye saved my life. Ye dinnae ken why ye let me touch ye."

"And what of you?" she fired back, lashing out to deflect the hurt that nigh choked her. "You tie my hand one moment, then you kiss me the next. You eye me suspiciously and guard that missive as if you'd give your life for it, then you touch me as if you *cared*—"

Her throat closed, but not before the worst possible word slipped out. Sabine swallowed hard, her face growing hot.

Colin stilled before her, an exhaled breath escaping between clenched teeth.

"Ye're right," he said at last, another rumble of thunder chasing his words.

For a long, heart-wrenching moment, Sabine believed he meant that he did in fact care for her. But then he went on.

"I *would* give my life for that missive. Ye had me fooled there for a moment, lass. Nay, no' with yer schemes and ploys to get to the letter. Ye fooled me into believing that we were the same."

She shook her head slowly as if she could make him stop, but he went on.

"We both have our missions, dinnae we? We'd both use whatever means necessary—including seduction—to fulfill our assignments. But the difference is, at the end of the day, I ken where my loyalties lie. I fight for the King of Scotland and for the freedom of my country and people. What do ye fight for, Sabine? Coin?"

His sharp eyes cut into her, examining her with keen intelligence. She could no longer muster the energy to mask the tempest of emotion that undoubtedly played across her face. Out of well-worn habit, she reached for the chain around her neck, seeking its comfort.

"Nay, no' coin, for I believe yer master keeps most of it," he said, his gaze slicing into her. "For his approval then. For a kind word from him, despite the fact that he hurts ye."

Her hand leapt away from the necklace as if it had burned her, even as her stomach dropped to her feet. How had he discerned so much? At the words that cut right to the truth, right to her heart, something cracked within her.

"Fabian cares for me!" she shrieked, her voice breaking. "He takes care of me. He would never abandon me—not like *you!*"

She shoved against his chest as hard as she could, but he barely budged. Tears blurred her vision as she looked up at him.

In that moment, she didn't know if she wanted Colin to disappear, never to tangle with the delicate threads around her heart again, or for him to wrap her in his steely embrace and never let go.

Through her tears, she saw his granite features crack as he gazed down at her. Pain flared in his vivid blue eyes even as his face softened.

"Sabine," he whispered, his voice a low caress. "I-

I'm sorry, lass. I shouldnae have—"

A branch snapped behind her. Colin's head jerked up, his whole body suddenly going taut.

"At last," a familiar voice rang through the forest beyond Ruith.

Sabine spun, her gaze darting over the stallion's saddle into the thick woods all around.

The speaker emerged through the trees a stone's throw away, two huge shadows looming behind him.

"*Miles*?" she gasped. "What are you doing here?"

Miles stared at her flatly as he walked his horse a pace closer. The shadows on either side of his shoulders materialized behind him into two enormous warriors with identical grins curving their large mouths.

"Fabian sent me," Miles said softly.

Relief crashed through her. She barely noticed the hard, fat drops of rain that began to fall around them.

Fabian *did* care for her. He would never abandon her.

But as Miles and his two brutes continued to advance slowly, some instinct sent fear shivering up her spine.

Fabian said he'd never come for her in the field. And why would Miles need two warriors by his side if he was only retrieving her?

"Miles, what—" she began, icy premonition racing in her veins.

Before she could ask her question, he turned to one

of his thugs.

"This time it doesn't have to be clean. Just make sure they're both dead."

Chapter Twenty-Two

"**N**ay!"

Before she knew what she was doing, Sabine darted around Ruith to confront Miles.

Colin's hand shot around her waist and held her back.

"Sabine, get behind me," Colin commanded.

"Miles, what is this?" she demanded, ignoring Colin. Her gaze jerked between Miles, sitting calmly atop his horse, and the two brutes who were slowly dismounting at his sides.

Miles leveled her with a flat stare.

"Are you truly surprised? You were compromised. Fabian cannot risk exposure." Miles's dark eyes flicked a glance at where Colin stood behind her, still gripping her waist with one hand as the other reached for the sword that was strapped to Ruith's saddlebags.

"He...he always said that if I was found out in the field, or ran into any trouble, I would simply have to find him again." Sabine's voice echoed through her ears, suddenly sounding naïve and childish.

Miles snorted softly. "Aye, I can see how he'd want you to think that, pet that you are to him. But you've been playing with the adults long enough to figure out the truth by now."

Sickness roiled in her stomach and up the back of her throat as an agonizing realization dawned.

"He…he ordered you to kill me?"

"Aye."

"Because I was compromised in the field."

Miles nodded again. One of the brutes cracked his knuckles loudly, as if to make his impatience known.

"And…and that is all?"

She hated the sound of her small, weak voice in that moment, hated the gaping emptiness that opened around her.

"Aye, that is all."

How could that be all? She'd given her life to Fabian, and he was this quick to discard her? She risked herself with every assignment. She'd been blindly loyal to him even when he lashed out at her. By God, she'd even defended Fabian to Colin.

Fabian cares for me.

He would never abandon me.

Her own words revealed her foolishness, her error in trusting and believing in Fabian.

The carefully ordered pieces of her life—her training from street urchin to skilled thief, her assignments proudly accomplished, her unfailing loyalty to Fabian—scattered and crumbled like naught more than dead leaves in a wintery wind.

She had been wrong—about everything. Her

whole life was one long, unbroken lie—until this moment, when the truth rent her heart as sure as a sword.

The truth was, Fabian didn't care for her. Had he ever? If he could order her death just to protect against the threat of exposure, mayhap even his rare kindnesses had been a lie, a manipulation.

And she'd huddled in the palm of his hand at every step, desperate for a sliver of affection, afraid of being abandoned all over again.

The forest spun around her. Rain splattered her face, but it did not lift her from her torpor. Distantly, she registered that she'd sagged against Colin's solid body.

"No games," Miles was saying, his voice sounding far away. "You understand, Rollo? Rabbie? No toying with them. Just be quick about it."

Colin shook her. "Stay with me, lass."

Though blackness encroached at the edges of her mind, Sabine dragged herself back to nightmarish reality.

When her eyes focused once more, she found the brutes, Rabbie and Rollo, stalking toward them slowly. Colin brandished his unsheathed sword in front of her, making a barrier of steel between her and the thugs.

"Can ye stand?" Colin said, never taking his gaze from the approaching warriors.

"Aye."

"Then get behind me and stay there until I tell ye otherwise." His voice was firm yet calm. He loosened his grasp on her waist and she hurried to obey him.

Some of his composure seeped into her, and her mind unknotted slightly. All that existed was this heartbeat, then the next as the warriors closed in on them. Rain rustled the leaves all around them, making the whole forest seem alive.

She'd never truly been in a battle before. It was usually her way to avoid direct confrontation. Yet Colin's sudden calm and clarity was a comfort to her ragged nerves—until one of the brutes yanked his sword from its sheath on his back and launched himself at Colin.

Then everything came undone with horrifying suddenness.

Colin blocked the blow, the clang of the two blades echoed by another clap of thunder. Sabine had to leap out of the way as one of the twin warriors shoved Colin back.

He recovered quickly, but he only just had time to sidestep the other warrior's attack.

This was naught like the skirmish she'd witnessed in the stables. Then, Colin had moved with lethal grace, yet he'd inflicted no more damage than a broken nose.

Now, all three of the men fought savagely. Each blow was delivered with fearsome strength and deadly intent, and every narrow evasion saved a man's life.

The two brutes tried to circle him, splitting up in an attempt to separate her from Colin. His blade darted out like a snake, first at one and then at the other, forcing them in front of him.

One of the giants launched another attack, his blade illuminating in the flash of lightning overhead. Colin caught the edge of the sword with his own, then twisted his wrist so that he bound the other blade with his.

He pinned the first brute's sword to the ground, but just then the other charged, blade aimed at Colin's chest.

Colin just barely arched out of the sword's path. The blade passed by him without making contact, but the second giant still barreled toward him. Colin took a shoulder to the chest and tumbled backward.

A wordless scream of terror ripped from Sabine's throat as she flung herself out of the way of Colin's careening body. He landed on the ground with a grunt but had no time to recover his footing, for the brutes set upon him once more.

He rolled just as one of the warriors' blades sank into the muddy ground where his head had been a heartbeat before.

"Get on Ruith's back!" he barked even as he regained his feet, blocking another blow.

Sabine scrambled through the mud and leaves toward the black steed, but even as she gained ground, she caught sight of Miles moving in on her. He reined his horse around the bristling melee made by Colin and the twin warriors as they fought on, angling himself toward Sabine.

Just as she reached Ruith, Miles loomed over her, drawing a short blade from his boot.

"Miles, nay!" she cried, stumbling back against Ruith's saddlebags.

Her plea was met with a flat, uncaring stare that chilled her very soul.

As he raised his dagger, an idea exploded through her mind. She dove a hand into the saddlebag behind her. When her fingers closed around the heavy sheath of her dagger, she yanked it free.

She lifted the dagger, still sheathed, over her head just as Miles's blade came down.

Reverberations from the impact of the blow traveled all the way down her good arm and into her hurt shoulder. Still, she'd managed to keep Miles's dagger from cleaving her skull in two.

He snarled in frustration, drawing back for another attack. Instinctively, Sabine dropped, rolling under Ruith's belly.

Miles growled again at her evasion, his horse stepping wildly as he yanked on the reins.

Frightened that Ruith would spook as well and trample her, she continued her roll, coming to her feet on the other side of the huge stallion.

Just then, a heart-stopping bellow tore through the forest. Sabine's throat seized as fear for Colin lanced her, but when her eyes found him, he was dragging his blade from one of the twins' chests.

The other giant warrior roared with rage.

"You killed my brother! You'll pay, you bloody bastard, I swear it!"

As the brute launched himself with renewed energy at Colin, Sabine's attention was jerked back to Miles when he cursed softly.

His gaze was still locked on Colin and the remaining twin as they circled each other slowly.

Trembling, Sabine wrapped one hand around the gilded sheath and gripped the dagger's handle with the other. Her left arm was still so cursedly weak. She gritted her teeth, willing her injured arm to cooperate.

Her left shoulder throbbing in protest, she at last managed to unsheathe the dagger. She ducked under Ruith's belly again, hoping the well-trained warhorse remained steady.

When she'd cleared the horse's belly, she jerked to her feet, dagger raised at Miles.

He started at her sudden appearance, tearing his gaze away from Colin and the warrior. Before he could react, though, she jammed the dagger deep into his thigh.

Miles screamed and kicked out, connecting with her stomach. She was thrown back, the dagger going with her in her tight grasp.

Sabine slumped against Ruith's side and fell to the ground. This time, the stallion could not help but dance sideways, nickering in distress. Miles's horse was even more spooked. It sidestepped and tossed its head, its hooves stomping toward Sabine.

She screamed again, flinging herself farther under Ruith.

"Sabine!"

Colin's ragged shout was filled with terror, but at least it meant he was still alive.

As she rolled away from both horses, amazingly avoiding all eight hooves, Colin roared a fierce battle cry. His war cry was quickly followed by the strangled scream of the other warrior.

She looked up to find blood spurting from the giant's neck as he toppled backward. Colin was already sprinting toward her, his blade dripping with dark blood and rainwater.

He hardly slowed when he scooped her up, still barreling toward Ruith. When he reached the stallion, he slammed his sword into its sheath and tossed her onto Ruith's back.

Colin launched himself into the saddle behind her. At that moment, Miles's horse reared wildly, flinging him to the ground in an unnaturally-shaped heap. Miles's scream was cut off by a low, sickening crunch.

She could not tell if Miles was still alive, for Colin spurred Ruith forward hard. The stallion exploded into a gallop at his master's command, crashing through the rain-drenched forest.

Sabine dared one glance behind them as they plowed onward. A flash of lightning illuminated the darkening woods, but all she saw was the gnarled outlines of the trees as they sprinted away.

Chapter Twenty-Three

A roiling fog of emotion clouded Colin's mind as he drove Ruith on. He could hardly feel the cold, pelting rain or the dull, distant aches in his body. Even Sabine's slight form before him in the saddle barely cut through the storm in his own head.

And what must she be feeling? She huddled against him, her body yielding to the arm he'd wrapped around her waist to hold her steady in their desperate flight west.

Her master—the bastard's name was Fabian—had tried to have her killed. The man she'd devoted herself to so completely, despite his cruelty to her, had abandoned her like so much refuse.

As Ruith galloped beneath him, the harsh words he'd spoken to Sabine drifted back. He'd pushed her away after indulging in his lust, coward that he was. Then he'd thought to throw her devotion to Fabian in her face.

She'd been so sure of Fabian's loyalty to her, of his caring for her, when she'd lashed back at Colin. He'd seen the deeper fear in her eyes, though. Fear of being abandoned again, like she was as a child.

Aye, Colin had abandoned her in turning so cold and distant after their morning of shared pleasure. He'd been too tangled in his own confusion over what they'd done to realize that he was hurting her.

But far worse, Fabian had forsaken her as well—the one person in whom she'd placed all the innocent faith of an orphaned child. The one person she said had ever cared about her.

Yet if Colin faced the pain and fear he'd fled from this morning, there was no denying the truth. Despite Fabian's desertion, Sabine was not alone, nor was she uncared for.

Colin pushed down the fresh swell of confusion that thought produced. He cared for a bloody spying, thieving Englishwoman—and he, one of King Robert the Bruce's fiercest warriors, a member of the Bodyguard Corps sworn to protect Scotland from all English threats.

Yet he couldn't be a coward any longer, by God. Aye, he'd made a damned fine mess of things, but he could no longer flee from his feelings for Sabine. She had to know that she was not alone, especially now.

But first, he had to get her to safety.

Ruith slowed, and Colin silently cursed himself. Bloody hell, he wouldn't be able to whisk Sabine away from danger if he ran his faithful stallion into the ground.

He reined Ruith in and let the animal catch his breath. They stood in a little clearing within the denser woods all around. Blessedly, the rain began to lighten, though dark clouds obscured the moon and thunder still rolled in the distance.

"Sabine," he murmured softly.

She jumped in his hold as if she'd only just now noticed they'd stopped.

Carefully, he untangled his arm from around her waist and slid from Ruith's back. He dropped the reins so that the horse could lower his head, still panting heavily.

When he looked up at Sabine, sharp fear lanced him.

She was in worse shape than he'd thought. The hood of her cloak hung uselessly down her back, her dark hair streaming with rainwater. Her gaze was fastened forward, a vacant look in her eyes.

The shaking of her hands drew his attention. He sucked in a breath at what she held.

Clutched in one hand was the elaborately gilded sheath for her dagger. In the other, she gripped the dagger's hilt, her knuckles white. The blade was darkened with blood.

"Sabine," he said gently. He slowly reached for her hands, wrapping each one in a tender grip. "It is over, lass. Ye can put the dagger away now."

Her head jerked and her wide-eyed gaze landed on him.

"Miles...I stabbed Miles in the leg." Her bottom lip trembled as she spoke, her tone distant and disbelieving.

"Aye, lass," Colin said quietly. "And ye likely saved yer life by doing so. Did ye…did ye see what happened to him?"

He wanted to go gentle with her, but he needed to know. The two giants who'd attacked him were both dead, he was certain. Yet he'd been so caught up in battling them that he'd failed to protect Sabine from Miles. He'd seen the man fall from his horse, but little else.

Sabine shook her head slowly. "His horse threw him. He went down in a pile that looked—"

She swallowed hard, squeezing her eyes shut. After a steadying breath, she managed to go on.

"I didn't see him move, but nor do I know if he is dead."

Carefully, he took the dagger and sheath from her trembling hands. He dragged the blade in the damp grass at his feet, then wiped away the rainwater on his breeches. When the dagger was securely back in its sheath, he extended it to her.

"Why dinnae ye hold on to that for now, lass."

She nodded numbly and tucked the dagger away in the folds of her wet, mud-covered dress.

"Will others come if Miles doesnae?"

Sabine's brows lifted in desperation. "Fabian is not one to leave loose ends."

"We'd better keep moving," he said quietly, scanning the meadow.

When he turned back to Sabine, silent tears mingled with the trickling droplets of rain on her cheeks.

He touched her gently, as if soothing a wounded animal. Cupping her cheeks, he turned her face toward him and tilted her chin down so that their eyes met.

"Sabine, listen to me. Ye are strong, lass. Ye will get through this. And I will help ye, I swear. We must get to safety now, but once we are on a boat, I promise to do everything I can to take away the pain."

Her distant gaze clouded with confusion at the mention of a boat, but she didn't ask about it. Colin took that as a sign of just how deep and dark the despair that had swallowed her was.

He caught up the reins and mounted behind her, urging the wearied Ruith on once again. He couldn't be sure how far they'd ridden in their flight from Fabian's men, but at least he could tell by the mountains that rose distantly beyond the trees off his right shoulder that they were still traveling west.

When they'd stopped before the storm had arrived, he'd planned to hunker down for the night, then continue on to Portpatrick with the hope of reaching the little port town on the morrow. But now with the threat of another attack on their heels, there was no time to rest.

He held Sabine close as the trees blurred in a dark mass around them. By God, so much had changed in the last sennight. He'd gone from fighting at the Bruce's side to take Carlisle to playing nanny goat to

Osborn, then he'd become the keeper of the beautiful but secretive English spy who was currently enfolded in his arms.

And now it appeared as though he was needed as a bodyguard after all, though he never would have imagined that he'd be applying his skills to protect the very thief who threatened the security of his King's correspondence.

If he were still attempting to deny his feelings for Sabine, he could justify beating back Fabian's thugs as necessary to his mission. The Bruce had sent him not only to deliver the missive to his brother, but also to ferret out those behind the compromise in his chain of communication. He'd found Sabine and still needed to deliver her to the Bruce so that the King could determine what to do with her, and what information she could provide on Fabian's organization.

Yet he could not pretend neutrality toward Sabine any longer. He'd acted on instinct alone when Miles and the two giant brutes had threatened her. And he knew deep in his chest that he would place himself between Sabine and anyone who dared attempt to hurt her again.

That realization drew his stomach into a tight knot. Aye, he'd broken his vow and allowed himself to care for another woman after Joan—and another woman who was a skilled deceiver. But it was too late to throw up his defenses now. Sabine needed him.

Distant flickering lights pulled him away from his

churning thoughts. The pinpricks of yellow light stood out against a backdrop of unbroken darkness. It had to be the tiny village of Portpatrick, set against the night-black sea.

Now Colin could only pray that he could get them on a boat to Ireland before Fabian's men could track them down once more.

Chapter Twenty-Four

Colin dropped several coins into the drowsy stable lad's hands.

"See that he is verra well cared for," he said firmly, patting Ruith's neck. "I'll be back in a matter of days, and I expect to see him content as a pig in slops and his coat gleaming, ye understand?"

The stable lad, who wasn't really a lad at all, bobbed his gray head. "Aye, milord. We'll see to the animal's every care. Ye needn't worry."

With a curt nod and another stroke of Ruith's neck, Colin hoisted his saddlebags over one shoulder and turned back to the stable's doors. Sabine stood just at the edge of the flickering lantern light looking like a ghost.

She was so pale and fragile, her cloak hanging heavily around her shoulders and her ruined dress clinging wetly to her slight frame. Those wide, dark eyes looked haunted as they gazed at naught.

He needed to get her warm and dry once they could secure passage to Ireland. But more than that, he needed to get her talking, crying—anything to help her crawl from the black hole she'd sunken into and start her toward healing.

Taking her hand, he gently pulled her away from the stables and toward the sleepy little village's docks.

The storm that had blown in from the west was finally starting to clear, and streaks of moonlight fell through patchy clouds. In the pale light, he squinted at the row of dark ships that bobbed and groaned quietly against the wooden docks.

His gaze landed on a long, thin birlinn. The ship would be perfect for a swift crossing to Ireland. As he drew Sabine nearer, though, he realized that the birlinn, built for speed and transporting men, would require a crew of at least two dozen men to work the oars when the large, square sail was lowered.

Colin strode on past several more birlinns and larger vessels before his gaze landed on a small, squat cog at the far end of the docks. Judging by its round, deep hull, the cog was no doubt used for cargo runs. That extra room below deck would be perfect for allowing Sabine to rest. And the whole ship looked small enough to be sailed with only a skeleton crew.

When they reached the far end of the docks, Colin released Sabine and stepped up to the cog's high wooden sides.

"Anyone here?" he called, rapping his knuckles atop one of the oak gunwales.

The little ship rocked gently alongside the dock, the lap of water against wood the only sound breaking the still night.

Then the faint hiss of metal being unsheathed from leather whispered through the air.

Without thinking, Colin bolted in front of Sabine, one hand coming around the hilt of his sword.

"Who is poking his nose around my ship at this black hour?" The gruff voice drifted from a large shadow that suddenly rose from the cog's deck and moved toward them.

"Hold, man, I mean no harm," Colin snapped, keeping his grip firm on the hilt but willing himself not to draw.

The shadow stepped into a beam of moonlight, revealing a gnarled, barrel-chested man holding a long dagger. The man eyed them critically under lowered eyebrows that were the same color—copper streaked with white—as his hair.

"What's this about, then?" the man asked, shifting his narrowed gaze over Colin.

Colin's mind sped ahead as he opened his mouth. The man was already suspicious and on guard. If Colin tried to force him to set sail for Ireland, undoubtedly the salty old sailor would have no problem escalating the situation. They didn't need trouble, just a quick passage out of here—now.

Colin lifted his hand from his sword and raised it disarmingly, sliding a friendly smile onto his face.

"Och, my apologies for rousing ye," he said lightly. "We would have been to Portpatrick at a decent hour if it hadnae have been for this cursed weather."

The man still held the dagger aloft, though he didn't make a move toward them. Instead, he waited in silence, the line of his mouth turned down in a frown behind a bushy copper beard.

"Ye see, my wife and I need to reach Ireland with all haste." He stepped aside so that the man could see Sabine. "She's Irish, ye ken, and her brother is set to wed on the morrow."

"If ye need transportation, ye can catch the ferry in the morning," the man said gruffly. His grizzled featured shifted slightly from suspicious to annoyed, though—a sign of progress.

"Aye, well, that's the problem," Colin said with a sigh. "We were supposed to be there yesterday, but this damned rain made the roads slow-going. I fear what my wife's mother will do to me if we miss her son's wedding."

The man's snort was vaguely pitying for Colin's plight, but he still seemed unmoved.

"And of course my mother-in-law is eager to see her only daughter now that a bairn is on the way."

Colin felt Sabine stiffen next to him as the man's eyes shifted to her.

"It is early yet, but my mother-in-law insisted we attend the wedding before my wife cannae travel."

The man's gruff façade softened ever so slightly. "The wee lass looks half drowned."

"Aye, as I said, we were caught in that blasted storm. I'd hoped to get her warm and dry, but the town's inn is full, and we are behind schedule already…"

Colin slipped an arm around Sabine, drawing her protectively to his side. He let his heart-wrenching plea hang in the air as the old sea dog considered them.

The man slid the dagger into the sheath on his hip, then rubbed his bearded cheek in thought.

"We were planning on setting sail at first light, since we received the last delivery we were waiting on this evening."

He looked out over the dark water, which was silvered with moonlight.

"I dinnae like to sail at night," he muttered. "But the seas will be calm now that the storm has blown off."

"We'll compensate ye for the trouble, of course," Colin said apologetically. He lifted the pouch on his belt and let the noise of the heavy coins clinking together fill the air.

The sound of money was the final straw. The man's eyes lost all trace of suspicion as he assessed the pouch. He was a cargo transporter, after all, a trade where coin controlled all but the weather.

"Arran! Keith!" the man barked over his shoulder. Turning back to Colin and Sabine, the man said, "When the ship is full of her cargo, we sleep aboard. Never can be too sure about the men snooping around on the docks at this hour."

"Oh, aye," Colin said, giving him a wide grin. "Ye

never can be too careful."

The man snorted again, clearly enjoying Colin's good humor despite the fact that he'd been taken for a troublemaker little more than a heartbeat before.

After a moment, two more men stumbled bleary-eyed onto the cog's deck, looking in confusion between Colin and the man.

"I'm Duff, the captain of this vessel," the old man said proudly. "This here is Arran, my brother, and his son Keith." Duff motioned toward the one called Arran, who looked identical to him except with a slightly less weathered appearance. The younger lad, Keith, was tall and thin, but bore his father and uncle's coppery hair.

Colin removed the entire coin pouch from his belt and tossed it across the gunwale to Duff.

"I cannae thank ye enough, and I'm sure my mother-in-law would give ye her thanks as well for seeing her daughter safely to the wedding."

Duff caught the pouch and hefted it appreciatively.

"My wife needs to rest," Colin added, making his kindly voice a hair firmer.

"Ye can both go into the hold," Duff replied. "We three will have our hands full with the crossing. Ye'll be undisturbed, I assure ye."

"We are grateful," Colin said, no longer needing to pretend sincerity.

He scooped Sabine into his arms and lifted her over the ship's high gunwales, then threw his legs over after her.

As Keith and Arran set about untying the cog from the dock, Duff led them to the middle of the deck. He bent and lifted up a large section of planking, revealing a dark hole that led down to the cargo hold.

"There's a lantern down there. Once ye have it lit, I'll close ye in. Just mind that ye dinnae light my cargo and ship on fire," Duff said with a gruff bark that must have been a laugh.

Colin helped Sabine into the hold, then jumped down after her.

The weak moonlight streaming from the hole in the deck provided just enough illumination for him to fumble his way toward where a lantern hung from the low wooden planking overhead. Removing his flint from the saddlebags over his shoulder, he sparked the candle to life.

"Just shove the boards aside if ye need aught," Duff said from above. "Keith, the sail! Arran, ye take the tiller while I—"

His barking orders were cut off as he dropped the board covering the hole. With the planking down, all the sounds from abovedeck were muted. Colin and Sabine were suddenly encased in a silent, dim little world within the hold.

Colin looked around. The hold was indeed nigh full with its cargo. Piles of canvas sacks covered almost every inch of the cog's flat hull, and most of the piles rose to the wooden planks overhead.

The familiar, earthy scents of wool and leather filled the hold. No doubt if Colin opened the sacks, he'd find both materials in great quantity there.

Toward the front of the ship, there was a little empty space just before the hull curved upward. He took Sabine's hand and guided her toward it, having to stoop as they neared the prow.

Colin removed his length of plaid from the saddlebags, then dropped them to the planks below. Drawing the plaid around Sabine, he gently lowered her down with him.

"Sabine," he said softly. "I ken ye are in shock and still hurting, but please, talk to me."

He swept a damp lock of hair away from her face. "Ye are safe now, lass. I am here."

She blinked up at him, her eyes wide and vulnerable in the dim lantern light. At last, she dragged in a breath and parted trembling lips to speak.

Chapter Twenty-Five

Sabine wasn't sure if it was Colin's gentle hand on her cheek or his whispered words that roused her from the pitch-black chasm that had swallowed her.

Somehow, her tongue managed to form words.

"I am the greatest fool that has ever lived."

Colin's tawny brows lowered and his mouth flattened. "Nay, ye arenae a fool, lass."

"Aye, I am. My whole life has been a lie, and I was the last to know." The words burned hot in her throat as shame washed over her.

"And Fabian is responsible for that, no' ye." He took her hands in his, the warm roughness of them penetrating the numbing cold in her limbs. "Ye were just a child when he found ye, is that right?"

She nodded, unable to speak around the lump in her throat.

"He took ye in from the streets. He raised ye and made ye feel loyal to him."

He'd remembered what she told him all those days past, even though he'd been suspicious that she was lying.

"How were ye to ken that he'd turn on ye when ye

were no longer of use to him?" The question was spoken softly, yet Sabine could see an angry muscle twitch in his jaw.

She wished she could direct her pain and hatred at Fabian as well, but all she could muster was anger for herself. She'd defended Fabian to Colin even as the man she'd thought of as a father was plotting to kill her.

"Mayhap I couldn't have known what sort of man he was then, but I'm no longer a child. I remained loyal to him despite everything he's done to hurt me."

That muscle jumped in Colin's jaw again. He held her with a grim gaze. "What exactly did he do to ye, lass?"

Sabine's mind crashed through more than a dozen years of smiles, praise, and kindness, spiked with slaps, thrown objects, screams of rage, and words meant to leave scars as surely as a knife did.

"He...he taught me to read and memorize. He praised me when I did well, and hit me when I didn't."

Colin flinched but didn't interrupt. His hands squeezed hers gently, so she went on.

"He gave me my dagger and sent me on my first assignment when I was nine. As a child, it was easy to move in crowded streets or inns unnoticed. I excelled at my work, and he told me he was proud of me."

She had to force down the bile that rose in her throat at what came next.

"When I was fourteen, he told me that I was no

longer a child, that I had to start using different tactics to retrieve the missives, records, and documents he needed. He made me dress differently, walk and talk differently. I had to...had to be able to tease men, dangle myself in front of them to get what I wanted. Once, Fabian locked me in a room without food for a sennight. It took me that long to realize he expected me to charm a meal from the man guarding the chamber door."

Aye, that had been a lesson she would never forget. The gnawing hunger, the faintness, the spinning head and empty stomach. She'd learned to lie, to play the part of the coquettish woman, quickly and effortlessly after that.

"Did he...did he make ye follow through with yer flirtations as well?" Colin asked, his voice hard and low.

Sabine exhaled slowly. "Nay, for he said I couldn't risk myself in that way. I had to move quickly, tell a heart-wrenching or enticing tale—just enough to get close to my mark—and then disappear with the information I was sent for. He told me to guard myself carefully, for men would use me and discard me."

Her voice broke on the last words. She dropped her gaze from Colin, feeling too exposed, too vulnerable. Hadn't Fabian been right about that part at least? Colin had been kind and gentle with her, yet he'd pulled away after he'd taken his pleasure from her.

Colin's hand suddenly cupped her chin. "Sabine, look at me."

Reluctantly, she dragged her eyes up to his. They were dark and filled with storming emotion as he held her gaze.

"Fabian is wrong," he rasped. "No' everyone is so cold and uncaring. I ken I hurt ye, but ye need to believe that it was no' yer fault."

She shook her head, unable to get words out around the lump in her throat.

"I didnae pull away because I had gotten what I wanted from ye. And I will never toss ye aside as Fabian has." He struggled for a moment, a battle waging across his hard features. "I was a coward," he murmured at last. "I have been afraid, too—afraid of caring for ye."

Shock flooded her, sweeping away the pain and shame for a blessed heartbeat.

"What?"

He held her with his searching gaze, a soft smile touching his lips. "I care for ye, lass. Wrong as it might be, I do. I cannae deny it."

She let the words spread warmth through her aching heart for a long moment before a question arose in her mind.

"Why were you afraid?"

Pain flashed in Colin's eyes, but he didn't turn away. "Someone once broke my trust—broke my heart. Someone betrayed me, as Fabian has with ye, lass."

"Tell me," she whispered.

Colin dragged in a breath and released it slowly through his teeth. "I joined the Bruce and the fight for Scottish independence from England nine years past. I thought the whole thing a grand adventure—noble and exciting, as most young men imagine war to be."

Colin's eyes grew distant with memory as he went on. "I had no reason to doubt that life in the Bruce's army would be any different than life back home on MacKay lands. Everything had come easy for me before then. Aye, my da wasnae always well, but he had my mother and sister to look after him. We had enough to eat, we had a roof over our heads, and I had a woman who loved me."

Sabine's chest involuntarily squeezed. Was it simply the thought that Colin's perfect youth had been destroyed in some way that left him guarded and suspicious? Or was it the thought of him loving another woman, even in his past?

"Her name was Joan," he continued, his voice turning hard. "She was the most sought-after lass in the entire clan. She was quick with a smile or a bat of the eye, though she wouldnae let any of the men chasing her bind themselves to her—until me. I wooed her, and she agreed to wed me, but first we were handfasted."

Sabine could very well imagine that no woman could deny Colin when he used that heart-stopping smile or let his dancing blue eyes imply something wicked. What would that carefree lad have been like? She suddenly wished she could have known him then, before the world had turned them both hard and un-trusting.

"What does it mean to be handfasted?"

"It is a Scottish tradition. We were bound together for a year and a day. At the end of that time, we were expected to get married, though we could break the agreement if we found we didnae suit."

A dark shadow crossed his features and he paused, seemingly lost in memory, before going on.

"No' long after we were handfasted, I joined the Bruce in the Lowlands to help him beat the English back from the borders. I wasnae able to return to MacKay lands for almost a year, but I remained faithful to Joan. I kenned it would be hard on her, for she so enjoyed other men's attention. But she vowed that she wanted only me, and I believed her."

"But…but she betrayed you," Sabine murmured.

"Aye. When I finally managed to return home, I found her rolling in the hay with another man—a man who had once been my closest friend. While I'd been away fighting for Scotland, she'd grown bored and decided to turn her charms elsewhere."

Colin dragged a hand through his mane of golden hair. "I vowed that day never to be taken in again, never to be duped by honeyed words and whispered promises."

His eyes were hard chips of blue in the low light. "I felt lied to, made a fool. But I also realized that charm could be a tool—a weapon—to manipulate people, as

Joan had manipulated me. I've wielded that weapon in the service of the Scottish cause for independence ever since."

Sabine swallowed. It hurt to think that she'd been on the receiving end of his calculated charm when Colin smiled at her or touched her, but she understood him now. He was like her—though in truth the weapon of lies and charm was actually more of a shield. It kept others at a safe distance and protected against the fear of being hurt.

"What became of Joan?"

"She married the man I found her with, partly to appease her parents once word spread about her actions. Last I heard, she is still seeking other men's attention, for she cannae be satisfied with being loved by only one man. It seems a fitting punishment for both of them—they are alone even in marriage to each other."

"And you?" Sabine breathed. Eight years was a long time to carry around such a burden. Did the pain still haunt him?

"I left home and rejoined the Bruce's army. I threw myself into the war, and distinguished myself both on and off the battlefield. Few ken about Joan, so I am thought to be a merry, even-keeled man by most— always the one with a quick smile or an easy word."

"But in truth you are hiding a deeper pain," she murmured.

"I prefer it that way."

A silence fell between them, broken only by the muffled lap of the sea as the ship cut through the water.

"Ye see, ye are no' the only one to be taken in by a deceiver," Colin said at last. "But I ken that ye have suffered worse than I. Joan only broke my heart. Fabian hurt ye in so many more ways."

He exhaled slowly between his teeth. "And ye are no' a fool for trusting the only person who's ever shown ye a sliver of kindness, lass. I am the real fool, for I have let one lass's actions eight years ago make me suspicious and guarded. My own cowardice led me to hurt ye, and I never want to do that again."

"If you are a fool for being suspicious, then I am a fool for trusting. Even when Fabian was cruel, I remained loyal to him."

"Nay, lass," he said softly. "Yer willingness to trust is a strength, no' a weakness. It shows that ye still believed in the goodness of people, despite what Fabian tried to make ye think. That takes far more courage than mere cynicism."

His words struck her like a powerful blast of cool, clarifying wind.

Aye, she'd trusted Fabian, even when he'd hurt her. He'd made her afraid of the world beyond his controlling embrace. He'd kept her isolated and constantly seeking his approval.

Yet even with all his insistence that only he would ever look out for her, Colin had held her gaze and told her that he cared. While Fabian sought to have her killed for the slightest threat to his own safety, Colin had risked his life for her.

"I'm sorry I pushed ye away," he said, brushing the backs of his fingers across her cheek. "I dinnae want to live as I have for the last eight years any longer. I dinnae want to hurt ye with my pride or my suspicion anymore. And I dinnae want ye to hurt yourself for Fabian's wrongs. It wasnae your fault."

Sabine drew in a breath as if it was her first. The ancient stone wall that Fabian taught her to build around her heart began to crumble.

"It wasnae yer fault," Colin repeated, soft but firm.

A sob rose up from her chest and escaped her lips, then another.

"It wasnae yer fault."

Each time she heard the words, another stone fell and the truth pushed its way through the cracks. In a way, though she'd grown into a woman, a part of her had always remained the scared, abandoned child she'd been when Fabian found her.

He'd kept her that way, she realized now. He'd praised and then berated her, showered her with gifts and then beat her so that she was always frightened, always believing she was on the verge of losing the only person who loved her.

"It wasnae yer fault."

The last bits of the old wall fell, and Sabine let go and wept.

She wept for the innocent child she'd once been.

She wept for the wrongs she'd committed when she'd been willing to do aught for Fabian.

She wept for all the years lost to him and his lies.

And she wept in joy, for now that she finally saw the truth, she was free of Fabian, free of her past, and free to make a new life for herself.

Colin's arms came around her in a fierce embrace, dragging her against his chest. He buried his face in her hair and murmured to her, though she could hardly understand the words over her own sobs.

After the hard tears had passed, her breathing slowed and she nestled against Colin's chest. Never had she felt so safe than she did in Colin's arms.

Without thinking, she lifted her head and brushed her lips against his.

He stiffened and froze. "Ye have been through much this day," he murmured. "I dinnae want ye to do aught ye'll regret in the light of morning."

Even though his words warned her against the desire that suddenly coursed in her veins, she could feel his manhood growing hard where she pressed into him.

"I won't regret this," she said, holding his gaze steadily with hers.

"I dinnae ken if I will be able to stop once we start," he rasped, liquid blue heat flickering in his eyes.

This was no game, no tease. She was making this decision for herself and no one else. "For the first time in my life, I feel free—and I choose this. I choose *you*, Colin."

Her words must have driven deep into his heart, for his eyes flashed with emotion the second before his mouth claimed hers.

Chapter Twenty-Six

At Sabine's words, Colin's heart felt as though it had sprouted wings and threatened to fly out of his chest.

She chose him.

He'd felt exposed, vulnerable, when he told her about Joan. Yet once he'd spoken the words, he realized what a fool he'd been for letting the events of the past control him. And his pain could not compare with hers. He'd been spurned by a lover, while she'd been betrayed by the only person she had, a person willing to kill her.

He'd feared that as raw and wounded as she was, what little he could share in her pain, what little he could do to alleviate it, would do naught.

But she was stronger even than he'd known, for if she could care about him, then Fabian had never truly been able to change her at the core. She'd lived through hell, but she'd come out of it free and with the capacity to care, to trust.

The fact that she put that trust in him humbled him more completely than anything he'd ever experienced.

He kissed her, trying to communicate his awe at

her strength without words.

But as he deepened the kiss, he knew his feelings went far beyond respect and admiration. He was falling in love with her.

Her fortitude, her bravery, her trust in him.

Her ability to be vulnerable even after living through so much.

Everything she'd been through that had made her the scarred yet strong woman she was.

Aye, he was falling in love with her. And he needed to show her in the most basic way.

His fingers found the clasp on her damp cloak and quickly unfastened it. Her hands tugged his tunic from his belt even as he began unlacing the ties on her dress.

He paused to pull his tunic over his head while she wriggled free of her dress, managing to use both her arms without wincing in discomfort.

Once he'd discarded his belt and boots, he turned back to her clad only in his breeches.

Her gaze roamed over his form, and his blood pumped hotly at the look of hungry anticipation in her eyes.

Gently, he eased her back onto the plaid he'd wrapped her in earlier. He crouched over her and took the hem of her shift in hand.

With deliberate slowness, he raised the hem an inch, then another. By God, he could feast on the sight of her creamy skin and slim, coltish legs for a lifetime.

He lifted the shift past her knees, then up her silky

thighs until he revealed the dark triangle of hair protecting her womanhood. How he longed to stop and taste her in that moment, to feel her quiver with pleasure against his tongue.

He forced himself onward, determined to see all of her in the soft lantern light. As the hem skimmed past her narrow waist, she shivered. Then it cleared the high, pert mounds of her breasts, each topped with a perfect rosy nipple he'd tasted once before.

She lifted her arms, the left one lower than the other, belying the stiffness that must still remain there. When at last the shift slipped completely free of her, he devoured the sight of her like a man half-starved.

She was perfect. Her dark hair splayed wildly against the green and blue of his plaid, her skin pale and delicately flushed. Those wide, dark eyes fastened on him, a look of unguarded trust shimmering there.

His gaze landed on the necklace she still wore, which pooled in the hollow of her throat. A gold ring was attached to the chain, a small, dark emerald catching the lantern light.

Sabine stilled. Slowly, one hand came up and traced the necklace.

"Fabian gave it to me," she whispered. "He wears its match. He told me when he gave it to me that it bound us together for life."

Carefully grasping the ring and chain, she lifted her head and slipped the necklace off. She gently tossed it toward their feet, and it landed on the crumpled pile of her dress.

Her depthless, searching eyes locked on him once more, and she gave him a little nod.

He descended on her, no longer able to control himself. He claimed her lips in a searing kiss that sent his blood hammering in his veins. His hands found her breasts, and his mouth captured her moan of pleasure.

Their tongues tangled erotically, but the need to kiss her everywhere was powerful enough to make him draw back. His lips found her neck, her earlobe, the tender hollow at her throat.

He moved lower, circling one breast slowly even as she arched up to him, silently begging him for more. At last, he captured one pink, taut nipple between his lips and laved it. She bucked and moaned, her fingers turning to claws on his shoulders.

As her hands rose to tangle in his hair, he dropped lower still, tracing the delicate skin across her stomach. Gooseflesh followed his lips in a trail toward that place he so longed to kiss, to taste.

When his mouth brushed the soft curls covering her womanhood, she gasped, but her legs fell open instinctively, beckoning him on.

She was already so wet for him. The realization sent his cock surging against his breeches and his bollocks aching with need.

Settling himself between her knees, his tongue found that spot of pure pleasure. Sabine inhaled again, her whole body stiffening in taut ecstasy as he circled and tasted, teased and laved her.

Slowly, he slid one finger and then two into her tight passage. He didn't want to hurt her when she took him inside, but she was an innocent, untried to such an invasion.

To his relief, she moaned in pleasure as he worked his fingers inside her, his tongue still swirling over that perfect spot. Her hips began to undulate in the instinctual rhythm of lovemaking, and her breath hitched in her throat.

Just as he felt her knees begin to tremble around his shoulders, he withdrew. By God, he wasn't going to last very long, so fiercely did he want to drive into her.

But nay, he had to go slow for her, had to make it perfect.

He yanked off his breeches, his cock springing free. Despite the sudden freedom, his manhood ached all the more, for he gazed down at Sabine and his heart nigh stopped.

She lay against his plaid, panting with need and legs spread before him. Her eyes locked on him. They shimmered with desire in the low light.

Colin lowered himself between her knees, his cock nudging her entrance. He nearly lost control when the tip of his manhood made contact with her damp folds, but he forced himself to hold still.

"Are ye sure, Sabine?" he ground out.

"Aye," she said.

He began to move forward, but something flickered behind her eyes that made him freeze again.

"Colin?" she murmured. "Don't hurt me."

His heart broke into a thousand pieces in that moment. Emotion tightened his throat as he gazed down at her, vulnerable and trusting him with her body, her heart.

"I never will," he rasped, low and rough.

She held his gaze and gave him a slow nod.

Slowly, deliberately, he eased forward so that he entered her a hair's breadth at a time.

He had to grind his teeth against the urge to thrust forward, to claim her fully.

Her wince at the invasion slowed him even further. When at last he'd driven to the hilt, she inhaled but didn't push him away. He stayed still, letting her adjust to his size as he stretched and filled her.

When the tightness in her delicate features eased slightly, he drew back, then slid forward once more.

She gasped again, but this time pleasure mingled with discomfort in her eyes. He ground into her, slowly circling his hips to let her feel all of him. Then he took her mouth in a penetrating kiss.

Her knees relaxed around his hips and she moaned with wordless need. He built a gradual rhythm then, his tongue mirroring the thrusts of his cock as he claimed her.

Soon, her hips rolled in time with his, and her breathing grew shallow. He slipped a hand between their bodies, finding that spot just above where they were joined. He was immediately rewarded with a breathy moan that was almost his undoing.

He gritted his teeth, willing his body not to come undone just yet. He wanted her to soar to the heights of pleasure first, to yield to the ecstasy of their joining before he lost his threadbare grip on control.

He hitched their rhythm, and suddenly her body coiled like a spring. She cried out, arching up into him as her limbs trembled in release.

Her core tightening around him was his undoing. His control snapped. With a rough thrust, he buried himself completely inside her, his release coming hard and hot.

He collapsed over her, catching his weight on one elbow to avoid crushing her with his body.

As he rolled to the side and pulled her into his arms, their eyes met.

No words were needed in that moment, for the raw emotion that shimmered in her gaze cut straight to his heart.

He wondered fleetingly before dropping his head onto his plaid and letting exhaustion claim him if she saw in his eyes the emotion that brimmed within him.

Love.

Chapter Twenty-Seven

S abine woke when the lantern swung with the rocking of the sea, casting candlelight across her eyes.

She lay in Colin's warm, hard embrace, nestled in a pile of his soft plaid. The dim cargo hold was filled with the comforting, earthy smells of wool and leather and a faint trace of Colin's masculine, piney scent.

Her body ached and hummed deliciously. No wonder Fabian had warned her against giving herself to a man. The feeling was as intoxicating as a fine wine running through her veins.

Careful not to disturb Colin, she slid from his arms and sat up. She gazed down at his relaxed form.

His skin glowed softly in the lantern light, but beneath the smooth bronzed exterior lay ridges of chiseled muscle. The golden bristle along his hard jawline glinted in the low light. His chest rose and fell gently, casting shadows in the valleys between the stacked muscles banding his stomach with each exhale.

His manhood lay dormant now between his powerful legs. Memories of what they'd just shared rushed back, causing heat to rise to the surface of Sabine's skin.

Mayhap this was the other reason Fabian had insisted she keep herself innocent. Now that she had given herself to Colin, she felt an inextricable pull toward him.

She brushed a lock of tawny hair from his forehead. Nay, that wasn't quite the truth. Sharing pleasure hadn't caused the invisible ties that bound her to him, she admitted. She cared for him. The pleasure they'd shared was simply the expression of what she bore in her heart.

He stirred slightly in his sleep, and the light caught the whiter flesh of an old scar across his broad chest. Sabine leaned forward and noticed for the first time that his bronzed skin bore several scars, some white with age, and others still faintly pink.

No doubt he'd earned those scars serving his King and country. All of a sudden, Colin's harshly spoken words before Miles's attack rushed back to her.

Ye fooled me into believing that we were the same.

Sabine swallowed and squeezed her eyes shut, but the string of words unraveled in her mind anyway.

But the difference is, at the end of the day, I ken where my loyalties lie.

Blood hammered in her ears as shame flooded her.

I fight for the King of Scotland and for the freedom of my country and people.

She dragged her eyes open to stare down at his still form.

What do ye fight for, Sabine?

Aye, Colin had his loyalties perfectly figured out. He was a man of honor, a man committed to King and country. He bore the scars to prove it.

And what of her? She'd devoted her whole life to Fabian, but it had all been a sham, a lie based on one-sided loyalty.

She'd made a fool of herself in trusting Fabian. She'd always thought herself an untrusting person, for Fabian had taught her to be cautious, guarded. People would run roughshod over her if she let them, he'd told her.

Yet mayhap all along her problem was that she was *too* trusting. Colin had called it a sign that she still bore a heart, that she still had the capacity to care for others, but what had that belief, that willingness to trust, gotten her? It had kept her bound to Fabian through his rages, through his subtle manipulations of her thoughts and feelings, through the missions with naught in return but a sliver of his so often withheld praise.

Sabine quietly scooted away from Colin and retrieved her discarded shift. As she pulled the shift over her head and down her body, she tried to straighten her tangled thoughts, but to no avail.

Her gaze fell on her necklace, which glinted dully on top of her dress. She let her finger brush the cool metal, something she'd done hundreds of times to soothe herself. But the feel of the necklace against the pad of her finger now only served to remind her of Fabian's betrayal.

Was she too trusting? She'd already made the error of throwing her faith behind Fabian. Had she just made the same mistake with Colin?

She stifled a moan of frustration at herself. Without Fabian telling her what to do, what to think, she couldn't even discern the truth. He'd made her this way. He'd tied knots of confusion and mistrust in her mind and heart to keep her compliant. But now she needed to undo the tangled mess he'd left within her on her own.

The ship rocked again, sending the lantern, which hung on a hook from the planks overhead, tilting sideways. The candle sputtered as it cast angled light across the hold.

Sabine rose and padded to the lantern. She straightened it with one hand and the candle's flame steadied. Bracing her feet against the ship's gentle pitching, she looked over at where Colin lay in repose.

But her gaze snagged on the pile of his hastily discarded clothing next to her dress. On top lay his tunic, which he'd removed so hurriedly that he'd yanked it off and tossed it aside inside out.

The candlelight caught on a faint seam on the inside of the tunic.

Sabine's stomach twisted.

It was the secret pocket sewn into the tunic to carry—

The missive.

Chapter Twenty-Eight

Without thinking, Sabine took a step toward the tunic, her gaze locked on the place where the missive lay tucked away.

But the thought of doing Fabian's bidding drew her up sharply. He would want her to read the missive. Wasn't that the reason she was here with Colin now? If she hadn't realized that Colin bore the missive she'd been sent to read, she would have fled back in the village's stables, leaving Colin to fend off the half dozen inn patrons she'd set on him.

The only reason she was here now was because she'd decided in a flash of determination to remain with him and try to recover the missive's contents—for Fabian. For his praise and his pride in her.

She would never serve Fabian again, she vowed bitterly. But as her gaze flitted up to Colin, uncertainty twisted like a knife in her belly.

I ken where my loyalties lie.

His harsh voice once again echoed through her mind. Colin was loyal to King Robert the Bruce and his cause for Scottish freedom—not her. They were still enemies, despite the passion they'd just shared. She was an English thief—a spy, in truth, though she'd rejected the accusation when he'd thrown it at her—and he was a Scot, a warrior with a clear mission.

He'd asked her before she'd given herself to him if she was sure this was what she wanted. He'd warned her that she might regret her actions in the light of morning.

Sabine knew in her heart that she would never regret what they'd shared—but would he?

Though he thought himself cold and scarred from Joan's betrayal, he was an honorable and good man. He fought with principles. He'd devoted his life to his King, which meant that they would always be enemies.

She'd already made the mistake of granting her loyalty to a man who could not return it. Would she make the same mistake again?

What do ye fight for, Sabine?

She only had herself, now. Aye, she cared for Colin—more than cared, if the squeezing of her heart was any indication—but she needed to look out for herself. Information was power—both Fabian and Colin had told her that. And Sabine vowed never to be powerless again.

Dragging in a ragged breath, she crouched before Colin's discarded tunic. She watched him for a slow count to fifty, but his breathing remained even and his lids motionless.

She lifted trembling fingers to the seam on the inside of his tunic. To an untrained eye it would look like a simple fold in the material, but Sabine had encountered enough hidden pockets to discern its true purpose.

She slid a finger into the seam and wormed it deeper into the pocket. Her fingertip brushed waxed parchment. As she inched the little packet out of its hiding place, she kept her eyes locked on Colin.

When she slipped the waxed parchment free, she let herself breathe deeply for a moment as she tried to slow her pounding heart.

Her discarded dress was in reaching distance, so she fumbled for the dagger Fabian had given her in its folds.

Holding the dagger and the packet of parchment to her thudding chest, she rose and went to the lantern. She lifted it from its hook and set it on the flat hull, settling herself so that she blocked most of the light from landing on Colin.

The dagger flashed in the candlelight as she silently slid it from its sheath. She swung open the little door on the front of the lantern, once again checking over her shoulder that the light did not disturb Colin.

She'd done this more than a hundred times, and yet not even on her first assignment had her hands shaken this badly.

Sabine sucked in a deep breath, mentally ordering her hands to calm and her nerves to unknot. If she trembled, she might break the seal or singe the missive.

The light was slightly brighter now with the lantern's door open. She lifted the waxed parchment, carefully studying how it was folded so that she could recreate it exactly when she replaced it in Colin's tunic.

Muscle memory at last took over, and the usual composure that stole over her as she worked finally slowed her pulse.

With delicate fingers, she opened the wax parchment and removed the missive from its folds. She tilted the seal toward the light, but she knew instantly that it bore the King of Scotland's mark, just like the one Osborn had carried.

She held the tip of her dagger into the candle flame, counting off until she knew it was heated precisely. Then she slid it under the seal.

The seal lifted suddenly, but it did not break. Exhaling silently, Sabine set the dagger aside and unfolded the missive.

She read it once through rapidly, a trick Fabian had taught her. If she'd ever been caught in the field or had been short on time, she was supposed to get a general impression for a missive's contents, even if she didn't have time to memorize all of it. Though Fabian's clients didn't pay as much for those impressions, Fabian always said that it was worth it to save her neck.

Sabine pushed aside the memory, now soured with the knowledge that Fabian only cared about her life so long as it was of use to him.

Lifting her eyes back to the top of the missive, she read slowly, studying each word in relation to the others so that it was branded on her mind.

> *I have heard rumblings from your isle. Be warned, brother, de Burgh is not your only enemy. He seeks to lure you south to Louth, but he is no doubt up to something. Hold your position in Inniskeen. If Edmund Butler has joined de Burgh, he leaves the north vulnerable. This could be your chance to strike. The local lords in the north are with you.*

The missive wasn't signed, but it didn't need to be with the King of Scotland's seal on the outside. The Bruce's message didn't make sense to Sabine, though she got the impression that it had to do with the King's brother, Edward Bruce, and his fight to secure Ireland for his cause.

Disquiet slid through her like a cold breeze. When Colin had accused her of being a spy, he'd told her men's lives hung in the balance when she gave information to Fabian. She'd never deliberately paid attention to the contents of the missives she read, but now that she did, she understood what Colin meant.

She has fought against contemplating the implications of what she'd done as a thief—a spy. Fabian had told her not to fill her head with such worries, lest she grow confused and falter at a crucial moment in an assignment. She realized now that it was just another one of Fabian's manipulations to keep her obedient—and keep information flowing through him to his clients.

If this message had fallen into Fabian's hands, to whom would he have sold it? Would it have cost Edward Bruce and his men their lives?

And for what purpose? To quash the Scots' fight for freedom? To secure England's leash around Scotland's neck once more?

Sabine hadn't thought of herself as helping England bring the Scots to heel, yet now she saw that in delivering information to Fabian, who then in turn sold it to powerful English noblemen, that's exactly what she'd been doing.

That realization chilled her, for it meant that she had been responsible, albeit inadvertently, of depriving others of their freedom.

She'd never truly appreciated just how valuable freedom was until a few hours ago when she'd finally mentally rid herself of Fabian's shackles. Suddenly she deeply understood the Scots'—and Colin's—dedication to the cause of independence.

Now that she felt the weight and power of the missive trembling in her fingertips, she thanked God that she hadn't given the information to Fabian. Nor would she ever, she vowed.

Sabine reread the missive once more to ensure that she'd locked away each word in her mind.

But why did she need this information for herself at all? She'd thought to protect herself with it if Colin changed his mind and took back his tender words in the morning. Yet in a flash of clarity, Sabine knew with every fiber of her being that she could never use this missive against Colin.

It didn't matter if he regretted his honeyed words and loving touches in the light of day. It didn't matter if he turned her over to the Bruce to be hanged as a spy. She would never betray him in his quest for freedom.

With a resigned exhale, she carefully folded the missive.

Just then, there was a low murmur and the soft rustling of wool behind her.

Sabine started so hard that the missive fell from her fingers. She spun around, clapping a hand over her mouth to muffle a fearful gasp.

Colin rolled over on his plaid, muttering something in his sleep.

Sabine could barely register the fact that his words were nonsensical, the murmurs of slumber, over the blood rushing in her ears. He still slept deeply. He hadn't just caught her reading the King's missive.

Her initial panic revealed something horrifying to her, though. Despite just vowing in her mind never to betray Colin, she *had* just betrayed him. In reading the missive, she'd betrayed his trust, broken his faith that she wouldn't deceive him anymore.

Just as dread had her stomach sinking to the hull's boards, the ship rolled sharply.

Sabine went tumbling backward. A tall stack of canvas-covered wool broke her impact against the hull's side, but she dropped gracelessly to her hands and knees against the planks.

The ship's motion smoothed, and she slowly began to rise to her feet.

Her gaze fell on where she'd dropped the missive several paces away.

To her horror, the candle had fallen out of the open lantern when the ship had rolled. The flame had caught the edge of the missive and now the parchment was ablaze.

The world seemed to tilt sickeningly again, but this time it wasn't because the ship rolled on a wave. Sabine scrambled forward in desperation. When she fell before the missive, it was more than half swallowed by the flames already.

She had naught to snuff the flames with. She was clad only in her shift, with no boots or even a thick piece of cloth to snuff the fire. Helplessness swamped her for a heartbeat. Then she snatched up the metal lantern itself, bringing down its square base on top of the burning missive. She ground the lantern into the hull's planks, frantic to stop the flames.

When she lifted the lantern, bile rose in her throat and she feared she would be sick.

The candle, which still sputtered on its side nearby, revealed that only charred ash and blackened scraps of torn parchment were left of the missive.

Oh God, nay. Please, nay.

With numb fingers, Sabine picked up the candle and placed it back in the lantern. She tried to scrape together a few of the least burned pieces of parchment, but it was hopeless. There was no righting it now.

He would know.

Colin would know of her betrayal. Whether she was brave enough to confess it to him or not, eventually he would discover that the missive was missing, and then all his worst fears about her would be confirmed.

As if she were sleepwalking, she gathered the blackened ashes and sprinkled them behind one of the many stacks of canvas-covered goods. She rubbed at the darkened spot on the planks with the heel of her foot until no trace of ash remained.

Then she slowly refolded the waxed parchment that had protected the missive. She slipped it back into Colin's tunic and turned the garment right-side out so as not to draw attention to the hidden pocket.

She was a coward, she thought through the numbing fog of shame and dread. Yet as she glanced at him, peaceful in sleep, she didn't have the courage to confess what she'd done.

He would discover it soon enough.

And then the delicate web of trust they'd threaded between their hearts would be destroyed forever.

Chapter Twenty-Nine

The cargo hold was dim, the candle having long ago burned itself out, when Colin woke. Without the warming pre-dawn sky as his guide, he wasn't sure how late he'd slept.

The hold was empty, the expanse of plaid next to him cool to the touch.

How he'd longed to wake with Sabine still tucked against him. He would have slid his fingers through that veil of sable hair, trailed his hand down her curving back, and shown her how much the night had meant to him with a searing kiss.

But she was gone. She must have gone abovedeck for some fresh air.

Was she as tangled in the implications of what they'd shared as he was?

Truth be told, Colin was relieved he still needed to reach the Bruce's brother in Ireland and deliver the King's missive. At least that task was clear. Beyond that, he had no idea what to do.

Should he drag Sabine to the Bruce to be drilled for information and punished for her role in Fabian's network of thieves? It was his duty as the Bruce's loyal soldier and a member of the Bodyguard Corps to identify and eliminate all threats to King and country. Yet he didn't truly believe Sabine was guilty. Aye, she'd delivered information to the Bruce's enemies. But she'd been a victim of Fabian's schemes as well.

Should he set her free, then? To do so would be to fail in his mission to ferret out those responsible for compromising the King's correspondence. The darker truth, though, was that Colin hated the idea of turning her loose, if only because it meant that he would likely never see her again.

Twice now, he'd told the lie that she was his wife. Despite all the reasons why he should not, he liked the feel of it. And the idea of her carrying his bairn made something go soft in his chest.

Colin cursed. His emotions were clouding his thinking. But damn it all, he'd gone too deep with Sabine to simply ignore his feelings for her.

He dressed slowly, chewing on what the future held. When at last he'd donned his clothes and tucked away the plaid in his saddlebags, there was no more avoiding facing her. He wouldn't cower belowdeck like some shamed bairn. They had too much that needed discussing.

When he lifted the planks that covered the cargo hold, weak gray light spilled in. He hoisted himself up, his gaze scanning the ship's deck.

Duff stood at the stern, one hand resting on the tiller. He nodded his white-copper head at Colin, then returned his eyes to the sea. Arran and Keith were adjusting the sail to capture the slight wind ruffling over the gunwales.

Colin's eyes went to the bow. His chest seized involuntarily.

Sabine stood with her back to him, her gaze fixed on the water. Her unbound hair twisted in the briny air, a dark, rich contrast to her pale skin. Though she still wore the same mud-covered, abused green wool dress, she might as well have been wearing the finest silks and jewels, for she looked like a beautiful queen to Colin.

He approached slowly, not wanting to disturb her thoughts. She seemed intent on gazing beyond the bow toward the open water. The sea was relatively calm, though the sky clung low to it, gray with the promise of yet more rain.

"Have ye spotted land?"

She jumped slightly at his softly spoken words. She turned her head partially over one shoulder, but she kept her chin tucked so that their eyes didn't meet.

"Nay, not yet."

She kept her voice low so that the others wouldn't hear her English accent. Apparently the lass did have some limits, for Colin had lied that she was Irish, yet mayhap she could not carry the accent.

He stepped closer so that there was no risk of her voice being snatched by the wind and drifting to the three crewmen.

"Last night was…" he began gruffly, suddenly feeling like a green lad. "It meant a great deal to me."

Her gaze darted up to his for the briefest moment. His heart twisted at what he saw in the depths of her hazel eyes.

Regret.

Hot pain tore through him. He'd been so busy chewing on what to do with the lass that he forgot his own words of warning to her last night. In the thin gray light, it was obvious that she regretted what they'd shared. He'd taken her innocence, and now she wished she could take it back.

"Sabine," he began softly. "I hope…I want ye to ken that…"

She swallowed, turning her gaze back to the sea.

Slowly, he reached out, brushing a hand down her back. She stiffened under his touch.

"Sabine, please, just tell me what I've done. What is wrong, lass? I swear I'll try to make it right."

He noticed then that her hands gripped the bow's gunwales, her knuckles white with the effort. He lifted a hand to touch her again, but let it drop before it reached her.

Keeping her head forward, she spoke quietly.

"Are we still enemies?"

Colin let out a slow breath. Of course she would fear that last night had changed naught for him. She was still his captive, and he was still charged with turning her over to the Bruce. But something *had* changed last night. He needed to tell her the truth of his feelings.

He struggled for the words for a long moment.

"I dinnae ken if we are enemies anymore," he said at last. "I believe Fabian is the true enemy—to both the Bruce and ye. Ye were just his pawn, lass. He used ye, hurt ye."

He swallowed the rage that bubbled up in his chest at Fabian's treatment of her. By God, he would never let anyone hurt her again.

"Ye need to ken…" he went on, his throat ragged. "Ye need to ken that I care for ye. I…I'm falling in love with ye, Sabine."

He'd said it. Though the words had threatened to lodge in his throat, now that they were free, they rang sure and true.

Her head snapped around, her eyes going wide. But then a terrible shadow fell across her features. Shame. Regret. Fear.

"Oh, nay," she whispered. "Nay, please do not say that, Colin. Please do not love me."

Her throat closed and the last words came out a choked rasp.

Hurt and confusion flooded him. "Why no', lass? It is the truth. I thought we agreed to be honest with each other."

She squeezed her eyes shut. A tear escaped and slid down her wind-pinkened cheek.

"Aye, we did," she said.

A struggle waged across her face for a long moment. She opened her mouth as if to force out difficult words, but then her eyes dimmed and lowered in defeat.

"You cannot love me," she said, keeping her gaze downcast. "I am not worthy of your love."

"Sabine." He took her chin gently in his hand and raised it so that he could hold her gaze. Another tear slid down her cheek. He wiped it away with his thumb, searching her eyes. "I dinnae ken what ye mean, or what happened between last night and this morn. I ken that we both bear shame in our pasts, that we have both been hurt, but—"

A fresh wave of anguish washed across her features. "You don't know me. You don't know what I'm capable of. If you did, you would hate yourself—and me—for your love."

Colin shook his head firmly in denial, but he struggled with what to say. Something had indeed happened last night, but while his feelings had rooted deeper into his heart, doubt had grown in hers. He racked his mind for the words to break through the walls she was erecting between them.

Just then, his gaze caught on something glinting around her throat.

The necklace Fabian had given her.

Cold dread sank in his stomach. She must have slipped it back on after they'd made love.

"What is this?"

Her gaze darted down. "It is not what you think."

Colin pulled the reins tight on a sudden flash of anger, keeping his voice level. "Did ye change yer mind then? Are ye still devoted to Fabian after all?"

"Nay!" she blurted. Her hurt eyes met his, and he saw the truth of her denial in their depths. "Nay," she repeated softly. "But I put it back on to remind myself of my past...so that I will never forget the shame of my mistakes."

"Sabine, dinnae punish yerself so. I—"

"Land ahead!" Arran's gruff bark cut Colin off.

He jerked his gaze over Sabine's shoulder. Sure enough, a misty green landmass emerged from the thick clouds ahead.

The little crew flew into a flurry of activity.

"Keith, have the oars ready when the docks come in sight," Duff shot from the back of the ship. "Arran, ye'll be on the sail. And lad," he called, pinning Colin with a look. "We could always use a stout back and an extra pair of hands on the oars if ye're willing."

Colin looked at Sabine, but she'd lowered her chin once more, locking her eyes on the deck's planks.

"Aye," he said, reluctantly turning from her. "Glad to help considering all ye've done for us."

Colin took up his task alongside Keith, lifting the long wooden oars from the hold and positioning them in their oarlocks for the final stretch of water between the cog and the docks. Sabine stayed at the bow to avoid being in the crew's way. She never once met

Colin's searching gaze.

Something was amiss, but there was no time to prod Sabine for answers or craft the perfect words to draw her from her sadness.

Ireland loomed.

And so did Colin's duty.

Chapter Thirty

They were met at the docks by a wall of Scottish warriors.

Despite the men's fearsome scowls, suspicious looks, and the hands resting on their sword hilts, Colin found the scene strangely comforting. It was good to be among warriors again.

Most of the men wore breeches in the style of the English and Scottish Lowlanders, but several had colorful clan plaids slung over their shoulders or draped around them like cloaks. It almost felt like being back in Scotland among the Bruce's army.

"What is yer business here?" one of the men demanded, striding down the length of the dock. His narrowed, ice-blue eyes took in the cargo ship, the crew, and Colin and Sabine.

"I am sanctioned to trade along the Irish coast," Duff replied, pulling a scrolled piece of parchment from the pouch on his belt. He held it up, showing the Scottish traders' guild seal to the warrior.

"And ye?" the Scot said, shifting his gaze to Colin.

Duff began to repeat the lie Colin had given him last night, but Colin interjected.

"Mayhap I can explain everything once I get my wife on solid ground," he said quickly. "She is carrying my bairn, and the seas seem to have unsettled her stomach this morn."

The warrior eyed them for another long minute before at last giving them a curt nod of his dark head.

Colin hoisted his saddlebags on one shoulder, then extended his hand for a firm shake with Duff, Arran, and Keith. "Thank ye again," he said before swinging his legs over the gunwale and landing with a thump on the docks. He lifted Sabine over after him, who mutely nodded her thanks to the crew as well.

Tucking her arm under his as an attentive husband would do, he walked her down the docks and toward the wall of large Scottish warriors.

"Does yer wife need, ahem, privacy?" the man who'd met them at the end of the docks asked, casting a wary look at her.

"I need to speak with ye away from the others," Colin said bluntly, dropping his voice.

The man turned icy, apprehensive eyes on him, his dark brows lowering. If he'd had more time and his wits about him, Colin would have chosen a tone and words that drew less suspicion, but as it was, speed was of the essence.

Luckily, the warrior nodded again and motioned them forward. They walked through the wall of warriors and away from the docks toward a tall stone tower that Colin guessed was used for watching the sea for approaching vessels.

The man opened the door to the tower and motioned for them to head up the spiral stone staircase to the right.

Colin could feel tension radiating from Sabine, but he urged her up the stairs, following close behind.

When they reached the top, two broad Scottish warriors turned from the arrow slits in the stone wall where they'd been looking out over the water.

"Stand down, men," the man said as he moved into the small space behind Colin. "Give us a moment."

The two warriors glanced at each other, then lifted their eyebrows at Colin and Sabine, but finally they nodded to the man who must be their superior and shuffled to the stairs.

When the two warriors' footsteps faded from earshot, the man turned to them, his gaze sharp and cold.

"The only reason I am affording ye such leeway is that I detect a Highland brogue on yer tongue, man," he said. "Explain yerself before my generosity is spent."

Colin squared his shoulders. "My name is Colin MacKay. I am working in the service of our King."

The man's eyes widened a hair's breadth, recognition flickering across their pale depths.

"Colin MacKay—ye mean the Colin MacKay who is in the Bruce's direct council?"

"Aye, the same. I've been sent by the Bruce to deliver a message for his brother."

A slow smile began to spread across the man's face,

chasing away the hardened warrior who'd been glaring at them a moment before.

"I've heard of ye, but it's good to finally meet ye in person." The man extended a hand toward Colin. "I am Kirk MacLeod."

Now it was Colin's turn to feel his eyes widen with recognition. He clasped Kirk's extended forearm and gave it a firm shake.

"Ye are in Edward Bruce's inner circle, are ye no'?"

"Aye. Glad to hear ye've heard of me as well."

Kirk MacLeod had been in Robert the Bruce's service for many years. When the Bruce sent his brother Edward to Ireland in a quest to unite all Celtic peoples against the English, Kirk had been hand-selected to serve as Edward Bruce's right-hand man. Though Edward Bruce hadn't formed a similar organization as Robert the Bruce's Bodyguard Corps, Kirk was nevertheless among a small and tight-knit group of elite warriors whom the Bruces kept close to their sides.

"Are ye a MacLeod of the isles?" Colin asked.

"Aye," Kirk replied. "Is a MacKay Highlander acquainted with one of my kin?"

Colin smiled. "Angus MacLeod. He's been looking out for me in the Bruce's army for nigh nine years now."

"The old bear. Angus is a distant uncle of mine."

"It is good to meet ye," Colin said, sobering. "I wouldnae mind updating ye on how yer uncle fares at some point, but my business is pressing."

Kirk's face once again fell into its hard lines. "Aye. Ye'll need to reach Edward quickly then."

Colin nodded, but Kirk hesitated, shifting his gaze to Sabine.

"And the lass?" he asked, his eyes keen as he scrutinized Sabine. "Is she with us?"

Conflicting emotions twined together to form a knot in Colin's stomach. He glanced at Sabine, who stood stock-still behind him. Her compressed lips were faintly lined in white.

"I'll vouch for her," Colin said at last. "There is much to explain, but later."

Kirk nodded curtly and turned to descend the tower stairs. Before following, Colin tried to catch Sabine's eye to give her a reassuring look, but she dropped her gaze to the stone floor.

When they stepped from the watch tower, Kirk was already barking orders to the warriors stationed there.

"Henry, fetch us three horses. Darrach and William, return to your posts in the tower."

The men were quick to do their leader's bidding, though several sent sideways looks at Colin and Sabine.

When the one named Henry appeared leading three large horses, he shot an openly suspicious look in Colin's direction.

"Milord, are ye sure ye can trust this man? Mayhap ye should bring an additional contingent to keep watch over them—and protect yer back."

Kirk snatched one of the reins from Henry's proffered hand and swung into the saddle. "This man is Colin MacKay, of King Robert the Bruce's inner council," he said loud enough for all those nearby to hear. "The King trusts this man with his life, so therefore I do as well."

Murmurs rippled through the gathered warriors. Colin felt the stares of many men land on him.

Henry extended him the reins to another horse, his eyes wide. As Colin accepted the reins, Henry gave him a bow.

Colin left his horse standing before the tower for a moment to help Sabine mount her own steed, then swung into his saddle.

"Be vigilant, men," Kirk called to the warriors.

The soldiers called ayes in response, but someone's voice rose above the rest.

"*Manu forti!*"

One of the warriors in the front of the group placed his fist over his heart, then lifted it toward Colin. "*Manu forti!*" he said, taking up the call.

Soon all the warriors had pounded their chests with a fist and then raised their hands to Colin, shouting the same phrase.

Sabine reined her horse close to his, leaning over so that her low voice would be heard over the chants.

"What are they saying?"

Colin's throat had tightened with emotion at the display his fellow Scottish warriors had given him. He swallowed, turning to Sabine.

"*Manu forti* is the MacKay clan's motto. It means 'with a strong hand.'"

"But why? Why are they saluting you?"

Colin felt a humble smile curl his lips. "Like Kirk, they have heard of my service to King Robert. These warriors are honoring me with this send-off."

Sabine's eyes rounded, and something that looked like anguish flashed there before it quickly disappeared. "I…I didn't know just how important you are to your country—to your cause."

Pride swelled in his chest as he shifted his gaze from Sabine to the men, all from different clans, with the MacKay motto on their lips and their fists raised in salute. Aye, he'd fought for his place at the Bruce's side and would never take the honor of that place for granted.

Kirk spurred his horse and set a southwesterly course. Colin followed Sabine after him, watching her hair ripple with the horse's strides. As the warriors' chant faded behind him, the dark foreboding that had plagued him since he first met Sabine descended again.

Aye, he was the Bruce's loyal servant. But what did that mean for Sabine's future?

Chapter Thirty-One

As a sea of off-white canvas tents emerged in the distance, Sabine had to clench her teeth to keep them from chattering in fear.

She'd been on dangerous assignments before. She'd had to knock out men twice her size and pray that they remained unconscious as she worked. She'd even once had to drug an English nobleman so that he would sleep soundly as she rummaged through his stacks of missives and ledgers.

But never had she ridden directly into the middle of an army—an army that would likely tear her limb from limb when they found out that an English spy was in their midst.

Colin had said that he would vouch for her, but he would undoubtedly be the first in line to tighten the noose around her neck when he discovered that the missive he'd been sent to deliver was gone.

As inconspicuously as she could, she let her eyes dart over the landscape in the hopes that some out, some escape, would present itself before they reached the cluster of tents.

Like the northern regions of England and the Scottish Lowlands, Ireland was lushly green. Softly rolling hills carpeted in emerald grasses were broken up by clumps of trees and the small tract lands of farmsteads.

The vast expanse of tents was tucked in a valley between two larger hills. A stream trailed through the middle of the camp. In the overcast light of the late afternoon, Sabine could see that the camp swarmed with the activity of warriors, who were mere black dots from this distance.

Nay, there was no way to escape now. Coward that she was, she'd hoped for a fleeting moment that she could simply flee from what she had done to Colin, but she would have to bear the consequences now.

"I hope I havenae pushed yer wife too hard today," Kirk said over his shoulder to Colin. "What with her carrying a bairn, we shouldnae have ridden so hard, but ye said yer business is urgent, and Edward Bruce is preparing to move his camp."

Colin cleared his throat before answering. "Her name is Sabine, and she isnae my wife, nor is she with child."

Kirk spun in the saddle, gaze sharp on the two of them.

Colin held up a staying hand. "It is complicated, but I still vouch for her. Mayhap there will be time to explain some day."

Kirk's dark brows remained lowered, but he grunted after a moment and turned forward in the saddle once more. "Aye, mayhap."

Sabine felt herself sink a little deeper into the pit of shame engulfing her. All the lies, all the secrets in her life seemed to have tangled themselves around her neck. With each of the horse's strides drawing her closer to Edward Bruce's camp, she felt the strings tightening.

As they reached the outskirts of the tent village, Sabine's pulse quickened. Kirk had spoken true—the camp buzzed with activity as Scottish warriors lowered tents, loaded wagons, and harnessed horses. Edward Bruce was preparing to move.

Kirk sent up a whistle, and a younger lad appeared to take their horses' reins.

Even before Sabine's boots had squelched in the churned mud, Kirk was striding into the heart of the camp.

"We've been stationed here for a fortnight," he said over his shoulder to Colin. "Edward has been waiting for word from his brother, though he began to fear that his last missive asking for counsel didn't reach the King."

Sabine ducked her head, wincing. She hadn't been privy to any missive sent between Edward Bruce and the King, though she wouldn't put it past Fabian to have intercepted it.

To her utter relief, Colin shook his head and spoke. "Nay, the Bruce received Edward's missive, but we were in the middle of a siege on Carlisle castle in the Borderlands. He sent me with all haste once he'd crafted his message in response."

Kirk nodded, leading them deeper into the maze-like paths between the tents. "Let us hope that the message ye bear is of some aid. When this cursed weather hasnae pinned us down, the Irish forces still loyal to the English have."

Sabine quickened her step to try to keep up with Colin and Kirk's long strides. Canvas tents swirled all around her, but she hardly noticed, for her mind shot back to the contents of the missive.

Hold your position in Inniskeen.

Was this Inniskeen, then? If it was, Edward's decision to move would be going against the Bruce's advice to remain.

De Burgh is not your only enemy.

What did that mean? Would Edward be walking into a trap if he moved?

Sabine's blood hammered in her ears. Her dread at Colin learning of her betrayal was chased away by the deepening realization that the information she bore in her head could save men's lives—or lead to men's deaths, depending on what she did with her knowledge.

The thought sent an icy chill down her spine. Before she could contemplate the implications of the information she carried, however, Kirk made a sharp turn and suddenly came to a halt in front of a tent that was taller and longer than the others around it.

He murmured something to the guard posted outside the tent, who then slipped between the canvas flaps. A moment later, the guard re-emerged and motioned them all inside.

Sabine tried to swallow the fear that rose in her throat, but it lodged there, nigh choking her.

The interior of the tent was slightly dimmer than the overcast evening outside, though a candle flickered on a wooden table, creating a warm glow within. The table was strewn with what appeared to be several maps, though Sabine couldn't make them out from where she stood.

Before she had time to scan the rest of the tent's interior, a man stood from a chair positioned near the table and strode toward them.

Edward Bruce. It had to be. Though Sabine had never laid eyes on King Robert the Bruce, she'd heard that his physical appearance matched his role as warrior-King. He was said to possess a large frame, graying russet hair, and keen dark eyes.

The man before her lacked the gray in his reddish-brown hair, but otherwise, he fit the King's description as only a brother could.

Edward was tall—as tall as both Colin and Kirk, making Sabine feel like a sapling surrounded by towering oaks. He wore chainmail over his tunic as if he were about to step into battle, though his head was uncovered.

He was likely only a handful of years older than Colin, but his eyes bore traces of strain around them.

His gaze skittered over them to Kirk, a russet brow lifted in inquiry.

"This is Colin MacKay, milord, and Sabine, his…a trusted companion." Kirk frowned, but luckily for Sabine, he didn't shoot her another one of his cutting stares.

"Colin MacKay," Edward Bruce said, a weary smile lifting one corner of his mouth. "My brother speaks very highly of ye."

"Thank ye, milord," Colin said, bowing deeply.

Remembering herself, Sabine dropped into a low curtsy, suddenly ashamed of her mud-covered, travel-worn dress and boots.

"Let's no' waste time with formalities," Edward said, motioning them both up. "Ye have word from my brother."

"Aye," Colin replied. Without further preamble, he reached under the neckline of his tunic and moved his hand over his heart.

Sabine's breath suddenly came shallow, making the room tilt slightly. It was happening. Colin would know what she'd done in a matter of moments, and then her life—and his love—would be over.

She heard the faint crinkle of waxed parchment as Colin's fingers dug in the hidden pocket sewn into his tunic. He withdrew his hand, and in his grasp he bore the protective wrapping that had once concealed the missive.

Colin extended the little packet of waxed parchment to Edward Bruce's waiting hand.

"We'll leave ye, milord," Colin said, turning to the tent's flaps.

Edward waved at him distractedly, making Colin halt. "Aught that I ken, Kirk kens as well. I imagine it is the same between ye and my brother, Colin." He glanced at Sabine for a heartbeat, but then seemed to disregard her. "And if ye trust the lass, then so will I."

Sabine's heart hammered against her ribcage, unable to tear her gaze away from the parchment in Edward's hand.

Slowly, he began to unfold it.

At last the wax paper lay open—revealing naught but air within.

Chapter Thirty-Two

"What is the meaning of this?" Edward Bruce barked.

Both Kirk and Colin stiffened on either side of Sabine at his sharp tone.

The room spun faster around her, but then it suddenly stopped. A strange calm came over her. She wouldn't have to look away from Colin's searching blue eyes anymore. She wouldn't have to hide the truth of her betrayal. It meant watching Colin's heart be ripped out, and knowing she was responsible, but at least there would be no more lies between them.

"What is amiss, milord?" Kirk said, taking a step forward.

Edward held up the empty waxed parchment wrapping.

"There is no missive here," he snapped, his dark eyes pinning Colin.

"Nay," Colin breathed.

Sabine looked up at him, as if seeing him through the mist of a dream. He would never forgive her for this. Yet her heart still stretched toward him. She loved him, she realized with a start.

Colin shoved his hand back into the neckline of his tunic, his hand fishing wildly in the hidden pocket within. A moment later, he yanked the whole tunic off his head. He gripped the front where the jaggedly sewn line marked the path of the sword that had almost sliced his chest in two.

The tense air within the tent was split with the sound of rending fabric as Colin tore his tunic apart.

"Nay," he panted again, staring down at the strips of wool in his hands.

The look of devastation in his eyes cut Sabine to the quick. He'd failed at his mission—because of her. Men would die—because of her.

But she could still make up for some of the destruction she'd caused. Nay, she couldn't undo her betrayal of Colin in reading the missive. But she could help him in the cause that was most important to him.

Squeezing her eyes shut to block out distractions, Sabine opened her mouth and dragged in a deep breath.

"*I have heard rumblings from your isle. Be warned, brother, de Burgh is not your only enemy.*"

"Sabine, what are ye—"

"What is the meaning of this?" Edward demanded again, cutting Colin off.

"*He seeks to lure you south to Louth, but he is no doubt up to something. Hold your position in Inniskeen.*" Her brows lowered as she concentrated on the words. She'd learned how to hold them exactly right in her head, but Fabian didn't usually interrupt her when she began reciting them.

"Bloody hell," Kirk breathed off to her left. Colin sputtered for words on her other side, but he could not form any.

"If Edmund Butler has joined de Burgh, he leaves the north vulnerable. This could be your chance to strike. The local lords in the north are with you."

The final words echoed through the tent, which had fallen eerily silent as she concluded the recitation.

Slowly, Sabine opened her eyes.

Kirk stared at her in stunned confusion. Edward Bruce's brows were lowered and his mouth tight as he waited for an explanation.

And in Colin's vivid blue eyes she found the bottomless agony of betrayal.

"Nay, Sabine," he whispered. "Ye didnae—"

The words stuck in his throat and he was unable to continue, but the look he gave her might as well have been a knife burying itself in her heart. Hurt. Distrust. But worst of all, she saw resignation steal across his features.

"I-I opened the missive from the King," she began, her voice barely audible even to her own ears. "I read it and memorized it."

Edward Bruce's eyes rounded in rage. "Ye're a bloody Englishwoman!" he bellowed.

Belatedly, she realized that her English accent made her words all the more damning to the three

Scots.

Edward took a rapid step toward her, closing half the distance between them.

Kirk bolted forward as well, though he angled his body slightly so that his shoulder jutted in front of Edward, as if to protect Sabine from any rash actions on Edward's part. Still, his gaze was as cold and cutting as a shard of ice as he looked at her.

"Who in bloody hell are ye, lass?" he demanded, his voice chillingly level.

"As Colin said, my name is Sabine. I am—was—a thief…a spy, though I never considered myself such."

Edward's eyes widened even more until she could see white all around the dark center. His nostrils flared with fury.

"It was my job to steal documents—accounts, ledgers, but mostly missives—and either deliver them to my boss, or memorize the contents and let them continue on so that neither the sender or the receiver would know that the information had been compromised," she went on quickly.

"Ye *vouched* for this woman?" Kirk asked, turning to Colin.

Colin's features hardened, a wall dropping over the anguish in his eyes. "I thought I could trust her."

"I am not loyal to my boss any longer," Sabine said, looking between the three men for a sign that they would believe her. "I realize now that I have been a prisoner to him—to my own fears." At the hard stares that met her, she hurried on. "Colin has shown me what it means to be loyal, honorable, to truly care about a noble cause. I see now the value of freedom, and I want naught more than to help."

She turned to Colin as she spoke the last words, unashamed to let him see the truth in her eyes. She silently pleaded with him to understand, but he turned away, giving her the hard expanse of his bare back.

"Is this some sort of trick?" Edward demanded.

"Nay," she said quickly. "The words I spoke were exactly as they appeared in the missive bearing King Robert the Bruce's seal, I swear on my life."

Edward's face darkened. "Yer life is verra much at stake, lass, make no mistake."

Sabine had to swallow, but she nodded her head. "I understand. And I did not recite the message in the hope that it would change your handling of me." She dropped her head. Suddenly the weight of all the events of the last sennight caught up with her. "I...I know that you must do what you see fit with me. I delivered the message only because I wished for you to have the information. It may save many of your men's lives."

Edward let out a slow exhale through his teeth. At last, he spoke. "I need to think on this situation. No action will be taken against ye, woman—no' yet, anyway—until I sort things out more fully. Colin, can ye see that the lass is secured somewhere?"

Colin lifted his gaze to Edward. "Aye, milord."

"And Colin," Edward said grimly. "I dinnae want the lass harmed, but nor do I want her to have a chance to escape."

"Understood, milord." Colin's voice was hard and flat as he turned cold eyes on Sabine.

"And our plans to mobilize, milord?" Kirk asked quietly.

Edward eyed her for a long moment before answering. "Tell the men to hold our position for now. We'll see what tomorrow brings."

Kirk nodded and strode around Sabine toward the tent's flaps.

With his features set in granite, Colin stepped in front of Sabine.

"My guard will show ye to an empty tent where ye can secure the lass," Edward said, turning away.

Sabine prayed that she would find even the faintest trace of gentleness when Colin wrapped a large hand around one of her wrists.

But in his firm hold, she felt only his cold disgust.

Chapter Thirty-Three

So numb with shock was Colin that he hardly noticed where Edward Bruce's guard was leading him.

He blindly followed the burly warrior through the maze of tents, oblivious to their surroundings. The only thing he could seem to focus on was the delicate bone of Sabine's wrist, which he held in his grip.

She was so slight that if he'd wanted to, he could have snapped the bone with little more than a squeeze and a twist. Yet even after all she'd done, the thought of hurting her made his stomach roil with sickness.

It wasn't until the guard halted in front of a small canvas tent and turned to Colin with a length of rope extended in his hand that his mind sharpened.

The full weight of Sabine's betrayal suddenly descended on him, cutting through the fog of shock. His worst fears had come true for a second time. She'd taken advantage of his misguided trust—and his love.

He wordlessly took the rope from the guard and entered the tent, pulling Sabine behind him.

The interior was dim, as the sun had set some time while they'd been with Edward Bruce. Dried hay covered the ground, keeping the wet grass and mud underneath at bay. A thick pole stood in the middle of the circular tent. Other than that, the space was empty.

Colin led Sabine by the wrist toward the pole. He positioned the pole between them, then carefully grasped her left hand along with her right and began binding her wrists together around the wood.

He'd tied her before, but this felt different. He'd told her he loved her. He'd lain with her, trusting her to sleep in his arms after they'd made love.

He worked in silence, keeping his gaze on her trembling hands as he secured the rope.

"Ye can stand up or sit down as ye please," he said, finishing his knot. "I'll have the guard bring ye water and bread as well. Ye should be able to get them to yer mouth even with yer hands like this."

"Colin, I—"

"If yer left shoulder begins to hurt ye," he said, ignoring her pleading interjection, "I'll reposition ye. But ye will remain bound."

He turned to go, but her quavering voice stopped him.

"Please," she whispered. "Please, just let me explain."

Colin pivoted slowly on his heels, forcing himself to look Sabine in the face.

Her delicate features were contorted into a mask of desperation. Tears shone in her wide, imploring eyes. She didn't fight against her constraints, but rather clutched the pole as if her legs were about to give out.

"Why did ye do it?" he rasped, breaking the thick silence between them.

Sabine's slim throat bobbed as she struggled wordlessly.

"I…I feared that in the light of day, you would realize you'd made a mistake," she said at last, her voice reed-thin. "You'd regret making love to me, telling me that you cared—that you loved me. You'd remember that you are a Scottish warrior fighting for freedom, and that I am your captive English spy."

Colin's heart twisted cruelly. It had been the same fear he'd had for her—that she would regret giving herself to him, that she would turn away from him.

"I feared that I had fooled myself again," she went on, "that I would come to learn with time that I'd misplaced my trust in you, just as I did with Fabian. I believed in a moment of panic that I only had myself, that I could only trust myself. And you yourself told me that information was powerful. I thought to read the missive and stow its contents away in my mind so that if I ever needed to protect myself—from Fabian, or from you—that I could use the information as a shield."

Colin exhaled slowly. In a distant corner of his mind, he understood her logic, albeit tainted by fear— fear that Fabian had instilled in her. But the angry, hurt voices screaming at him drowned out that whisper of understanding.

"So ye fucked me and then waited until I slept to open the missive. Clever," he bit out, tasting bile as he spat the foul word.

She flinched as if he'd struck her. Aye, he'd intended to hurt her, but now he hated himself for it. Self-loathing mingled with hot fury, bubbling dangerously in his stomach.

"I didn't use you in that way," she whispered desperately, tears slipping freely down her pale cheeks. "You must believe me."

He wanted to, damn it all, but the pain and anger were too great within him.

"Why didnae ye return the missive to my tunic, as ye ken well how to do? Wouldnae it have been easier to use the information to your benefit if I didnae ken ye had it?" he demanded.

"It was an accident. I didn't mean to destroy the missive," she murmured. "When I read it, I grew frightened, for I finally realized just how powerful—and deadly—such information could be. And I realized that I'd betrayed you in opening it."

She dragged in a breath, squeezing her eyes shut for a moment. "In truth, I don't know what I might have done if the missive hadn't caught fire when the ship rolled and the lantern tipped over."

Colin felt the slightest twinge of relief to hear that she hadn't intentionally burned the missive to keep it from him. He quickly shoved the feeling down, though. How could he even be sure she was telling the truth about it being an accident?

"I'd like to think that I would have confessed my actions immediately and begged your forgiveness," she went on. "But I proved a coward after the missive burned. I knew I couldn't keep it from you forever, but I could not face the pain of telling you what I'd done."

"And now?" he asked quietly. "Why did ye tell Edward Bruce what the missive contained?"

"I spoke the truth earlier," she said. "I was afraid of what would happen if that information fell into the wrong hands. And though I have never fought for any cause before, I believe with all my heart in the fight for freedom. I want to help you."

He narrowed his eyes on her. "Is this some sort of trick? Will ye try to escape and pass this information along to Fabian? Or was it yer true mission all along to infiltrate the Scottish army here in Ireland?"

He gestured toward the necklace that hung around her neck as if it proved his suspicion.

"Nay," she breathed, her eyes widening. "I will never give my loyalty to him again."

"It seems that I still cannae tell when ye are lying and when ye are telling the truth," he ground out harshly.

She gasped as if he'd struck her again, but then she exhaled slowly and met his eyes. "You have every right to distrust me—to hate me. I know how greatly I have hurt you. I betrayed you…as Joan did."

"Dinnae speak her name to me," he hissed, spinning on his heels and giving her his back.

"Colin, please!" Sabine cried out. "I wish there was some way I could make you understand—make you believe me."

He dragged his gaze over his shoulder and their eyes locked.

"I promise never to lie to you again," she said, holding his gaze with her tear-filled eyes.

"It's a wee bit too late for that," he murmured, turning away once more.

Her fingers clawed the air uselessly as she strained against her bonds to halt his exit. Soft fingertips brushed against his back, which was still bare since he hadn't had time to don a new tunic after tearing his apart.

"Please," she moaned. "No more lies between us, I vow it."

He spun back to her, the emotion he'd fought so hard to keep leashed at last breaking free.

"No more lies?" He snatched her bound wrists in his hands, taking a swift step closer. "What of yer kisses, yer sighs of pleasure? I saw in yer eyes when I made love to ye that ye cared for me. Was that a lie, too?"

"Nay, that wasn't a lie," she breathed, her pain-filled eyes unwavering on his. "I more than care for you. I love you."

Something cracked deep in Colin's chest.

Like lightning, he closed the remaining distance between them. Half-mad with the storm of emotion breaking within him, he claimed her mouth in a searing kiss.

The salt of her tears mingled with the sweet honey of her mouth. She moaned, opening her lips to his invading tongue, surrendering to him.

Her nails sank into his chest as she looked for purchase, but he hardly noticed their bite. Need consumed him—need for Sabine, only Sabine.

His hand buried itself in her silky hair as he deepened the kiss. He tilted back her head, taking everything she would give him with savage hunger.

Blood roared in his ears and hammered in his veins. His cock strained toward her against his breeches, his skin aflame with unquenchable desire.

Through the blaze of passion and the storm of emotion, he felt the truth of all she'd said deep in his bones. She barred naught from him. She was utterly vulnerable in her submission to him in this moment.

In a blinding flash of clarity, he saw into her heart. Saw the pain, the fear. And saw the love and trust she bore for him.

Colin tore his mouth from hers, ripping his hands away as he forced himself to step back.

"Nay," he breathed raggedly. "Nay, I cannae. I cannae trust ye. I *must* no'."

Sabine sagged against the thick pole, her face crumpling in agony. She clung to the wood as she sank to her knees in the straw.

"Colin," she whispered, tears once again welling in her eyes.

He turned and strode from the tent, her heartbroken sobs echoing in his ears.

Chapter Thirty-Four

S abine winced when the tent flaps were thrown back and bright morning light shattered the darkness within.

Slowly, she lifted herself from the hay-covered ground. Her whole body ached, but it wasn't from sleeping on the ground or from the rope that bound her to the tent's pole. Nay, it was from the sobs that had racked her body all through the night until at last she'd collapsed, spent and trembling.

She slid her hands up the pole slightly so that she could raise a palm against the sharp light pouring in at the front of the tent.

A large, dark form stood silhouetted in sunlight between the tent's open flaps. For a heart-stopping moment, she thought it was Colin, but as her eyes adjusted, she realized that it was the guard who'd escorted them here last night.

The guard stepped into the tent and silently set about untying Sabine's hands.

"What is happening?" she croaked, her voice rough from crying. She swallowed and tried again. "Where are you taking me?"

"Edward Bruce wishes to see ye," the guard replied gruffly, not looking at her.

Sabine's stomach dropped like a stone. Edward must have taken the night to consider what to do with her, and now he'd decided on his judgement.

"W-what does he have planned for me?"

The guard didn't answer as he unwound the last of the rope from around her wrists. He wrapped a thick hand around her upper arm and lifted her to her feet as if she weighed naught.

Fear surged through her veins. Had she been sentenced to death for spying? Would such a harsh judgement come so swiftly? And what of her punishment? Was she being dragged to her death at this very moment?

She tugged against the guard's hold, but she might as well have been trying to move a mountain. His grip was firm and unwavering as he pulled her toward the tent's flaps.

Sabine had to throw a hand up to shield her eyes once more as they emerged into the harsh light of morning. The activity from the evening before had ceased, though several soldiers stared at her as she was marched through the maze of tents.

She straightened her spine and clenched her teeth in the face of their looks. If she was going to her death, she might as well try to be brave.

She smoothed her battered dress, but the garment was far from looking presentable to stand for judgement. When she lifted a hand to her face, her eyes were swollen from crying herself to sleep. Her hand slid down to her lips, which trembled slightly. So much for being brave.

When they reached Edward's tent, Sabine dragged in a breath, at last finding her courage. She'd done wrong, she knew. She'd hurt people, mayhap even cost people their lives when she'd worked for Fabian. And she'd betrayed the one person who'd ever truly loved her. She could only pray that someday, Colin would find a way to forgive her after she was gone.

The guard held back the tent flap and released her, motioning her inside.

On wobbling legs, she stepped into the tent.

Kirk stood to the left, his arms crossed over his chest and his eyes unreadable as they took her in. Edward Bruce was bent over the wooden table in the middle, his attention focused on the maps strewn there.

And Colin stood off to the right.

When their gazes locked, she inhaled. Dark purple shadows sat under his eyes as if he hadn't slept a wink last night. His tawny mane of hair sat unbound and disheveled around his shoulders. Golden bristle covered his hard-set jaw. Like Kirk, his eyes were unreadable as his gaze swept over her.

Edward straightened from the table. "We've had some news, lass, and I thought ye had a right to hear it."

News? Sabine wasn't sure what Edward meant, but she nodded unsteadily.

"A few of my scouts traveled south to Louth overnight, where I'd planned to relocate my men. I've been keeping an eye on Richard de Burgh, though he hasnae made a move in over a fortnight. De Burgh still holds his position just south of Louth, but my scouts noticed some strange activity to the west."

Edward stepped around to the front of the table, then propped himself on its edge, all the while holding her with his gaze.

"Apparently, another force had assembled in alliance with de Burgh—a force led by Edmund Butler."

Sabine gasped, her mind skittering back to the missive she'd memorized.

De Burgh is not your only enemy…

He seeks to lure you south to Louth…

Hold your position…

Edmund Butler has joined de Burgh.

"My scouts say that Butler and his army were moving in the dead of night to avoid detection. They must have learned that I was mobilizing my forces and had hoped to ambush us," Edward went on.

Sabine's heart leapt inside her chest. "So…so the message I delivered. It…it…"

"It saved the lives of countless numbers of my men, lass," Edward said, straightening from the table. "Yer words proved true."

The air suddenly rushed from her lungs as relief crashed over her. The inside of the tent spun wildly, and her trembling legs gave out from beneath her.

She crumpled toward the ground, but before she reached it, Colin's strong arms wrapped around her, lifting her and cradling her against his chest.

His warm, piney scent brought her back from her swoon. Her arms involuntarily looped around his neck and she clung to him, silently praying that he would never let her go.

"I...I helped," she breathed.

An unfamiliar warmth spread from her chest through her limbs. It was pride, she realized—pride that she had done something to help people rather than harm them, pride that she had played a small part in Scotland's fight for freedom.

"Aye," Edward said, drawing her attention. "And I plan on taking my brother's advice as well. We are headed north, for Butler's alliance with de Burgh leaves the region undefended by Irish troops still loyal to England. As my brother says, the locals there will welcome us now that the English are away." Edward smiled faintly. "Robert will no doubt be greatly pleased at this victory."

"I'll give the order, milord," Kirk said, stepping forward. As he strode around Colin, who still clutched Sabine in his arms, Kirk tilted his head slightly to her. The small display of thanks sent a fresh wave of pride through her.

"Can ye stand?" Colin's voice rumbled softly through his chest and into hers.

"Aye," she said reluctantly.

He set her carefully on her feet, but kept one hand gently wrapped around her elbow to steady her.

"As far as I'm concerned, ye should be thanked for yer help in avoiding the trap Butler laid for me," Edward said, "though I gather I dinnae ken the full extent of the web ye are tangled in."

"W-what will you do with me, milord?" Sabine asked.

Edward rubbed a hand over his eyes and sighed. "To be honest, I dinnae ken, lass. I've asked Colin for his opinion, but he has been strangely silent on the matter."

She gazed up at Colin. A storm rolled across his sea-blue eyes.

He cleared his throat. "I havenae given my opinion because I fear that…that I am too emotionally ensnared in this situation to have a clear view of things. I am no' sure if I can form a fair course of action."

Edward's gaze sharpened as he looked from Colin to Sabine. He grunted, though Sabine thought she detected a slight curve around the corner of Edward's mouth.

"I see. Well, since my brother is the one ye must ultimately report to, I am tempted to let him decide what the correct path is in this situation. Do ye believe yerself fit to take the lass back to the King for final judgement, Colin?"

Colin's Adam's apple bobbed as he swallowed, his face drawn taut. "Aye, milord."

"Good," Edward said, walking back around his table. "I would invite ye to stay and rest from yer journey for another night, but I want to mobilize my men and head north as soon as possible. We'll no' be here in a few hours' time."

"I understand, milord. I can be ready to depart immediately." Colin glanced at Sabine, his gaze filled with unspoken concern. "Do ye have the strength to go on, lass?"

A little tendril of hope tried to push its way through the rubble and ash in Sabine's heart.

She'd prayed that Colin would find a way to forgive her, but had assumed that would only happen after she'd been sent to death. Yet the traces of tenderness he showed toward her allowed her hope that mayhap there was still a chance to earn his forgiveness before she faced whatever judgement the Bruce would have for her. Even the pain in his eyes revealed that he still felt something for her. The thread of hope budded, taking hold in her chest.

"Aye," she said softly. "I am strong enough to go on."

Chapter Thirty-Five

As the days slipped by, Colin watched the light of hope that had glowed in Sabine's eyes back in Edward Bruce's tent slowly fade.

It was his fault, damn it all. Yet he could not let himself succumb to his love for her.

He told himself it was wrong to love his enemy, wrong to believe her after all her lies and deceptions. But the truth that would not be stifled in his heart was that he was afraid. He feared that if he let himself love her, the loss of her to the Bruce's judgement would be his final undoing.

His mind had run itself ragged over the last four days as he tried to guess what the Bruce might do with Sabine.

She could be hanged for treason without hesitation. She could be imprisoned for the rest of her life as punishment for stealing missives. Colin still believed the Bruce would not resort to torturing her, though she would be ordered to reveal all she knew about Fabian and his organization.

He didn't let himself dwell on the possibility that the Bruce might show leniency given the fact that she'd saved countless lives in Edward Bruce's army. Just as he let her hope die slowly in the face of his silence and distance, he quashed his own hope that things could end well for them.

They'd made the crossing back to Scotland uneventfully. The ferry used to transport both men and livestock had been slow but effective enough in getting them to Portpatrick.

Colin had retrieved Ruith from the town's stables. The stallion looked as glossy and well-fed as Colin had ever seen him, and he thanked the stable master for the animal's care.

Then they'd set out heading east toward Lochmaben. Sabine made no attempt to escape. She seemed resolved to facing her fate in Lochmaben.

Although they likely could have stayed at inns along the way, Colin simply couldn't muster the energy to smile kindly at an innkeeper or form another lie about traveling with his wife. So they kept off the roads and to the woods, making camp in silence each evening.

The nights were long and cold sleeping across the fire from Sabine, but the days on horseback with her were far worse. Having Sabine pressed between his legs, their hips moving together with Ruith's strides, had him gritting his teeth and praying for a swift journey to Lochmaben. He cursed his traitorous body for its undeterred desire for her.

But far more painful than denying his physical need

for Sabine had been turning a cold shoulder to her when she tentatively placed her hand on his forearm, or when she gazed into his eyes with unguarded hope written on her delicate features.

Each time he brushed off her touch, or shifted his gaze away, or let the silence sit heavy and black as a storm cloud between them, he saw the light dim slightly in her eyes. He knew she hoped that a seedling of love still budded in his heart. Aye, it did, but it grew in poisoned ground. He could never let it take root.

On the fifth day after they'd departed from Ireland, Colin guided Ruith slightly to the south. Sabine seemed to come out of the torpor that had settled over her during the long stretches of silence. She straightened slightly in the saddle before him and looked around.

"Why are we going south?" she asked softly.

Colin unclenched his jaw. "We are near Dumfries. I dinnae want to draw too close in case we are recognized."

"Oh," she replied. Laden silence settled over them once more.

Colin scanned the forest for a good place to make camp. Somewhere in this tangle of woods, he'd chased Sabine down and taken her captive. How could he have known then that she would be the one to capture him, mind, body, and soul?

He shoved the melancholy thought aside as he dismounted and helped her from Ruith's back. She touched his hands where they were wrapped around her waist.

"Colin…" She looked up at him with a plea in her hazel eyes.

This would be one of their last nights together before reaching Lochmaben. If he had aught to say to her, now was the time.

Colin fisted his hands and jerked them from her waist, turning away.

"Colin!" she said again, her voice rising with desperation. "You promised never to hurt me."

He turned back to find her breathing hard, her eyes ablaze with frustration. It was as if something had finally snapped in her.

"You promised never to hurt me," she repeated, "and yet you have been so cold, so distant since—"

"Since I learned that ye'd read the missive." The words came out wearily, for Colin felt more heartsick than angry.

"Aye," Sabine said. "And though you seemed to soften toward me that morning in Edward Bruce's tent, I feel like—" Her voice strained, growing thin. "I feel like I am being abandoned all over again. First by whatever family I had as a child, then by Fabian, and now by you."

The thought of being compared to that bastard sent a sudden bolt of hot anger into Colin's gut. Yet somewhere in the back of his mind, he knew the anger should be at himself, for he'd hurt her with his selfish withdrawal.

"We cannot go on like this," she went on. "Please, just talk to me. I know there is still love between us."

"What would ye have me say, Sabine?" he ground out, feeling his tight rein on control suddenly slipping away as raw emotion surged within him. "That I still love ye? Aye, I do. But it doesnae make a difference."

"Why not?"

"Because I am still turning ye over to my King's judgement!" he barked. "Because ye are still my enemy, whether I want it to be so or no'."

"But why has that made you so cold to me?" she demanded. "I know I must go before the Bruce. I know I have done wrong. I feel as though I am finally doing *right* in facing the consequences of my actions, and in—" Her voice caught, but she forced herself onward. "And in loving you."

"What would ye have me say?" he asked again, his own throat tightening. "Mayhap I cannae stand the thought of loving ye, only to lose ye."

Her eyes rounded in surprise at his words. He, too, was shocked at the raw admission. He dragged in a breath, trying to steel himself against the storm threatening to break within his heart.

"I am afraid, too," she said quietly, holding his gaze. "When the guard came to fetch me to Edward's tent that morning, I feared that I was to be executed right then."

She shook her head slightly as if to rid herself of the dark memories before going on.

"And I am afraid of what awaits me at the Bruce's hands. I am afraid to lose you. But that doesn't change the fact that I love you."

He drew in a sharp breath at the vulnerable honesty of her words.

"I don't know what the future holds," she said, her voice barely above a whisper. "But I'm willing to take a leap of faith, to risk loving you anyway."

All at once, the old scar deep in Colin's heart tore open. Her softly spoken words might as well have been a sword driven straight into the wound that had never quite healed.

He'd been afraid for so long—afraid to trust, afraid to love, and all because he'd been hurt once many years ago.

Aye, Joan had broken his heart, broken his trust with her betrayal. But that had been eight long years ago. Why did one woman's actions still control him so profoundly?

He'd shaped his whole life around avoiding trusting people again, avoiding being hurt. All the charm, the lighthearted smiles and flirtatious winks, had been naught more than a shield, he realized. He used them to keep people at bay, to protect himself from ever truly caring about someone again.

Yet Sabine had broken through that shield. She could bring him to his knees with a word or a kiss. Despite everything standing against them, love had taken hold in both their hearts.

Colin stood on a precipice. Behind him was the life he'd known—a life of charm and manipulation, of guarding his heart against threats. A familiar life, but a lonely one.

Before him lay the vast expanse of the unknown—a future where he may lose Sabine, but one in which he let himself fully love her. He knew in a flash of clarity what he wanted—nay, what he needed.

"I broke my vow no' to hurt ye," he rasped. "And for that I must beg yer forgiveness. It seemed safer to retreat, to withdraw from what I felt than face the risk of opening my heart again only to be hurt—to have ye torn away. But I see now how selfish I've been, fleeing into myself, fleeing from what lies between us."

Tears shone in her eyes as he spoke. She nodded slowly for him to go on, her throat bobbing with a hard swallow.

"Ye humble me with yer bravery, lass," he murmured, touching her velvety cheek with his thumb. "Ye of all people have every right no' to trust or love. Yet ye bestow both upon me. I... I want to take that leap of faith with ye."

A heart-rending smile broke over her face as the tears slipped freely down her cheeks.

"I willnae abandon ye ever again," Colin went on, forcing the words around the emotion tightening his throat. "I dinnae care that we are supposed to be enemies. I love ye, Sabine. I love ye."

She launched herself into his arms so forcefully that

the air rushed from his lungs. He buried his face in her rich tresses, dragging in the soft scent of her hair. His arms clamped her to him so hard that she, too, had the wind knocked from her.

As he squeezed her still closer, his heart twisted painfully. In a day or two, he would deliver her to the Bruce and he might never see her again.

"I have wasted so much time," he breathed, nuzzling her ear. "So much time that I could have been kissing ye, holding ye, telling ye just how much I love ye."

"I don't know what the future holds for us," Sabine whispered, her voice muffled against his shoulder, "but I will not waste another second we have together. I love you too, Colin."

"Aye, no more wasted time," he said, drawing back from her.

She gazed up at him, love shining in her green-gold eyes.

"I need ye, Sabine," he said, his voice growing husky. "God, how I need ye."

Something shifted in the air around them, and all at once Colin's blood flared with desire.

Longing flickered in the depths of Sabine's eyes as well. Her lips parted, her breath growing shallow with anticipation.

That was all it took to snap Colin's control.

He dipped his head, taking her lips with his.

Chapter Thirty-Six

S abine opened under Colin's kiss, beckoning him in. Their tongues danced, a sensual promise of what was to come.

His hands were everywhere—in her hair, on her back, around her waist. He couldn't seem to get enough of her.

Nor could she get enough of him. She tangled her fingers in his silken gold mane, then let her hands drag across his broad shoulders to the hard plane of his chest. She could feel his heart hammering just below her fingertips. That heart beat for her, she knew with a swell of elation, just as hers beat for him.

His mouth left hers, only to brush kisses along her cheek and down her neck, then back up again until he found her earlobe tucked within her hair. He nipped her there, sending ripples of pleasure through her. When his tongue darted out to lave her earlobe, she shivered in delight.

She tugged his tunic from his belt, eager to feel his warm, taut skin. Her hand slipped under the tunic, and the muscles of his stomach bunched at her touch. She wanted to stroke every inch of him, taste him as he had so erotically tasted her.

Her hand dropped from beneath his tunic and found the thick, hard column of his manhood straining against his breeches.

He sucked in a sharp breath as she cupped him.

"Easy, lass," he hissed. "Else I'll spend myself in my breeches before I get this damned dress off ye."

He yanked urgently at the ties running down her back. When they loosened, he practically ripped the dress down her shoulders.

He froze, his gaze locking on her left shoulder where her shift exposed her skin.

"Did I hurt ye?"

"Nay." She rolled the shoulder experimentally. She'd regained almost all of her range of motion, and there was no more pain, only a bit of stiffness. Though bruises still marked her shoulder, they'd faded from purple to faint green. "It is almost completely healed."

"Good, because I dinnae ken if I can be gentle," he growled.

Another shiver of anticipation rippled through her.

He tugged her dress the rest of the way down her hips and legs until it lay in a limp pile at her feet. Wrapping his hands around her waist, he lifted her out of the pile and set her off to his left away from Ruith.

Working swiftly, he dug his plaid out of his saddle-bag and turned back to her. His gaze devoured her like a man half-starved.

With a quick flick of his wrist, he unfurled the

plaid, never taking his eyes from her. Then he moved like lightning, closing the distance between them.

His mouth fell on hers once again, his hands peeling away her shift. She pulled at his tunic until he finally broke their kiss just long enough to rip the garment over his head and toss it aside.

Her hands worked his belt as she felt cool air touch her bare breasts. The belt fell away just as Colin bent, flicking his tongue over one nipple.

She gasped, her legs swaying. Colin's arms came around her, holding her steady as he claimed first one breast and then the other with his hot mouth.

Need pulsed through her like liquid fire, pooling between her legs.

"Now," she panted. "Please, now."

He pushed her shift all the way to her feet, then scooped her up, pressing her against the granite wall of his chest.

In two steps, he'd reached the plaid where he'd spread it on the forest floor. He laid her down gently, yet his hands, which clenched her fiercely, belied the urgent need that mirrored her own.

He crouched over her, unfastening his breeches. When he pushed the garment down his lean hips, his cock sprang free, jutting long and hard from his body.

She stared at him, enthralled by the raw masculinity of his form. Where he was hard, she was soft. Where she was slim, his muscles stacked thickly.

He must have seen the captivation in her eyes, for

he growled low and wordless, then moved over her.

To her surprise, though, he dropped to the plaid next to her on his back, then wrapped his hands around her hips and lifted her on top of him.

Knees straddling his hips, she braced her hands on his chest, a question forming on her lips.

"*Bloody hell*," he hissed. His gaze roved over her, his fingers digging into her hips as he ground against her.

The question fled her mind as she realized what he intended. She felt exposed, straddling him as his eyes singed every inch of her flesh, but she also felt wanted, needed, treasured like never before.

One of his hands found her breast, stroking and teasing. She moved restlessly against him, looking for relief from the sweet torture of his touch.

"Aye, that's it," he rasped, moving his hips with hers.

His cock was wedged between them, pinned to his stomach by the folds of her womanhood.

She moved again, rubbing that perfect spot against the hard column of his cock.

His groan mingled with hers at that.

His cock slid between the damp folds of her womanhood, sending frissons of pleasure through her at the fuller contact.

"I cannae take any more," Colin ground out through clenched teeth.

He lifted her hips slightly, taking his cock in hand and guiding it to her entrance. But then he returned his hands to her hips, waiting with a strained look on his face.

Sabine felt a thrill rush through her. Colin was barely holding onto his control, letting her take him in.

She eased down slowly, gasping as he filled her. Colin panted, but his hands remained light on her hips.

Sabine's head fell back as she took him all the way in. She teetered on the line between pain and pleasure as he stretched her with his invasion.

But when his thumb dropped and he found that nub of pure ecstasy, she tumbled headlong into pleasure's grasp.

Instinctually, her hips began to move, rolling against him.

"Aye," he panted, meeting her rhythm with his thrusts.

His other hand left her hip and found her breast once more. His touch sent her careening upward toward the heights of rapture. Pleasure coiled tight within her, then suddenly sprung as her release crashed over her.

Colin's hands clamped onto her hips as he drove up into her hard. He shuddered, his voice echoing her cry of ecstasy as he came undone after her.

Sabine wilted onto his chest, her breathing ragged as she drifted down from the heavens.

"I love ye," he panted, his arms enfolding her.

"I love you, too."

They lay like that, bodies spent and limbs tangling

in his plaid on the forest floor, until the sky dimmed and the air turned faintly blue with evening.

At last, he stirred beneath her.

"Ye'd best get dressed before it grows cool."

Regretfully, she lifted her head and met his gaze. "Aye, I suppose so."

In silence, they rose and retrieved their discarded clothes.

As Sabine tightened the ties on her gown, fear stabbed her belly. What if Colin would grow cold again now that they'd returned from the luscious haze of pleasure and had to face reality once more?

As she turned toward Ruith, Colin caught her arm gently. He moved in front of her, locking his gaze on her.

"Dinnae fear, lass," he said. He must have been able to read her apprehension in her eyes. "I'll no' retreat again—ever. We'll find a way through this, I vow it."

Hope pushed back the uncertainty in her heart. "Thank you for that."

He dipped his head, brushing a tender kiss to her lips.

"Fabian would be so disappointed in you, Sabine."

Sabine whipped her head toward the familiar voice.

Miles stood a few dozen paces away, flanked by ten enormous men.

Sabine's scream died in her throat as the men lunged toward them.

Chapter Thirty-Seven

It was like a nightmare that wouldn't stop replaying before Colin's eyes.

Miles's men surged forward, just as before.

Except this time, there were ten of them rather than two.

Colin threw himself toward Ruith, where his sword protruded from one of the saddlebags. He yanked the sword free of its scabbard and bolted in front of Sabine just as a blade descended toward her head.

He caught the blade with his own, fighting against his opponent's strength. With a mighty push, he threw the sword back just in time to block another attack.

Sabine stumbled out of the way just in time as Colin spun and landed a deadly blow to his attacker's stomach.

Hot pain burned across his upper arm as a sword sliced through his skin. He pivoted and avoided the far more lethal thrust of another blade.

He dispatched a second man with a swipe of his sword across the man's exposed throat.

There were too many of them, though. The remaining eight warriors formed a circle around Colin, closing in slowly.

Battle lust roaring in his ears, Colin steeled himself for the next strike.

But just then Sabine's scream tore through the forest, high and terrified.

The circling warriors melted away as his vision honed in on her. She was on the ground near Ruith, attempting to scramble away from Miles, who loomed over her.

Miles's hand darted out, latching onto her hair. He dragged her to her feet, drawing another cry of pain and fear from her.

"Nay!" Colin bellowed. He lunged forward, only to feel the sharp slash of a blade across his thigh, forcing him to halt.

Miles dragged Sabine against him despite her wild attempts to escape his hold. Reaching down, Miles unsheathed a dagger from his boot and pressed the edge of the blade to Sabine's throat.

Sabine stilled, her eyes rounded with terror.

"It was nice knowing you, girl," Miles murmured softly.

Time seemed to slow as Miles began to draw his hand across her neck. In the blue twilight, a dark, thin ribbon of blood blossomed underneath the dagger as the blade bit into her throat.

"Nay!" Colin roared again.

He was too far away. He couldn't save her. He'd failed.

He hardly noticed the blade arching through the darkening sky toward his own neck.

"Wait!"

Sabine's high, shrill cry tore through the forest.

Miles's hand stilled in its progress. At Miles's hesitation, the blade angling to separate Colin's head from his shoulders also froze mid-air.

Miles stood motionless for a long moment. At last, he lifted the dagger an inch from Sabine's throat.

"I have naught against you, girl," he said flatly. "You always completed your assignments and never caused me trouble. I suppose I can grant you a few last words before you die."

Sabine's eyes were so wide that Colin could see white all around them in the dim light. Her gaze darted to him, her breath coming in short gasps.

"I...I have information that Fabian will want to hear before he kills us."

Colin's stomach fell to his feet even as his heart ripped in two.

"Sabine! Nay, dinnae—"

"He will be most pleased with what I have to say," she went on, her gaze still locked on Colin even as she spoke to Miles. "But if you kill us now, he'll never learn about the contents of the missive I intercepted."

Miles considered in silence. But then he brought the dagger's edge to Sabine's throat once again.

"It was from Robert the Bruce!" Sabine blurted.

Miles froze again, and Colin could see his dark

brows lift in surprise.

"I intercepted the *real* missive from the King of Scotland, not the dupe he sent to throw us off the true mark," Sabine rushed on.

"Fabian wanted both you and the man dead," Miles said slowly. "But he may prefer to hear what you have to say before he has your throats slit." He shrugged his thick shoulders as if he'd come to a decision. "He can do what he wishes with you once I've delivered you, so I suppose it makes no difference."

Miles removed the dagger from her neck and slid it back into his boot.

"Sabine," Colin breathed, disbelief rending his heart. "How could ye?"

Her lips moved, but no sound came out. He squinted through the dusky twilight, focusing on her mouth.

Please, she mouthed, *trust me*.

Colin felt more than saw one of the warriors rise up behind him. Something blunt made impact at the base of his skull, and the whole world went black.

Chapter Thirty-Eight

S abine squinted at the unassuming cottage as Miles reined his horse to a halt. Though it was dark, she could see that it was little more than a hovel, completely isolated in this small clearing in the woods.

They'd ridden hard all through last night and today. The sun had set several hours ago, but when it had been up, she'd used it to gauge their direction. Miles had taken them east, but then turned south midday. If they hadn't crossed the border with England already, they were close.

Sabine sniffed the air. Over the scents of pine, mud, and decaying plant life, she smelled the sharp tang of brine. They must be near the sea. If she had to guess, she'd say they were a few hours' ride northwest of Carlisle.

"What is this place?" she demanded as Miles dismounted stiffly.

Miles remained silent as he unbound her wrists from the pommel on her saddle. She'd been given the horse of one of the two men Colin had killed.

He pulled her down from the horse's back, then motioned for two of his men to fetch Colin.

Colin lay draped face-down over the second dead man's horse. As the hours of hard riding had slipped by, Sabine had grown increasingly worried that he might never wake.

When the two men took his arms and dragged him down, he stirred ever so slightly.

Sabine exhaled and murmured a prayer of thanks. He wasn't dead, though he seemed close enough. She needed him to come to his senses, for the sketch of a plan she'd formed over the last day would never succeed if he didn't have his wits about him.

"Continue on to Carlisle," Miles snapped at three of the other warriors.

The men nodded and spurred their horses east. That confirmed Sabine's suspicions about their present location, but she still didn't know why they were here. Was this a safe house of some sort? A waiting spot?

Miles limped back to his horse. He untied Ruith's reins, which he'd wrapped around his own horse's saddle, then awkwardly hobbled toward another of the men.

"See to the horses," Miles said, thrusting Ruith's reins at the man. "And take special care with this one."

Ruith nickered and sidestepped, and the warrior had to jerk hard on the reins to gain control of the stallion.

"Are you sure you want that one, Miles?" one of the men holding Colin asked. A few of the men chuckled low.

Sabine hadn't noticed it when Miles and his small army of warriors had first attacked, but over the last day, she realized that he limped badly and one of his arms seemed almost useless. He also bore a bruise on the side of his head, which disappeared into his dark hair.

Apparently, he hadn't come away from the fall from his horse as unscathed as it had seemed at first—the fall she and Ruith had partially caused.

"He is mine," Miles growled. "I claimed him. He just needs to be broken to me."

As one of the warriors gathered the horses and led them to a small barn just off the cottage, Miles motioned the others forward. He wrapped a tight hand around Sabine's arm, though she didn't fight against him.

Just then, the cottage's door swung open and soft candlelight spilled out. A figure stepping into the door-frame, illuminated from behind.

"Is it done?"

A chill raced down Sabine's spine at the voice.

Fabian.

He must have changed locations again, for she'd never seen this cottage or this patch of uninhabited forest before.

"Nay, milord, but I can—"

"What is this?" Fabian snarled as Miles pulled her into the pool of candlelight around the door.

"The girl says she has something to tell you," Miles

went on evenly.

"What could she possibly—"

"I read a missive from Robert the Bruce," Sabine said, willing her voice to remain steady. "The one you sent me after in the first place. Although the King's messenger bore a dummy missive, the messenger's bodyguard carried the real one."

Fabian's gaze sharpened on her for a moment, then turned to Miles.

"Why did you bring me the man alive? I thought I made myself clear."

"And I made myself clear to Miles," Sabine cut in before Miles could respond. "I told him that we were both to remain alive until you've heard what I have to say, or else I don't talk."

"I'll gladly kill both of them now if you aren't interested in the girl's message, milord," Miles said flatly. "I just thought that you'd want to have...options."

Fabian's hand rose to his meticulously manicured goatee as he considered.

"Bring them in," he said at last with an annoyed wave. He turned and strode into the cottage without waiting for them to follow.

Sabine breathed a silent sigh of relief. Buying more time in front of Fabian was only the first step, however.

As Miles pulled her into the cottage, she craned her neck over her shoulder.

"Colin," she said sharply. "Colin, wake up."

He groaned as he tried to lift his drooping head.

The men carrying him by the shoulders were none too gentle. She would have cursed them for dragging him so roughly into the cottage, but it seemed to rouse him from his stupor a bit more.

Miles continued to pull her toward the back of the cottage. Inside, a fire blazed in a small hearth and a few candles sat on a simple wooden table. There was a cot in one corner, but little else. The accommodations were surprisingly humble, considering how much Fabian enjoyed surrounding himself with finer things.

Miles led her to the back of the cottage. She realized belatedly that there was a single door in the wall, leading to an attached chamber she hadn't noticed from the front of the hovel.

As Miles tugged her into the small chamber, he turned and spoke over his shoulder.

"Wait out here," he said to the remaining two warriors who weren't carrying Colin. They nodded silently and took up position on either side of the door.

Miles moved her aside so that the two men who held Colin could drag him into the chamber as well, then booted the door closed behind them.

Only after she assured herself that Colin had opened his eyes and was beginning to get his feet under him did she allow herself to look around.

Like the cottage's front room, this one was small and humble. There were no windows, and the low thatched roofing, which most of the men's heads nearly brushed against, made it feel even smaller.

The only distinguishing feature of the room was the large wooden desk on the back wall. It was completely covered with stacks and piles of parchment, just as Fabian always kept his work space. Two candles were perched in holders on the front corners of the desk, casting flickering light over the otherwise bare room.

"I see you have taken a step down in the world," Sabine said to Fabian's back as he strode toward the desk.

His shoulders stiffened. Then slowly, he pivoted on his heels. His face was smooth as he walked toward her.

Without preamble, he slapped her hard on the cheek.

"The only reason your tongue can still waggle, you little bitch, is because you have piqued my curiosity," he said calmly.

"No longer pretending to care about me, then?" She turned her head back to him, holding his stare defiantly. She knew the truth now. He'd used her, manipulated her, but she would never be afraid of Fabian again.

A slow, cruel smile twisted his lips behind his goatee.

"Oh Sabine. You are most entertaining—far more so now than you were as a sniveling, scraping little urchin who wanted naught more than to please me."

Sabine clenched her teeth to keep from flinching at

his words. She had to remain strong, to stay focused and not let the pain of Fabian's cruel disregard blind her.

"But you were far easier to control, then," he went on, turning his back on her and ambling toward the desk once more.

"We found this on her, milord," Miles said, releasing her to step forward. He pulled Sabine's dagger from his belt and tossed it on the desk.

Fabian snorted as he glanced at the dagger. "You always were a sentimental one, keeping everything I ever gave you." His gaze slid over her. "You even still wear that necklace."

The ring Fabian had presented to her after her first mission felt as though it burned her skin where it hung on its chain. Sabine wouldn't bother telling him that she still wore it to remind herself of where she came from and who she used to be—someone she'd never be again. Let him think what he would.

"But enough of this," he said, all the amusement dropping from his voice. "Tell me what the missive contained."

"I have conditions," Sabine shot back.

Fabian smiled again, but this time it didn't reach his dark eyes. "And what would those be?"

"Let Colin and me walk away unharmed."

Fabian actually laughed.

"Christ, Sabine, I knew you were naïve, but I never thought you a dolt."

Her fists clenched with rage at her sides, but she kept her voice steady. "We will not make trouble or speak a word to anyone. You will never hear of or see us again. In exchange for our lives, you may have the information in Robert the Bruce's missive."

"Sabine."

Her gaze snapped to Colin as he rasped her name. Though the two men still held his arms, he bore his weight on his own feet. His head was steady, but his blue eyes were clouded with disbelief and apprehension as his gaze searched her.

In the short glance she could spare him, she tried to convey her plan through her eyes. Fearing raising Fabian's suspicion, though, she returned her attention back to him.

Fabian perched on the desk, stroking his goatee. "Your lover doesn't seem willing to agree to your terms."

"He will, for he doesn't want to see me dead."

"Bold little slut," Fabian said, his lips drawing back in a half-smile, half-sneer. "You fucked him, didn't you? What a waste of the perfectly good bargaining chip your virginity would have been."

Rage, pure and clarifying, burned through her. Yet somehow she wasn't surprised. Even Fabian's supposed protectiveness of her innocence had actually been for his own gain.

"You have my offer," she said, holding his stare.

Fabian turned to his desk and fiddled with one of

the pieces of parchment stacked there for a long moment.

"Very well," he said at last, turning his smile back on her. "Your lives for the contents of the missive—on the condition that if I discover you have broken your end of the bargain, I will kill you both in a most unpleasant and drawn-out way."

Colin suddenly surged against the men holding him. He bared his teeth, rage flashing in his eyes.

Good. He was regaining his wits, as well as his strength. But he would need more time.

"Agreed," Sabine said. "But answer a question for me first, as I am sure this will be the last time I ever see you."

Fabian spread his arms out magnanimously. "Ask away."

Sabine swallowed, forcing down the lump in her throat. "Before you sent Miles to kill me, I had been naught but loyal to you. I would have done aught for you. Why were you so quick to be rid of me without even giving me a chance to prove my loyalty?"

Fabian shrugged, his eyes gleaming. "You always were a tad too sentimental. It was a good trait for molding you into what I wanted, but I wonder if over time it would have proven problematic." He waved a dismissive hand. "But that is neither here nor there. You have always viewed me as a father, have you not?"

Unable to speak, Sabine simply nodded.

Fabian repressed a smile. "Just as I wished. But you

never understood the true nature of our work, dear, sweet Sabine. Oh, aye, you learned to deceive well enough. Men have always enjoyed your little fallen dove routine. But you never saw this for what it is."

"And what is it?" she breathed.

"A business. Not a family. Loyalty and caring have no place here. All that matters is the work." He cast a hand over the stacks of assorted slips of parchment. "When someone is good at the business, they may stay. If they fail, or become a liability, or compromise the business in any way—well, then they must be eliminated."

"Aye, I suppose I never understood that," Sabine said, her voice tight.

Fabian's smile widened. "You've already proven that." He flicked a hand toward her neck. "The fact that you're wearing that necklace, for example. Would you like to give it back to me? Mayhap throw it at me to be dramatic? You'd save me from having to make another one. Having them matched to the one I wear can be very time consuming. You see, I always give my newest recruits a copy of this ring and tell them they are special, just as I told you."

The taunting in his voice made sickness rise to the back of her throat. Even hating him for all he'd done, his words cut with fresh pain. She'd never been special to him. He'd never cared about her. She was only a tool to him—a tool he'd warped to his own devices, leaving her close to broken.

But not completely broken.

She watched Colin out of the corner of her eye. He was alert now, his body straining with barely contained fury.

"You've answered my question," she bit out.

"Then out with it," Fabian snapped. "What did the King's missive contain?"

Sabine dared a glance at Colin. His gaze was sharp and searching, no longer clouded with the lingering fog of unconsciousness.

Dragging in a deep breath, she opened her mouth to speak.

Chapter Thirty-Nine

Colin ground his teeth until his jaw ached to keep from bellowing at Sabine not to speak.

Aye, he didn't want to see her dead, but the betrayal of his King and cause could never be forgiven—not after all they'd shared.

Yet the last thing he remembered before the blackness had swallowed him in the forest was that she'd silently asked him to trust her. He'd told her he was willing to take the leap of faith with her. If that would be his end, then so be it, but at least he would know that he'd finally let love into his life again.

"The missive was bound for Ireland," Sabine began.

Colin dropped his head, praying for patience, praying for faith—praying for aught that would end this nightmare.

"The King was most displeased about his recent failure to capture Carlisle," she went on. "He said he could not rest until he'd secured that particular jewel for his crown."

Colin's ears bristled at that. The missive had said no such thing. Slowly, so as not to draw attention to himself, he lifted his head.

Fabian stood behind his desk, watching Sabine intently. A grin twitched at the corners of his mouth at Sabine's words.

Colin didn't try to mask the hot hatred that burned in his veins as he stared at Fabian.

"The King sent the missive to his brother, Edward Bruce, who is fighting in Ireland. He ordered Edward to return to Scotland so that his men could join the Bruce's forces. He wrote that with their combined armies, Carlisle would most certainly fall," Sabine said evenly.

Fabian's brows lifted and his eyes widened as pleasure stole over his face.

"Oh, that is a very valuable piece of information, indeed."

His hands flew into the piles of missives heaping atop the desk, sifting frantically through them.

"Those on the Irish front will want to know this, of course. The lords can begin drawing down their troops." He seemed to find a scrap of parchment he was looking for. He set it aside, then dove into the stacks once more. "And I'm sure Andrew Harclay will pay dearly to hear that Carlisle will be attacked again."

As Fabian dug frantically through the parchment on his desk, Sabine's gaze met Colin's. Her eyes slid to one of the candles flickering on the desk, then back to Colin.

He shook his head ever so slightly, unsure of what

she was trying to communicate.

Her gaze darted to the candle again, then shifted almost imperceptibly to the parchment-strewn desk. Then she returned her eyes to his, twitching her eyebrows. Her gaze flicked quickly to the two men who still held his arms.

Understanding struck him like a bolt of lightning. He jerked his head at her in refutation. It was far too dangerous. Neither of them had a weapon, and he was weak from fighting Fabian's men earlier. His head still throbbed, and both his upper arm and his thigh burned dully where they'd been slashed in the attack.

She held his gaze, then nodded slowly and solemnly.

"…will be pleased to hear of this as well," Fabian was saying, still eagerly searching his missives. He lifted his head as if he suddenly remembered that they were all still there. "Oh, and Miles, you can take care of these two now. I have what I need."

Miles stepped forward from where he'd stood behind Sabine and gripped her arm.

"You are breaking your word?" Sabine demanded.

"Stupid, stupid girl," Fabian said with a sad smile. "You still prove far too trusting. You honestly believed I would let you live? If it is any consolation, it isn't personal. It is just business."

Fabian returned his attention to his stacks of parchment, waving at Miles absently as if to hurry him along.

Miles bent, reaching for the dagger in his boot.

Just then, Sabine's foot shot out, kicking Miles in the leg he seemed to be favoring. Miles roared with pain and tumbled to the ground.

Sabine darted forward and knocked both of the candles over into the pile of parchment with one sweep of her arm.

In the heartbeat of confusion that froze the room, Colin struck. He ripped his left arm from one man's grasp and drove his elbow as hard as he could into the man's neck. The man collapsed, wheezing for breath through his crumpled throat.

He launched a punch at the other man holding him, but the man ducked. Colin sent a knee upward, catching him in the gut. With a hard shove, Colin sent the man careening into the hut's low plaster wall. The man's head connected with the wall with a sickening thud, and he fell motionless to the ground.

"Nay!" Fabian's rage-filled scream snapped Colin's attention back to the desk.

Both candles had caught on the heaps of parchment piled on the desk. The flames spread quickly, consuming the dry parchment with increasing intensity.

Sabine darted a hand through the flames, retrieving the dagger that lay atop the parchment.

Suddenly the door to the chamber was yanked open and two more warriors spilled in. Colin had to leap out of the way of their swinging swords, which drove him back.

"Colin!" Sabine shouted.

He spared her a glance, only to find her dagger sailing toward him. He caught it, throwing the gilded sheath aside as he bared the blade.

With a quick block and spin, he'd driven the dagger into one of the men's chests. He yanked the blade free as the man toppled, turning to the other one.

The warrior paused, assessing Colin before launching an attack. After all, three warriors plus Miles lay on the floor, either writhing in pain or motionless in death.

As the warrior circled him slowly, Colin darted a glance at Sabine. She was backing away from the blazing desk, which Fabian still stood behind. Fabian was frantically trying to save the parchment from the flames, but the fire licked across the entire top of the wooden desk.

"Nay!" Fabian screamed again, trying to tamp out the flames with his bare hands.

His fine silk sleeves caught fire, the blaze traveling swiftly up his arms.

Fabian shrieked wordlessly, waving his arms frantically to stop the flames. But in his wild motions, his arms brushed the roof's dry thatching. Fire immediately spread to the thatch, the flames hungrily consuming more fuel.

"Sabine, get away from there!" Colin bellowed just as the last warrior launched his attack.

Colin darted out of the way of the warrior's long

sword, letting the man's momentum carry him forward. As the warrior stumbled past him, Colin drove the dagger into his side, twisting it as he pulled it free. The man fell to the floor with a gurgling moan.

Colin swayed on his feet, his head spinning from the exertion. Nausea pulsed in his stomach in time with the throbbing at the base of his skull where Fabian's man had struck him. He forced his eyes to focus on the back of the chamber, where he could still hazily make out Sabine's form against the growing blaze.

Fabian must have lunged across the burning desk, for he lay atop it now, seemingly unaware that his entire tunic and vest were catching fire. Sabine struggled away from him, but she couldn't seem to free herself.

Through the roaring flames and the haze of sickness, Colin realized why Sabine had not fled.

Fabian had somehow managed to grab the necklace around her neck and was dragging her into the fire with him.

"You little bitch!" he screamed. "You will not escape me!"

Sabine clawed wildly at her neck, but the necklace choked her as Fabian pulled back on it.

Miles, who still lay on the floor nearby clutching his leg, began to drag himself toward Fabian.

Colin darted forward, kicking Miles in the temple where he saw the edge of a dark bruise disappearing into his hairline.

Miles silently slumped back to the ground, either unconscious or dead.

Sabine's scream had Colin lurching toward her. He reached for her, stumbling as his vision blurred from the fire, smoke, and his own dizziness.

"Colin!" She launched herself forward, straining against the necklace in Fabian's grasp.

Suddenly the chain around her neck snapped and she fell forward into Colin's arms.

"Nay!" Fabian shrieked. He rolled from the fiery desk onto the ground, but his burning clothes encased him in raging flames.

Taking Sabine by the hand, Colin staggered toward the door. He kicked the door closed once they were through, cutting off Fabian's blood-curdling screams and sealing him and his men in the burning chamber.

They stumbled through the cottage's main room and out the door into the night.

"What in—"

A warrior loomed from the small barn near the cottage, his stunned expression illuminated by the blaze racing along the thatched roof behind them.

Colin lurched forward, driving Sabine's dagger into the dumbfounded warrior. As the man slid to the ground, Colin took Sabine's hand once more and pulled her toward the barn.

He threw open each of the stall doors within until he found Ruith in the back, pawing at the ground and snorting in distress. With a sharp whistle, he sent all the horses bolting from the barn. They darted into the little clearing, then disappeared into the darkened woods.

Hands trembling with fatigue and dizziness, he helped Sabine onto Ruith's back, then threw himself into the saddle behind her.

Ruith eagerly dashed out of the barn at Colin's nudge. Colin spurred the horse into the trees, leaving the flame-consumed cottage behind them.

Chapter Forty

Sabine smoothed her sunflower-yellow skirts with clammy hands. The dress, though a little long on her, was a blessed change from the battered, stained green wool gown she'd worn before.

In the sennight since she and Colin had ridden, bedraggled and bleeding, into King Robert the Bruce's camp in Lochmaben, Sabine had known more kindness than in all the years of her life combined.

Sabine had been given a hot bath, and the camp's healer, a kindly, beautiful golden-haired woman named Jossalyn Sinclair, had seen to both her shoulder and the damage done to her neck.

Jossalyn had nodded approvingly at the set of Sabine's shoulder. She'd determined that the cut on Sabine's neck from Miles's dagger didn't need stitches, though she'd worn a bandage for the first few days in camp to cover the scratches and abrasions made when Fabian had choked her with the necklace.

Jossalyn had also somehow managed to produce the yellow dress Sabine now wore as well. And though she'd promised Sabine that she would see what she could do with her old gown, Sabine suspected that the bubbly, warm-hearted healer had surreptitiously burned the tattered, mud- and blood-stained garment.

"Are ye ready, lass?"

Sabine's head snapped up at Colin's low, soft voice. She stood from the cot she'd been provided and smoothed her dress again, though it didn't need it.

As she crossed the small space from the cot to where Colin stood in the open flaps of her canvas tent, she drank in the sight of him.

She'd barely seen him at all in the last sennight, and when she had it was usually from a distance. Under the pretense that they both needed to rest after their ordeal, they'd been given separate tents. Though Colin's injuries had been somewhat more severe than Sabine's, he was not kept in isolation as Sabine was. Besides Jossalyn, Sabine had hardly spoken to anyone in the camp. But she'd watched from her tent's flaps as fierce-looking warriors had come and gone from Colin's tent not far away.

She wasn't sure if her isolation or his visitations were a good or bad sign, but for a brief moment, the sight of Colin chased away her fears.

His tawny mane was held at the nape of his neck by a leather strip. He, too, wore simple but new clothes. A blue tunic that brought out the brightness of his eyes was belted over clean breeches and boots that covered his calves. His eyes were soft on her, but a muscle twitched in his jaw, belying the tension beneath his calm façade.

"As ready as I'll ever be," she replied.

He extended his arm to her as he held open the tent flaps. Sabine hesitated, looking around at the camp, which buzzed with Scottish warriors as they went about their daily activities.

"Dinnae be afraid, Sabine," Colin said softly. "I have already told anyone who will listen that ye saved my life. Ye've no enemies here—and if ye did, I would-nae let them harm ye."

Sabine's heart rose to her throat at Colin's protec-tiveness. "You saved my life as well, you know."

"Aye, well," he said, his lips curling with a soft smile. "We saved each other."

At his smile, it was as if the sun had suddenly bro-ken through thick clouds. Sabine's breath caught at being the recipient of such warmth and light. But all too quickly, the loving glow faded from his face and he clenched his jaw once more.

"We'd best no' keep the King waiting."

Sabine swallowed hard. Though she'd been al-lowed to rest and recuperate for the last sennight, the time had finally come to face the Bruce. She drew strength from Colin when she looped her arm in his, but she could not help the trembling of her knees as he guided her through the camp.

Colin must have felt her shaking, for he drew her closer and leaned down to her ear.

"The Bruce is a good-hearted, fair man."

Sabine didn't doubt it, for Colin would not pledge

his life to someone he thought cruel or dishonorable, yet she wouldn't allow herself to hope for a positive outcome. She'd done wrong in her past, there was no denying it. All she could do now was tell the King the truth and pray that he would have mercy on her.

As Colin led her through the canvas tents, Sabine was struck by how similar Robert the Bruce's camp was to his brother Edward Bruce's, though things appeared to be arranged for a longer-term stay here. She would have continued looking around except that Colin came to a halt before a canvas tent that was larger than the others.

Unlike Edward Bruce's one guard, four enormous warriors stood outside the tent. They must have recognized Colin, though, for with naught more than a nod from him, one of the guards pulled back the tent's flap.

Sabine's gaze skittered over the tent's comparatively dim interior as she stepped inside. Just as she might have guessed, the King's tent appeared both more permanent and somewhat more opulent than his brother's. Woven rugs covered the dirt ground, and several upholstered chairs sat scattered around the tent. Whereas Edward Bruce's tent had contained little more than a wooden table, this one was dominated by an ornately carved, large oak desk.

When Sabine's gaze landed on the man seated behind the desk, she went rigid and her stomach knotted.

The King of Scotland rose slowly, his dark eyes assessing them. Sabine yanked her arm from Colin's and threw herself onto her knees, dropping her head in supplication.

She saw Colin step forward out of the corner of her eye, and then to her complete and utter shock, he took the King's extended arm and shared a firm shake.

"It is good to see ye again, Colin. Ye gave us all quite the fright the way ye rode into camp a sennight past. Forgive me for no' speaking with ye sooner, but I've been kept busy."

"Thank ye, Robert," Colin replied.

Sabine couldn't help the hissing sound as she sucked in a breath. Had Colin truly just called the King of Scotland by his given name?

A large, weathered had suddenly appeared before her lowered gaze. In astonishment, her eyes beheld the hand, which bore a large gold signet ring on the middle finger. Even in the low light, she could see the warrior bearing a sword and shield on horseback etched in the gold. *The King's seal.*

Her gaze lifted to the brocaded arm and the broad chest all the way up to King Robert the Bruce's face. His russet beard was more liberally streaked with gray than Edward Bruce's had been, as was his hair. His face bore all the etchings of his struggles over the years, yet his eyes were sharp and inquisitive as they beheld her.

"Colin must no' have explained how I prefer to conduct my affairs in private company," the Bruce said. "Ye need no' supplicate yerself, lass."

Slowly, Sabine placed her trembling fingers in the Bruce's extended hand. He helped her to her feet, then tilted his head ever so slightly over her hand before releasing it.

Only then did she notice the other two men in the tent. One, a dark-haired man with nigh black eyes, was stepping toward Colin for a quick forearm grasp. He turned to Sabine and gave her a curt nod.

"Finn Sutherland," he said, his voice low and clipped.

Sabine dipped into a curtsy, trying to steady her knees under Finn's cool, wary gaze.

"Colin," the second of the two men said, stepping forward from the King's left. "It is good to see ye, man."

This man was just as tall and broadly muscled as all the others in the tent, though he bore a strangely curved bow over one shoulder. His hair was as dark as Finn's, but his eyes were a sharp charcoal gray.

Unlike Finn's staid greeting, this man pulled Colin in for a hug. Colin actually smiled as he returned the embrace, pounding the man on the back.

"I am Garrick Sinclair," the man said, turning to Sabine.

Sabine had halfway dropped into another curtsy when she faltered. "Sinclair?" she murmured, looking up at Garrick.

"I believe ye've already met my wife Jossalyn," Garrick replied, warmth suddenly entering his gray eyes. "She has already told me of her...fondness for ye."

Sabine felt her eyes go round. The Bruce's sweet, gentle healer was this fierce warrior's wife? And Jossalyn had spoken of her to him?

"P-please pass on my thanks to her once more for her care, and for this dress," Sabine managed.

Garrick nodded and then stepped back to the King's side.

"Now," the Bruce said, taking command of the room. "Why don't we all sit, as I gather there is much to discuss."

At the Bruce's suddenly serious tone, the knot in Sabine's stomach drew impossibly tighter.

Cold sweat sprung onto her palms as Colin guided her toward one of the upholstered chairs. Colin sat next to her, the two of them facing the Bruce, who was flanked on either side by Finn and Garrick.

"I understand yer name is Sabine, lass," the Bruce began. "But I havenae been informed of yer family name."

Sabine opened her mouth, but the words to explain her lack of family and her painful childhood clogged in her throat.

"She was an orphan, a foundling," Colin said, coming to her aid. "She kens naught of her family, for she was lifted from the streets of London as a child. And as for her family name..."

He looked over at her, his gaze searching.

"It will be MacKay—that is, if she'll have me, and if ye'll allow it, Robert."

Sabine's heart seized, and hot tears of surprise suddenly clouded her vision. She gave Colin a nod, not trusting her voice in that moment.

When she turned her misted gaze back on the three men before her, she found one of Finn's dark brows lifted questioningly and the King's eyes slightly wider than before. A small smile played on Garrick's lips. Mayhap Sabine had inadvertently let something slip as Jossalyn had seen to her wounds. Or mayhap Garrick had simply been the quickest to discern the invisible threads of love that bound Colin and Sabine together.

The Bruce cleared his throat. "I still need an explanation for what happened on yer mission before I make any decisions, Colin."

Colin nodded, then turned to Sabine. "Why don't ye start from the beginning?"

Drawing in a deep breath, Sabine did just that—but not from the moment that she met Colin, or the moment when Fabian had given her the assignment, but from the very beginning.

She spoke of what little she could remember of her childhood—hunger, cold, and uncaring faces looking down on her—and then Fabian's sudden rescue. She described Fabian's treatment of her, leaving naught of his mercurial moods out.

When she began describing her training and her

early missions intercepting missives, the Bruce stiffened in his chair. Finn narrowed his gaze on her, and she had to fight the instinct to shrink back from the cold hatred in his stare.

She forged on, explaining the turn her training took as she reached womanhood. The Bruce's mouth thinned, though for some reason Sabine sensed that his disgust was more directed at Fabian than herself.

By the time she reached the description of Fabian's assignment to intercept the missive she believed Osborn carried, the air in the tent hung thick with tension.

Blessedly, Colin came to her aid once more. He took over recounting how she'd found the blank missive, then how he'd tracked her down and taken her into his custody. Colin explained how he'd planned to hold her captive until he could deliver the real message to Edward Bruce and then return to Scotland to hand her over to Robert for questioning. The King nodded at this, stroking his beard, but he remained silent.

When Colin described how Miles and the giant twin warriors had attacked, bent on killing Sabine on Fabian's orders, Sabine's throat tightened and tears once again sprang to her eyes. Aye, Fabian's betrayal still hurt, as it likely would for some time yet.

Forcing down the emotion squeezing her throat, she spoke as Colin paused.

"I had never questioned my loyalty before then, sire," she said to the Bruce. "But I realized that I had misplaced my faith in the man I thought of as my father. Worse, I hadn't considered how my actions had hurt others. I thought of myself as a simple thief, little more than a pickpocket, though instead of coin I took information. Colin made me realize that my actions had consequences, and that while some fought for freedom, to protect their families and their homeland, I fought for naught but the love of a heartless man."

"And why do yer eyes brim with tears, lass?" the Bruce asked, his dark gaze examining her. "Are ye still loyal to that man? Do ye mourn having been caught?"

"Nay," she said, her voice strong and steady. "They are tears of anger—anger at myself. I haven't forgiven myself for giving my loyalty to such a cruel, manipulative man, nor will I for many years to come, I imagine."

"I believe her loyalty now lies with our cause, Robert," Colin said.

"Are ye mad, Colin?" Finn snapped, his black eyes flaring. "Ye expect us to believe that? She's an English spy, for Christ's sake."

Sabine inhaled and pressed her lips together at Finn's sharp words, but the Bruce held up a hand to silence the scowling warrior. The King's keen gaze shifted between Sabine and Colin.

"Explain yourself," he said curtly to Colin at last.

"She delivered yer message to yer brother just in time to save him from moving his men into an ambush," Colin said evenly. "She saved countless lives, possibly including yer brother's, Robert."

The King's eyes widened again as he turned to Sabine.

"It's true that I recited your missive, sire," she said quickly, "but I must confess that there would have never been a need for me to speak had I not read it and then accidentally destroyed it."

Finn muttered another curse, but the Bruce's attention didn't waver from her. "Go on."

Sabine told of how after Fabian's attack, she'd believed herself alone in the world, defenseless except in her ability to secure and memorize information. She left out the intimacies she'd shared with Colin, though she explained that because of Fabian's cruelty, she'd feared she couldn't trust Colin despite his honor and kindness toward her.

She described how the missive had caught fire, and how she'd known in a moment of clarity that no matter what happened to her, she needed to deliver the King's message.

"Men's lives depended on it," she said quietly. "Men who were fighting for the kind of freedom I had never known under Fabian's thumb."

Sabine couldn't interpret the long silence that followed her words. The Bruce and Garrick exchanged an unreadable look. Finn's features were still set in granite, though he no longer shot daggers at her with his dark eyes.

"Ye also have Sabine to thank for taking out Fabian, Robert," Colin said, breaking the silence. "She rid ye of a dangerous enemy."

Garrick leaned forward in his chair. "This I must hear."

"Fabian's men sprang on us no' far from Dumfries. The lass had a blade to her throat, and I was on my knees about to meet my maker," Colin said. "She tricked Fabian's men into leading us to him, then burned the filthy rat alive, along with countless stolen documents."

Garrick whistled low in astonishment. For the first time, Finn's steely resolve faltered and a look of genuine shock crossed his features.

"Is that true, lass?" the Bruce breathed.

"A-aye," she murmured. "I stalled him with a lie about what your missive contained, then knocked over the candles on his desk. Accidentally burning your missive actually gave me the idea. I knew there was naught that Fabian valued more than his slips of parchment—not even human life."

She turned to Colin, suddenly frightened. "I know I said I would not lie anymore, but I broke that promise when I lied to Fabian. I hope that someday you can forgive—"

"Lass," Colin said gently. "Ye saved my life with that lie—and ye protected the King's cause once again. There is naught to forgive."

Relief washed over her, but when she turned back to the Bruce, the slight frown behind his beard made her stomach twist once again.

"Are ye prepared to tell me everything ye ken about this Fabian and his organization?"

She nodded her head fiercely, but then stilled.

"What is it? Why do ye hesitate, lass?" the Bruce demanded.

"I will gladly tell you everything I know," she said quickly. "It is just...Fabian kept me isolated. I rarely ever saw anyone else in his employ, and spoke only with Miles, who died in the fire with Fabian."

The Bruce considered this for a moment. "But ye understand his techniques, do ye no'? Ye understand the tactics ye and I imagine others like ye employed in yer work?"

"Aye."

"We'll start there, then—no' now, but when ye've gotten some more rest."

"There may be others like Sabine still out there, Robert," Colin said grimly. "Or worse, others like Fabian. Yet I am still hopeful. With Fabian's death, the head of the beast has been lopped off. Without the head, whatever remains of his organization will likely crumble soon enough."

"We also still dinnae ken who paid the lass's boss for the contents of yer missive, Robert," Garrick said, his face darkening.

"Aye," the Bruce said. "It could be one of our old enemies gaining in strength and boldness, or it could be an entirely new threat. Be that as it may, the question remains: what am I to do with ye, Sabine?"

All eyes fell on Sabine. Her heart hammered against her ribcage and her breath grew short.

"I imagine that Finn would label ye a traitor and a danger to our fight against the English." The King flicked a glance at Finn, who only lifted a dark eyebrow, his features stoic.

"I also imagine that Garrick would call ye brave. As his wife is English, I believe he would have no problem allowing ye to join our cause."

Sabine blinked. She'd been so lost in her own fears and worries for the past sennight that she hadn't noticed that Jossalyn spoke with the same English accent she bore.

A larger thought crowded that one out, however. Was the Bruce saying that he was even *contemplating* not giving her the punishment of a traitor? Might there be a possibility that she would be allowed to join Colin in Scotland's cause?

Before she could consider that shocking possibility, the Bruce went on.

"And of course Colin loves ye, so I can gather where he stands. But I think I would like to let ye speak for yerself. What would ye have me do with ye, lass?"

Sabine's mouth fell open. She quickly clamped it shut, her cheeks heating at the rudeness of gaping at a King. It took her a long moment and several deep breaths to form words.

"I…I know I have hurt many people over the years

I spent serving Fabian. I may have even hurt you and your cause, sire, though I can't know with certainty."

Finn crossed his arms over his chest, a scowl on his face. Sabine hurried on before she lost her nerve.

"I was taught to steal, to trick people, to manipulate and lie. I wish I had not been molded so. I wish I could go back and change what I've done, what I was trained to become." Her voice grew thinner as she spoke until it was little more than a whisper.

Colin reached between their chairs and took her hand, squeezing it silently.

A flicker of pain crossed the Bruce's face. "Ye were just a child when Fabian took ye, lass. Ye were innocent before he hurt ye, before he used ye."

The Bruce cleared his throat, which suddenly sounded rough and thick. "I am sickened by those who drag women and children into warfare. This isnae the first time in this bloody war that the innocent have been made into either targets or weapons. Either way, they are the victims of men's cowardice and dishonor."

Sabine blinked back tears, so moved was she by the Bruce's words. She swallowed the lump in her throat, though, needing to go on.

"But the truth is, I cannot undo my past. Given that fact, all I can do is choose from this point onward how I will use my skills and abilities." She glanced at Finn, who still stared at her with hard eyes, but who listened nonetheless. "And I would choose to commit myself to you and your fight for freedom."

She held the Bruce's gaze steadily, showing him the truth of her words in her eyes. "I want to do good, and I've never encountered more good than I have in Colin. He has pledged himself to you, sire. If he believes in you and this cause, then I know that all you stand for, all you do, is honorable and just."

She heard Colin suck in a breath, but she kept her eyes on the Bruce. Something soft flickered across his gaze. One corner of his mouth lifted in an almost-smile.

"And where would ye start in this quest to do good?"

Sabine sat up straight, squaring her shoulders. "For starters, I would instruct you to dab a bit of pine sap along the seams of your missives. Then the seal could be lifted, but the parchment could not be opened without showing signs of tampering."

"What else, lass?" Garrick said, leaning forward with interest.

"I'd insist on working with your messengers to become more adept at watching for thieves and spies. Giant warriors aren't the only ones who can extract information," she went on. "Your man Osborn was too easily duped. Even Colin was fooled into paying me no heed when I first met him."

She clamped her teeth shut, suddenly realizing that she'd just criticized Colin in front of his King, drawing attention to his initial failing. To her shock, though, Garrick actually barked a laugh. Finn lifted a brow sardonically, shooting Colin a withering look, and the Bruce's lips twitched in what looked dangerously close to a smile.

Colin snorted, then sighed. "As ye can see, Robert," he said, "she clearly has much to offer."

"Aye, and there may even be a spot in the King's inner circle opening up since Colin cannae guard against a wee bonny lass," Garrick said with another laugh.

Colin shot a searing glare at Garrick, but before he could respond, the King held up a hand.

"Aught else, lass?"

Sabine pulled her lower lip between her teeth as she considered. "I'll do whatever I can to weed out what's left of Fabian's organization, and defend against such threats in the future. In truth, I hadn't considered the details, for I feared that my future would be short once you'd heard everything I'd done."

Once again, the Bruce's eyes went soft for a moment.

"I'm not sure how else I can help," Sabine went on, "but if there's one thing I've learned, it is that information is potent. Who has it, who doesn't, who wants it—all are powerful tools."

The Bruce suddenly stiffened in his chair, his gaze drifting away from Sabine and to the tent's canvas ceiling.

"I think ye've just given me an idea, lass," he said after a moment. A slow smile split his face. "A verra good idea."

Epilogue

Late September, 1315
Lochmaben, Scottish Lowlands

Colin held the reins as Andrew Harclay, constable of Carlisle Castle, mounted a gray palfrey.

"Farewell, Bruce," Harclay said, glancing down at the King, who stood by Colin's side, "I cannot say I'll miss you, but this has been most...interesting."

A fortnight earlier, Colin, Finn, Garrick, and a small force of select warriors had infiltrated Carlisle and taken Harclay hostage. Instead of attempting an all-out siege on the castle's impenetrable walls, they'd walked through the gates one by one during the village's harvest festival, then forced Harclay from the castle's protection.

Of course, they hadn't harmed Harclay. As a titled and knighted man, Harclay had been transported to Lochmaben where he'd been held with every comfort fitting his station until his ransom was agreed upon.

Besides, Colin thought ruefully, it served the Bruce's purposes to treat Harclay with all due respect.

The Bruce grinned up at Harclay as the man settled

himself in the saddle. "Aye," he replied. "A most fruitful visit ye paid me."

Harclay snorted, but grudging respect sat in his eyes. "An unwilling visit," Harclay corrected. "Yet I must admit that I am in awe of how well you have played this situation."

Colin guided the palfrey toward the edge of the Bruce's camp, making room for the Bruce to walk alongside Harclay's knee.

"Your actions have presented quite the puzzle to me this last fortnight. Your men captured me and brought me here ostensibly for the ransom payout," Harclay said, tilting his head toward the Bruce. "And yet upon my arrival you tell me that the Earl of Lancaster, the most powerful man in all of England behind only the King himself, has committed treason in attempting to form an alliance with you. More shocking still, you claim to have proof in the form of letters written in Lancaster's own hand."

The Bruce chuckled. Colin had been present when the Bruce had shown Harclay the damning letters, which had begged for the Bruce's aid in protecting Lancaster's bastard son.

Those letters had sent Ansel Sutherland, one of Colin's fellow Bodyguard Corps members, into England to watch over Lancaster's son. And Lancaster's double-crossing treachery against the Bruce had almost cost Ansel his life.

Ever since then, the Bruce had been looking for a

way to undermine Lancaster, and Harclay posed the perfect opportunity.

"I have been struggling to understand why you would make me privy to such information," Harclay went on. "After all, Lancaster was the man who knighted me eight years ago. His power threatens King Edward's. He is a formidable ally—and a dangerous enemy."

"And have ye puzzled out my aims, then?" the Bruce asked.

"I believe I have," Harclay replied. "Correct me if I err, but you know I am loyal to King Edward. Therefore in telling me of Lancaster's treason, you have now set me against Lancaster, for I cannot abide a man without honor, a man who would go against his King."

The Bruce nodded, another grin threatening at the corners of his mouth.

"But unless I wish to make known Lancaster's treachery to my King immediately—which I don't, for even as we speak, I fear that Lancaster's power may have already eclipsed King Edward's—you now hold something over *my* head, just as you hold knowledge of Lancaster's treason over his."

"Aye. If I were King Edward, I would be furious to learn of Lancaster's betrayal. But I would be even more irate to discover that one of my trusted men had knowledge of such a betrayal but didnae bring it to my attention." The Bruce patted the palfrey's neck, his dark eyes dancing as he looked up at Harclay.

"So now you have me in a bind, as well as Lancaster. And to top it all off, you've managed to extract two thousand marks for my ransom payment as well." Harclay shook his head slowly, that light of grudging respect once again returning to his eyes. "And that is why I say well played, Bruce."

"I would thank ye for the praise, but I cannae take full credit for the scheme," the Bruce said with a little bow. "Ye see that lass over there?"

Colin followed the Bruce's finger where he pointed behind them into the camp. Standing in a small grassy clearing between several of the tents stood Sabine.

Colin's heart lurched at the mere sight of her. Her sable hair hung unbound, shining richly in the slanting fall sunlight. She wore a sky-blue dress that hugged her slim yet shapely body. Before her stood Osborn, looking none too pleased to be engaged in conversation with her.

Over the past month, she'd slowly emerged of her shell, coming to trust more and more that she belonged in the Bruce's camp to help the King in any way she could.

So too had their love deepened as the trust they'd begun to build between them continued to grow. No longer did Colin have to force a smile to his face in order to charm or coax others, for at the mere thought of Sabine, his smile came naturally.

"That wee lass there reminded me just how powerful information can be," the Bruce went on. "And thanks to her, I have been devising all sorts of ways to use information to my advantage."

In response to the Bruce's wolfish smile, Harclay snorted and shook his head again.

"My men will see ye safely to the ransom exchange point," the Bruce said, coming to a stop as they reached the edge of the camp.

Just then, Garrick and Finn approached on horseback. Colin handed Harclay's reins to Finn, who nodded curtly.

Colin had some repairing to do on his friendship with Finn. Ever since Colin had proclaimed his intention to marry Sabine, Finn had been cool toward him—well, cooler than normal, for Finn was naturally a taciturn, guarded man. Still, Finn held an especially fervent distrust for the English ever since his family had been killed by English soldiers more than ten years ago.

As Garrick and Finn moved to either side of Harclay's palfrey, Colin stepped next to the Bruce.

"Are ye sure ye dinnae wish for me to go with them?" he asked under his breath.

"Nay, for I think ye will have better things to do today," the Bruce replied, a mischievous gleam in his eyes.

Colin lifted a brow at his King. "What are ye up to now?"

"I believe it is time for ye to wed yer woman," the Bruce said, waggling his russet-gray eyebrows at Colin. "We can arrange something in, say, a sennight—that is, if ye still wish to make her a MacKay."

Colin's heart swelled so greatly that he feared it would break his ribs. "Oh, aye, I do."

"Then ye'd best go tell her," the Bruce said, waving Colin toward Sabine.

He didn't need any further encouragement. He darted from the King's side and strode swiftly to where Sabine still stood with Osborn.

"…still dinnae understand why ye needed to hit me quite so hard over the head," Osborn was saying, his arms crossed over his chest and a sour scowl on his face.

"As I said, I apologize for that," Sabine replied, "but it is more important to me that you never allow some-one—"

Her words were cut off abruptly as Colin swept her off her feet and into his arms.

"What are you doing?" Sabine demanded, hazel eyes wide and lips parted in surprise as Colin began striding toward the tent they'd shared for the last month.

Colin ignored Osborn's grumbled complaints as they left him behind.

"I am taking my wife to our tent," he replied.

Sabine lifted a skeptical eyebrow, but then her whole face transformed with hope. "Does that mean that he—"

"Aye, the Bruce agreed to allow us to wed, though he is making us wait another sennight."

Sabine laughed as he shoved aside their tent's flaps and strode in. Colin's heart nearly stopped. It was the most beautiful sound he'd ever heard.

"I don't care if he makes us wait for a sennight or a month or a year."

"Is that so?" Colin said, setting her down on their cot.

"Aye, for I will love you no matter what, forever."

Colin's chest expanded as he took Sabine's mouth in a searing kiss. His love had grown so big that there was no more room in his heart for doubts or fears.

"Ye've stolen my heart completely, lass," he murmured against her lips. "And I love ye for it."

The End

Author's Note

As a writer of historical romance, it is my great privilege to weave together fact and fiction. In this book, I had the opportunity to set the love between the fictitious Colin and Sabine in the very fascinating and factual historical events of the summer of 1315.

In late June, 1315, Robert the Bruce attempted to siege Carlisle Castle. The castle sat just across the border in northwestern England, but the Bruce had grown bold after retaking much of the Scottish Lowlands from the English after the Battle of Bannockburn in 1314 (see my note at the end of *The Lady's Protector* (Highland Bodyguards, Book 1) for more on Bannockburn and England's ineffectual King, Edward II).

The Bruce's streak of victories finally ended with Carlisle. Though he marched ten thousand men from Lochmaben, they were unable to take the castle. More than that, nearly everything went wrong. Though it was no doubt an astounding failure, it is my invention that foul play or spying was involved.

The Bruce had left his siege machines (trebuchets, siege towers, and such) in Lochmaben, perhaps because he wanted to move with speed and assumed his huge force of men would be enough to overtake Carlisle, which was only defended by a few hundred men. However, when they tried to scale the walls, their ladders sank into the mud, and they were met with an onslaught of arrows and thrown rocks from those defending the castle. So great was the volley of arrows and rocks that one account from the time period notes that it was almost as if the castle defenders' stones bred and multiplied inside the walls.

After five days of attempting to scale the walls, the Bruce ordered a trebuchet and a siege tower (a structure as tall as the castle's walls that could be pushed next to the castle so that men could walk right over the walls) to be hastily constructed. They rained blows on the castle with the trebuchet for three days, but barely made a dent. And the summer had been so cursed with rain that the ground was boggy and muddy. The trebuchet, ladders, and siege tower all got stuck in the mud, rendering them immobile and useless.

The Scots then attempted to use a tactic that had helped them take Edinburgh castle a year before. On the ninth day of the siege, they focused their energies attacking the east side of the castle. Meanwhile, James "Black" Douglas, one of Robert the Bruce's right hand men, snuck around to the west side with a small group of men and attempted to scale the walls. But perhaps the English had heard of the tactic, for they fired arrows at Douglas and his men relentlessly until they were forced to retreat.

On the eleventh day, the Bruce decided to cut his

losses and abandon the siege on Carlisle. He and his men returned to Lochmaben frustrated, defeated, and likely muddy.

Although the weather seems like just plain bad luck, at least some of the credit for the Bruce's defeat should be given to Andrew Harclay, who is very much a real historical figure. Harclay was the constable of Carlisle Castle, and clearly ensured that it was well prepared and stocked for the Bruce's siege, despite having a much smaller force of men at his disposal.

Historians are divided on whether Harclay was simply lucky in defeating the Bruce at Carlisle, or if he was actually an intelligent, honorable man. Later in 1315, he was indeed kidnapped and held for ransom by Robert the Bruce, who extracted two thousand marks in payment for Harclay's safe return. One can only imagine what the two men discussed as the negotiations for ransom payment were made.

Without giving anything away (Harclay, Lancaster, and the Bruce's dealings with each other will continue to provide the backdrop for future Highland Bodyguards series books!), I will add that Harclay was knighted by the Earl of Lancaster, but eventually turned against Lancaster for making a secret alliance with the Bruce (again, you can learn more in my note for *The Lady's Protector*), thus committing treason against England's King Edward II. However, in a strange twist of fate, Harclay would later find himself in a similar situation, caught between the Bruce and

Edward II. You can't make this stuff up, people!

On to the war in Ireland. After the Scots' success at Bannockburn, the Bruce sought to chase his remaining enemies even further away, and divide England's troops, resources, and energies by bringing the battle to Ireland. Though there were other, complex reasons to take the fight to Irish soil, the one that fascinates me most is that the Bruce believed that all people of Celtic descent could be united against the English. He felt that the Irish (and the Welsh) had been subjugated in similar ways that the Scots had been by the English. Due to their shared ancestry, Celts across national borders could and should be united.

The Scottish invasion of Ireland proved difficult and problematic, however. Robert the Bruce sent his younger brother, Edward Bruce, to fight against the English, and those among the Irish who were allied with them, in May 1315.

I based the Bruce's missive and the strategic relocation of Edward Bruce's forces away from Louth and to the north on an actual event. One of the Scots' English-allied Irish enemies laid a trap for Edward, hoping to lure him into an ambush. Although the missive from Robert the Bruce was fictitious, somehow Edward Bruce avoided the trap and instead moved north, which had been left wide open. He claimed several towns and villages for his cause as a result of that fortuitous move.

After three years of hard-fought battles, however,

the Scottish cause in Ireland failed. They were unable to hold areas they'd conquered, and worse, they had sustained themselves by pillaging, which slowly turned the local people against them. Though the Bruce may have had both strategic and noble intentions for invading Ireland, ultimately the Irish people paid a steep price. Again, no spoilers (though you can always just Google it, I suppose!), but the war in Ireland also cost Edward Bruce dearly—that bit of history will come back for a later book in the Highland Bodyguards series!

A few smaller notes on the historical elements I included. When Sabine spun her first lie to Osborn and Colin, she said she was going to Lincluden Abbey. This is a real place that served as a nunnery in the medieval era, though it is only about a mile from Dumfries. I stretched the distance a bit to give my characters more time and space to roam.

The bridge I mentioned over the River Nith in Dumfries is also real. Devorgilla's Bridge was named after Lady Devorgilla de Balliol, the mother of King John Balliol, the short-term King of Scotland and Robert the Bruce's one-time rival for the throne. She had a wooden bridge built across the river in the middle of the 1200s, which was later replaced with stone.

In the Medieval era, as today, information was power. The transmitting, stealing, buying, and selling of information was no doubt on the minds of thieves, spies, and Kings alike. As far as I have researched, my portrayal of how a sealed message could be opened is accurate, though I never encountered anything on the "counter-intelligence" technique of using sap or tar on the flaps, as I mention at the end of this story. For more on the history of parchment, please see my note at the end of *Highlander's Return* (Sinclair Brothers Trilogy, Book 2.5).

Thank you for journeying back in time with me, and I hope you enjoyed reading my story as much as I did researching and writing it!

Thank You!

Thank you for taking the time to read *Heart's Thief* (Highland Bodyguards, Book 2)!

And thank you in advance for sharing your enjoyment of this book (or my other books) with fellow readers by leaving a review on Amazon and/or Goodreads. Long or short, detailed or to the point, I read all reviews and greatly appreciate you for writing one!

I love connecting with readers! Sign up for my newsletter and be the first to hear about my latest book news, flash sales, giveaways, and more—signing up is free and easy at: www.EmmaPrinceBooks.com

You also can join me on Twitter at:
@EmmaPrinceBooks.

Or keep up on Facebook at:
facebook.com/EmmaPrinceBooks

Teasers for Emma Prince's Books

Highland Bodyguards Series:

The Lady's Protector, the thrilling start to the Highland Bodyguards series, is available now on Amazon!

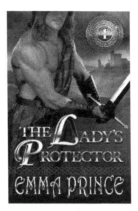

The Battle of Bannockburn may be over,
but the war is far from won.

Her Protector...

Ansel Sutherland is charged with a mission from King Robert the Bruce to protect the illegitimate son of a powerful English Earl. Though Ansel bristles at aiding an Englishman, the nature of the war for Scottish independence is changing, and he is honor-bound to serve as a bodyguard. He arrives in England to fulfill his assignment, only to meet the beautiful but secretive Lady Isolda, who refuses to tell him where his ward is.

When a mysterious attacker threatens Isolda's life, Ansel realizes he is the only thing standing between her and deadly peril.

His Lady...

Lady Isolda harbors dark secrets—secrets she refuses to reveal to the rugged Highland rogue who arrives at her castle demanding answers. But Ansel's dark eyes cut through all her defenses, threatening to undo her resolve. To protect her past, she cannot submit to the white-hot desire that burns between them. As the threat to her life spirals out of control, she has no choice but to trust Ansel to whisk her to safety deep in the heart of the Highlands...

THE SINCLAIR BROTHERS TRILOGY:

Go back to where it all began—with Robert and Alwin's story in **HIGHLANDER'S RANSOM**, Book One of the Sinclair Brothers Trilogy. Available now on Amazon!

He was out for revenge…

Laird Robert Sinclair would stop at nothing to exact revenge on Lord Raef Warren, the English scoundrel who had brought war to his doorstep and razed his lands and people. Leaving his clan in the Highlands to conduct covert attacks in the Borderlands, Robert lives to be a thorn in Warren's side. So when he finds a beautiful English lass on her way to marry Warren, he whisks her away to the Highlands with a plan to ransom her back to her dastardly fiancé.

She would not be controlled...

Lady Alwin Hewett had no idea when she left her father's manor to marry a man she'd never met that she would instead be kidnapped by a Highland rogue out for vengeance. But she refuses to be a pawn in any man's game. So when she learns that Robert has had them secretly wed, she will stop at nothing to regain her freedom. But her heart may have other plans...

Read Garrick and Jossalyn's love story (and meet Colin MacKay for the first time) in **HIGHLANDER'S REDEMPTION**, Book Two of the Sinclair Brothers Trilogy. Available now on Amazon!

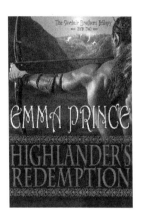

He is on a mission...

Garrick Sinclair, an expert archer and Robert the Bruce's best mercenary, is sent on a covert operation to the Borderlands by his older brother, Laird Robert Sinclair. He never expects to meet the most beautiful woman he's ever seen—who turns out to be the sister of Raef Warren, his family's mortal enemy. Though he knows he shouldn't want her—and doesn't deserve her—can he resist the passion that ignites between them?

She longs for freedom...

Jossalyn Warren is desperate to escape her cruel brother and put her healing skills to use, and perhaps the handsome stranger with a dangerous look about him will be her ticket to a new life. She never imagines that she will be spirited away to Robert the Bruce's secret camp in the Highlands, yet more shocking is the lust the dark warrior stirs in her. But can she heal the invisible scars of a man who believes that he's no hero?

Step into the lush, daring world of the Vikings with *Enthralled* (**Viking Lore, Book 1**)!

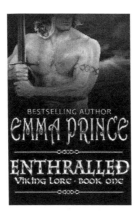

He is bound by honor...

Eirik is eager to plunder the treasures of the fabled lands to the west in order to secure the future of his village. The one thing he swears never to do is claim possession over another human being. But when he journeys across the North Sea to raid the holy houses of Northumbria, he encounters a dark-haired beauty, Laurel, who stirs him like no other. When his cruel cousin tries to take Laurel for himself, Eirik breaks his oath in an attempt to protect her. He claims her as his thrall. But can he claim her heart, or will Laurel fall prey to the devious schemes of his enemies?

She has the heart of a warrior...

Life as an orphan at Whitby Abbey hasn't been easy, but Laurel refuses to be bested by the backbreaking work and lecherous advances she must endure. When Viking raiders storm the abbey and take her captive, her strength may finally fail her—especially when she must face her fear of water at every turn. But under Eirik's gentle protection, she discovers a deeper bravery within herself—and a yearning for her golden-haired captor that she shouldn't harbor. Torn between securing her freedom or giving herself to her Viking master, will fate decide for her—and rip them apart forever?

About the Author

Emma Prince is the Bestselling and Amazon All-Star Author of steamy historical romances jam-packed with adventure, conflict, and of course love!

Emma grew up in drizzly Seattle, but traded her rain boots for sunglasses when she and her husband moved to the eastern slopes of the Sierra Nevada. Emma spent several years in academia, both as a graduate student and an instructor of college-level English and Humanities courses. She always savored her "fun books"—normally historical romances—on breaks or vacations. But as she began looking for the next chapter in her life, she wondered if perhaps her passion could turn into a career. Ever since then, she's been reading and writing books that celebrate happily ever afters!

Visit Emma's website, www.EmmaPrinceBooks.com, for updates on new books, future projects, her newsletter sign-up, book extras, and more!

You can follow Emma on Twitter at:

@EmmaPrinceBooks

Or join her on Facebook at:

facebook.com/EmmaPrinceBooks

77560810R00221

Made in the USA
Lexington, KY
29 December 2017